For Hire, Messenger of God

For Hire, Messenger of God

By *Art Burton*

For Lynne Murphy

Acknowledgements

First of all, I must mention my wife, Flame, and thank her for her patience and understanding when I would drift off into that other world populated by the characters in this book. She never gave up on my dream.

You will have noticed the dedication to Lynne Murphy. Lynne took the chance of being my first reader. She encouraged me to continue. Friends do that. She did more than just read. She took a red pencil and hacked and slashed at some of my favorite passages. It was hard on me, but a lesson that needed to be learned.

John Uhlman offered the first outside the family circle encouragement. He called me at home one night—a long distance call I should add—to tell me how much he enjoyed reading a draft of the book. John is the father of a friend of my son. We had met once or twice before. Not a total stranger, but far enough removed to be considered a disinterested observer. His call made me dig in and go for the finish line.

Proofreading is the bane of writers. I must thank Carol Obritsch, Bissy Grzesik, George MacDonald and Ruth-Ann Murphy for tackling this task for me. That being said, all the mistakes still lurking within are mine and not theirs. In matters of interpretation of grammar rules, I can be stubborn. Also, I can't resist the urge to fiddle with what should have been the final draft.

Not everyone is enamored by the electronic age. I thank my son, Peter, for pointing out the difference between an iPod and a Blackberry.

There is a great bunch of people collectively known as the Community of Writers with whom I shared stories, ideas and dreams at the Tatamagouche Centre over two summers. After an intensive week at this place, you could only come away inspired.

And finally, I have to mention Gail Bowen. If you know one of the most successful mystery writers in Canada, you would be crazy not to drop her name. Gail assured me that persistence and talent will pay off. Here's hoping.

I always look forward to any feedback from readers, both positive—especially positive—and negative. Writing can only improve with honest criticism. Tell me in person when we meet or email me at
artburton@eastlink.ca.

PROLOGUE

Jaun Miraze stood on the rise overlooking his vast coffee plantation. He felt the heartbeat of the central valley's most beautiful and productive coffee and orange growing region as he looked down on the Rio de Grande Canyon. As far as the eye could see, the trees, well, they were more of a shrub, groaned under the heavy load of coffee beans. The deep crimson of the ripening berries flowed like arterial blood mixing with the dark green of the leaves, glossy on the top, lighter and duller underneath. This year's crop would be the best he could remember, going all the way back to when he was a boy working for his father. Even the old, wizened production workers, who had been around forever, expressed their delight at the abundance this crop promised to yield.

Everything that goes into growing the perfect coffee bean had come together. Where in past years, the trees averaged about a pound and a half of berries each, which was considered adequate, this year they promised to bear three to four pounds. Praise be to the coffee gods.

The setting sun, reflecting off the shiny leaves of the trees, warmed his face before adding a reddish hue to the valley below. Despite the elevation, he felt no breeze and noticed no fluttering of the leaves. Instead an eerie stillness surrounded him. The calm before a storm, Juan thought.

He knew a category four hurricane had devastated Florida earlier in the week causing millions of dollars worth of damage. This storm now surged its way across the Gulf of Mexico in his direction. The experts said he had nothing to worry about. The storm would turn north before reaching his part of the world. They promised.

This storm was born in the Cape Verde Islands in the Atlantic Ocean days before. It had slashed its way across the Islands of the Caribbean leaving a scar of destruction in its wake. It dropped to a three as it crossed the narrow belt of land in southern Florida but now, as it surged across the warm gulf waters, it was back to category four and even had some predicting it would become a five.

Hurricanes typically move along a parabolic path which would cause this one to turn north over the gulf and back to the east coast and from there up towards Canada. Often, at the apex of the parabola, the hurricane stagnates, and as it re-curves in its path, both the wind intensity and forward movements may increase. Because of the combination of forward movement and circulatory motion, the strongest winds occur in the quadrant corresponding to the direction of the line of advance.

Fortunately for Juan, but unfortunately for the people of Texas and Louisiana, forecasters on the morning news had drawn this line into the Gulf and then twisted it northward, placing these unfortunate southern states directly in the path. Category four meant sustained winds of 200 kilometers per hour. Thank God they would have little effect here, but Houston, you will have a problem. Still, the air around Juan held a preternatural calmness. It had been hours since he had heard an updated forecast. As he stood there, he could sense a feeling of darkness building behind him. He swung his gaze to the east.

From his vantage point 2700 feet above the canyon he could see solid black clouds obliterating the eastern sky. The

Inter American Highway, about a kilometer away, suddenly faded from sight.

Rain started to bounce off his brown, leather cowboy hat, each hit making a pop like a silenced pistol. He pulled the hat down over his face and water started to flow off the brim landing in splotches on his boots. Suddenly the wind whipped across the tree branches forming intricate patterns like waves on the ocean.

Juan jumped into his Range Rider jeep, rolled up the windows and headed for cover. Before he completed the two kilometer drive to his house, the wind-slashed trees gave way to nature's assault causing their tops to sweep across the water-soaked ground as they swirled wildly trying to rip themselves free of their restrictive roots.

Tablespooned-size raindrops bounced so high off his engine bonnet that Juan could hardly see the road in front of him. Steering became difficult as the wind buffeted and shook the vehicle. He fought the steering-wheel to stay centered in his lane and then finally settling for staying centered on the entire roadbed. Already torrents of water filled the gutters. Juan knew this was going to be bad. Real bad.

Bad would be the understatement of the century. The renegade hurricane had inexplicably drifted off its typical parabolic path crashing over Mexico with its full fury leaving death and destruction in its wake. Countless lives were lost and incalculable damage to property incurred. The promising coffee harvest? It was just another broken promise.

Chapter 1

A slow smile spread across Robert Crosley's face as he lowered his binoculars. The cherry-red Cadillac approached the off ramp much too fast, as usual, and swung onto the exit at twice the posted limit of 45 km/h. This was Exit 6 off Highway 103 and led to the small but affluent beach community of Hubbards, Nova Scotia, home of Cadillac owner and driver Matthew Lane.

Caddy owners, especially rich ones, thought laws were for other people, lesser people. In reality there existed two sets of laws. Those of man, which money could help you circumvent and those of God, which play out for everybody in equal measure.

Matthew Lane had the money to get around man's rules and did so as often as he felt it necessary. Today's lesson for Mr. Lane presented the very basic rigidity of God's laws. Two tons of steel, rubber and leather travelling over 100 mph, or 160 km/h as they now called it, could not negotiate a ninety degree turn and remain upright.

Lesson two would deal with skulls and windshields, rib cages and steering wheels. Mr. Lane felt no obligation to obey man's law regarding seat belts either. He was no child. He would make his own decisions regarding safety. He actively decided against strapping himself into his car seat like a helpless baby. How convenient for Crosley.

Some days, Crosley mused, his job was just too easy. He leaned against a phone booth about a quarter mile from the interchange and waited. The early evening sun shone over his left shoulder and reflected off the windshield of the approaching car causing Crosley to squint into the Slimline field glasses. A slight, sea breeze blew in his face from the nearby Atlantic Ocean, just enough to keep the mosquitoes and black flies at bay.

The ramp looped down to a blacktopped, secondary road. The reduced speed requirement was to prepare you for the stop sign where the road and the ramp intersected. Large chunks of jagged granite left over from the explosions that carved this road out of the wilderness canyoned the roadway. A few skinny maple trees struggled to live amongst the boulders. Route 3 lay about 100 yards to the left of the exit.

Lane's grip tightened on the steering wheel as the car swayed, recovered and continued to speed around the partial clover leaf. The brake lights flashed a couple of times approaching the intersection and then the car leapt towards Highway 3 leaving a trail of black rubber from the smoking Michelins as all of its 460 horsepower was called into play. No metric-measured Cadillac for Mr. Lane, but instead one powered by a gas-guzzling 500 cubic-inch machine that even now inhaled its last few breaths of overpriced, overtaxed gasoline vapor as it roared towards its final destiny a mere 300 feet down the road.

The loud thrum of the engine combined with the howling of the tires sent a flock of small gray and white birds into a sudden burst of flight. Further in the woods, a mother deer and her two fawns stopped their grazing on the newly sprouted ferns, raised their heads, looked in the direction of the intruding sound and then bounded deeper into the forest away from human distractions.

As Crosley watched the drama unfold, he became aware of another car at the periphery of his vision. Its route, the opposite of the Cadillac, came from Route 3 towards Highway 103. The binoculars swung in a short arc centering the newcomer in its circle of vision.

"Damn," he said out loud. The outburst reflected no concern about the other car's occupants. Their life or death meant nothing to him, but rather expressed his desire to see his carefully laid plans carried out unaltered. He realized other cars could be on the road at supper time on a Wednesday evening, even this far from the city. He just hoped that no one else would be involved. He wanted all the publicity to be concentrated on his intended victim. Granted, it would take someone pretty prominent to upstage the death of Matthew Lane from the lead of every newscast in the province, the country, and indeed in the global community as well.

Crosley focused the glasses on the other car encroaching on his stage, a mid-sized, plain, almost utilitarian, black Ford carrying two people, a man and a woman sitting close together like teenage lovers. If fate selected this day to send this couple to their great reward, what did he care? Some people believed and believed with all their heart that everyone had a time to die and nothing could change that time. Crosley knew otherwise. He had chosen not only the time, but the place and the method for several people to meet their maker.

Perhaps this made him one of God's operatives in the eyes of these fatalists. He should have some business cards printed—Robert Crosley, Messenger of God. This thought caused him to give a brief, short laugh as events raced to a deadly conclusion before his eyes. To him, it all seemed to be unfolding in slow motion.

The driver of the Ford noticed the oncoming Cadillac as soon as he swung onto the secondary approach. The Cadillac driver grasped the steering wheel with one hand, the other hand flapped around in the air in a wild, frantic motion like a pendulum gone amuck. The car veered from one side of the

3

road to the other, as the steering hand performed the opposite action to the swinging arm, at the same time accelerating faster and faster as it continued down the road towards him. Two black snakes of burned rubber piled up like a stretched out curl on the road behind it. The Caddy driver's eyes shone like two toonies and were just as big. They darted all over the inside of the car with a savage but fearful look. The Ford driver would later describe it in his report as pure panic.

In the Ford, the driver's eyes were just the opposite—steady and calm. He looked away from the sure death heading his way, picked a spot on the side of the road and at the last possible second maneuvered out of harm's way by mere inches. His tires dropped over the shoulder into the loose gravel sending an arc of stones into the air as the car slewed and then climbed back onto the pavement. The car skidded to a halt. All this happened before the female passenger could scream out a warning: "Watch out for that car." Her voice lowered at the end of the statement as she realized her companion had already handled the situation.

"Crazy son of a bitch," the driver of the Ford said.

Now that the personal danger was past he could feel the cold sweat running down his face and back even though the temperature was still a sweltering 28 degrees Celsius.

"Jesus, that was close," he said. "Did you see that, Stell?" The question was rhetorical.

Already he could hear the increased roar of the Caddy's engine as the back wheels were thrust into the air, trying to pass the stopped front end of the car, the screeching of bending metal as said front end wrapped itself around a power pole and the shattering of glass as Lane's head crushed against the solid surface of the windshield. Then, gravity took over and the back wheels slammed into the ground again, regained traction, dug in sending a spray of gravel flying into the air and pushing the monster Caddy into the pole so hard that the racing engine was suddenly sharing the passenger compartment with what was left of Mr. Matthew Lane, filling the space vacated by his departing soul and various body parts.

The soul made its exit from the physical body as Lane's skull crashed into the windshield shattering the frontal lobe. This sent razor sharp splintered pieces of bone into his brain like pins into a pin cushion and caused instant death.

A millisecond later his ribs were crushed into the padded steering wheel of the big car. The padding failed in its intended purpose. The force was much too great. As the pieces of the skull pierced the brain, pieces of the ribs were letting the air out of his lungs and the blood out of his heart. But this had no effect. Lane was already dead. Another of God's immutable laws, he could only die once. There was silence. Silence interrupted with the occasional ticking of the hot engine as it cooled. A honeybee floated by the shattered windshield, oblivious to the carnage inside.

Crosley focused his attention on the black Ford. "Very impressive bit of driving," he heard himself say, "very impressive."

He watched the driver of the Ford jump from his car in time to catch the dying throes of the Cadillac as it pushed through the utility pole, snapping it like a dried stalk of straw. Hubcaps and motor parts rocketed over the bank and into the woods beyond like shrapnel from a cluster bomb. An information sign that had been snapped off in the initial collision tumbled from the sky in a spinning arc and broke one of the tail lights.

The main hulk of what had seconds before been the pride and joy of the late Matthew Lane hung speared on the bottom of the 12-inch brownish black, creosol soaked post.

The top part of the pole swung like a pendulum over the broad trunk cover which had somehow stayed shut tight throughout the ordeal. Four delicate strands of wire carrying several thousand volts of electricity held it in place. The post slowed in its motion and settled on to the trunk leaving a few elliptical scratches engraved in the red paint to mark it path. Lane's prized possession—his Caddy—was also a goner.

Crosley dropped a quarter into the pay phone beside him and dialed the number of "CMAD, All oldies, all the time." Thank goodness for underground telephone lines.

"News room," the voice on the other end answered. "This is the news tip line. What have you got for us?"

"I want to report an accident," Crosley said in a calm manner. "A big, shiny Cadillac, red in colour. Must be someone important. It looks like he's dead."

"Yeah man, where?" said the smooth baritone voice.

The announcers must man the phones when they're not on the air Crosley thought. "Hubbards. Between 103 and 3," he answered. "Didn't make the corner onto 3. Went straight across and snapped off a power pole." He paused and then continued: "Do I get paid for this information?"

"Sure man. Ninety-four dollars if this is the best tip of the month. What's your name?"

"Put down Marilyn Lane, Hubbards. My wife can use the money more than me." Crosley smiled at his little joke and broke off the connection.

He fed another quarter into the slot and dialed again. This number came from a business card he fished from his pocket, not the printed number on the front but one penciled in on the back.

"Tune into CMAD on your radio. You'll like the news," he said to the answering party. "And, oh yeah, deposit the rest of the money into the account."

Without waiting for a reply, he hung up.

Chapter 2

Detective Sergeant James McDonald looked back into the Ford at his girlfriend still strapped into the middle seatbelt of the front seat.

"Are you all right?" he asked.

Stella Martin sat staring straight ahead. A black ribbon of her shoulder length hair hung in front of her eyes in stark contrast to her pale, blood-drained face. One hand was slowly and unconsciously massaging her shoulder. He must have hit her with his elbow while avoiding the onrushing Caddy. After a brief moment, she turned towards the open door but not far enough to see out the rear window.

"I think so," she said. Her voice lacked conviction. "What about him?" She motioned towards the back. "He looked possessed by the devil himself. Did you see him?"

"Yeah Stell, I thought that too. Stay here, I'm going to check him out." The command, if that is what it was, was not necessary. She had no intention of going anywhere near the car or the deranged person in it. Her hands started to shake uncontrollably. Soon her whole body was jerking in time to the loud out and out sobs.

Jim reached in and patted her shoulder gently through the thin fabric of her white T-shirt. "I'll be right back," he assured her as he grabbed a first aid kit from the glove box. The tears continued to flow.

He steeled himself for the gruesome sight he knew awaited him. In his years driving a patrol car, Jim had seen his share of accidents. How many are your share, he wondered. One like this is more than a person's share. He noticed that his own hands had a slight shake to them also. Investigating an accident was one thing; this one damn near included him. Another coat of paint on either car and they would have been scraping together.

It didn't take years of experience to know that he was about to come face to face with death. McDonald's car had screeched to a halt about seventy feet from the accident scene. Reluctant to ruin what had been such a beautiful day, he started trotting down the road. Miracles occurred before and people walked away unscratched from what should have been sure death.

Often, these survivors were so drunk and thus so relaxed, they flopped around inside the car like rag dolls. There were no tense muscles trying to hang on to steering wheels only to have the wheel crush their chest. They just floated up over it, bounced off the windshield, folded down onto the floor like a dirty shirt and thus they somehow avoided death. But Jim had observed nothing relaxed about this guy. He presented the antithesis of relaxation.

About ten feet from the wreck, Jim slowed down. He approached the remains of the car with caution as he eyed the overhead wires. None had broken, yet, but he had no intention of taking any chances. Skillful driving had saved him once, no sense in getting careless now. The swinging pole was coming to rest on the trunk of the car. That would take most of the load so the wires would probably stay intact. Just don't rock the car, he reminded himself.

He stepped down into the ditch and climbed up the other side. The Caddy door had swung open and the engine had stalled. He reached in past the grisly remains of what had been seconds ago a living human being and turned off the key. The smell of burning flesh assaulted his nostrils.

Lane lay hugging the huge, hot engine that pushed through the firewall and into his lap from the impact of the high-speed collision. In life, he loved that power plant as much as anything else. He was proud of the way it jumped to obey his commands. He wanted speed, it provided it, no questions asked. Through it, he could assert his masculinity. Respond to any challenge on the open road or around town. Dominate anyone. It was fitting that they end up snuggled together like spent lovers.

"No sense adding a fire to this mess," Jim said as he extracted the key from the ignition. Lane didn't reply.

Jim pulled on some rubber gloves and went through the motions of checking for a carotid pulse. He found none. He leaned back out of the car and examined the Buxton key case in his hand. He could feel the rich, smooth texture of the soft leather. He unsnapped the opening and inside found the address he hoped would be there. Someone would have to tell the family, but not him. He experienced a sense of relief and then guilt for having the thought. Traffic accident deaths were a task for a patrolman not a detective. Guilty feeling or not, he couldn't deny his thankfulness. Somewhere a family's life would change forever with the upcoming knock on their door.

One last fire check and then he started back to his own car. He had better call this in before traffic got heavy. There would be photos to be taken of this stretch of road, measurements to make, reconstruction of the accident.

He looked up at the snaking black lines on the pavement as he returned to his own vehicle. Peel marks all the way to the stop sign. No brake marks. What possessed the Caddy owner to take off like that? He looked like the devil himself was in the car with him. Jim would be sure to mention to the investigators to have an autopsy done to check for substance abuse. He had detected no smell of liquor in the car, only burning flesh. He shivered as he opened his own car door.

Stella looked more composed. She had the police radio microphone in her hand.

"You won't believe this," she said. "When I called this in, the police dispatcher already knew about it."

"Not so surprising," Jim said. "There are a few houses up the road. Perhaps they heard the crash or could see something."

He looked around. No houses were really that close. There was a little store perched on the side of a hill about a quarter of a mile up the road, a red and white Coke sign hanging over the door, but no morbid crowd standing out front or headed this way attracted like flies to shit. Accidents always seemed to produce crowds.

"No," she went on, ignoring his interruption. "They had a call from CMAD in Halifax asking for confirmation." She shook her head in disbelief. "Someone phoned it in to the news tip line but didn't drop a dime to call the police, fire department or ambulance."

This time she did look back at the suspended wreck. "They didn't even show up here."

Another shiver went down Jim's back. His instinct as a cop kicked in. The accident happened less than two minutes ago and the radio station already had a report. This seemed suspicious to him considering how isolated the area was. He looked around again, only this time with a more investigative attitude. He slipped into homicide detective mode. Stella reacted to the change that came over him.

"You suspect something, don't you?"

Jim didn't comment. His mind recorded minute details. A phone booth sat in front of the store. It appeared empty but from this far away it was hard to tell. In the distance he could hear a siren. There must have been a car in the area for some other reason to arrive out here so quickly.

Three cars pulled off the ramp and stopped. Jim realized he was still parked on the roadway blocking both lanes. He got in, fired up the Ford and backed off the pavement onto the shoulder leaving the bright red Cadillac in full view of the others. The other cars pulled off also. The crowd was gathering, the spectacle waiting.

He reached over and put an understanding arm around Stella. "Are you all right?" he asked.

She nodded her head. "I guess so."

She looked back at the Caddy. "It all happened so fast. An hour ago we were laying on the beach at Bayswater soaking up the golden rays. As Browning or Wordsworth or someone once said: 'All was right with the world.' And now, look at this."

"That would be Mr. Browning," Jim said.

He leaned back and for a brief moment closed his eyes. He transported himself back to the fun and relaxation of the earlier afternoon. He reached for the cigarette package in his shirt pocket but it wasn't there, hadn't been for more than four years. At times like this he missed the comfort of a good smoke. That wasn't really true either. The taste of the last one he tried made him sick and had him wondering how he had ever gotten hooked on such a filthy habit.

Now his mind's eye drifted back to the blue sky, clean rippling sand and crystal clear water of the ocean. He could see Stell's nipples straining against the stretch material of her bathing suit as the cold surf splashed over her. Heard her squeals of delight as he dunked her under. Could feel the exhilarating feeling of rushing towards shore as he bodysurfed on a frothy breaker, water slip-streaming under his rigid body until his chest ran aground in the sand of the beach and the wave broke over his head.

He recalled the goose bumps pebbling his flesh as he made his initial advance into the cold water. Refreshing was the word most connoisseurs used to describe it. But in no time at all, the body adjusted to the water temperature setting up an afternoon of Atlantic delight, Maritime style.

They spent time alternating between lying on the beach, dodging the odd Frisbee and swimming in the ocean. He even started to build an elaborate sand castle, the kind where the vision in the mind of the builder outreaches the ability of the hands to produce.

At three o'clock, they paused for a picnic lunch in the adjoining park. Jim was always impressed with how Stell could put such a tasty basket of food together. Finished eating, they returned to the beach only to discover the tide had come in and undermined the foundation of their unfinished castle, leaving it in smooth, rolling mounds of sand.

They plopped down beside it and engaged in a long, gentle kiss as the next cold wave came and enveloped them. Both of them jumped up with a squeal. The water hadn't gotten any warmer. A couple of young teenage girls were looking at them with a contemptuous look which suggested old people their age shouldn't be acting like that in public or anywhere else for that matter. He was 36, she 34. The world was their oyster.

In 45 minutes and 30 miles, everything changed. Death sat in a wrecked car just behind them.

"You have to drop a quarter these days," Jim said in an attempt to lighten the mood a little.

Stella looked at him, confused.

Jim smiled at her. "You said they didn't even drop a dime to call the police. With inflation, these days you have to drop a quarter."

The smile he sought flashed across her face and then faded again as fast as it came. The fact that she could smile, even a fleeting smile, was a good sign.

The red, blue, red, blue flashing of lights reflected from the mirror into his eyes bringing him back to the present. The white RCMP cruiser with the rainbow colours slashing across the back doors pulled up behind the remains of the Cadillac. Jim opened the door, swung out and headed down the road again. His sandals scuffed along the hot pavement. His hands were thrust into the pockets of the dark green cargo shorts he wore.

He would just give a brief statement about what he had seen and get Stell the hell out of there. There would be lots of time later for a more detailed report. He pulled his hand from his pocket and glanced down at the key case. Maybe it wasn't leather, he thought. This was more like alligator hide. But that is a kind of leather.

His mind seemed to be searching for anything as a diversion from what he knew was still seared onto the now cooling engine. He had been a policeman for sixteen years. He had encountered too many bodies wrapped around engine blocks. Was it time to get out? This question came to his mind often in recent years. He had seen too much senseless loss of life. Despite that, the feeling of accomplishment which accompanied solving a difficult case still existed. Removing bad guys from the street still kept him rolling out of bed in the morning. He would never get used to the bodies; he would just accept that as part of the job.

"Yo, Scott," he said to the Mountie who was just stepping back from the open Cadillac door. He worked with the highway patrol man on other occasions and recognized him at once. "If you don't want to paw through the blood and guts looking for ID, this may be who he is. At any rate it's the owner of the keys."

Scott gave him a grim smile as he accepted the key case.

"Thanks Jim, but that's not necessary. I know Mr. Lane quite well. How long have you been here?"

"From the beginning," Jim said, "Genesis 1:1. Let's sit in your car and I'll fill you in." Then he lowered his voice so that only the Mountie and none of the curious onlookers craning their necks for a closer look at the gore could hear him. "I think there is something very strange going on here. Very, very strange." They proceeded back to the police cruiser as two volunteer fire trucks arrived on the scene, one a pumper, the other a rescue unit.

The paramedics from the rescue truck cautiously approached the open door of the now defunct Caddie. A quick check with their stethoscope told them their services were not required.

A fireman in a white helmet approached them. The others milled around not sure what to do. There were no signs of fire and no gasoline or other liquids spilled on the road. One of them started directing traffic around the area of the mishap. The others drifted over for a closer look at the wreck and its contents.

The Mountie stopped to discuss a plan of action with the fire chief. It was important not to compromise the accident scene but they wanted to get traffic moving as soon as they could. The traffic on Route 3 would be rerouted down a side road around the site. Signs would be posted at exits 5 and 7 advising that exit 6 was closed. The fire chief would handle all that.

The Mountie joined Jim in the patrol car.

"How come you know Lane, Scott?" Jim asked after they were seated inside. "Are you moving up through the social classes? Somehow Lane doesn't strike me as a down-home boy." Jim smiled.

"No, he was as rich as they come around here. Finding him wrapped around a power pole is no surprise, either," Scott Bowen said without responding to the smile. "He drove that tank like he owned the road. Maybe he did for all I know. He could afford it. I could never make a ticket stick and I gave him plenty.

"'You're wasting your time and mine, Sonny,' he used to tell me, and I guess he was right. But I kept writing them. He kept getting them fixed." His glance swung toward the red hulk. "Does this mean I won? The old bastard will fix this somehow and tomorrow I'll see him cruising down the road again."

"Only in your wildest nightmares," Jim said. They both nodded in agreement, quiet for a moment as they reflected on that truth.

"But," Bowen said, "there's more. About a month ago we were told to maintain a high profile in the Hubbards area in the evenings and on weekends. There was never any real explanation. We were just told to watch for strange or suspicious cars, you know, parked in remote areas or around the rich houses."

He cocked a thumb towards the Caddy. "He was the object of the interest."

Jim's interest level rose.

"Did you ever see anything?" he asked.

"Hell Jim, this is Hubbards and this is the summertime. Do you know what the only industry is here?"

"I don't suppose you mean fish processing."

"Not any more I don't. From June to September, there are more tourists and vacationers in this area than there are residents. The campground at the beach is filled with people from Halifax who spend the entire summer here and commute. There is a continuous and ever changing influx of strange cars, campers and trucks. Only some desk jockey who never leaves his office could ask us to be on the lookout for strange vehicles here at this time of the year.

"If this had happened an hour earlier, God knows how many cars would have been involved." He looked back up the road at the tire tracks crossing both lanes. "It was a good thing the old bugger always worked late. You were lucky he didn't clip you."

"Yeah, lucky," Jim said and then gave a brief description of what he had seen while Bowen filled in his report. The note taking stopped when Jim got to the part describing the demented look on Lane's face as he roared by. He gave Jim an "is this for real" stare, then shrugged and continued writing. Jim depicted a Lane foreign to the one the Mountie knew, but Jim suspected nothing really surprised the officer anymore.

Jim was not some wide-eyed nut case relating this description of events either, but a fellow police officer, a trained observer, a sergeant of the detectives at that. Jim knew Scott would emphasize that part in his report so that his superiors wouldn't think Scott had taken up fiction writing. Even as he related the events, Jim was questioning the self-doubts in his own mind about what he knew he had seen.

After he got out of the police car, he leaned back in the window: "If you find anything out of the ordinary, give me a call will you? I've never seen anyone drive like that in a car by himself. He was terrified."

"Sure," Scott said, "but you have way too much time on your hands if you're going to take an interest in a routine car accident. As gory as it is, it is still just routine, wild man driving or not. He was driving too fast, took out a power pole, smearing his face all over the windshield, now he's dead. Happens every day somewhere in the country. Routine."

"Not this one," Jim said. "Not this one."

Chapter 3

An involuntary shudder passed through Claude Jackson as he looked at the dead phone in his hand. The sounds of Beethoven's Sixth Symphony from the built-in stereo system filled the silence. A large Leo Mallet landscape hung alone on one wall, lit from above. The opposite wall contained a built-in bar fridge with the music producing Sony stereo system above it. Numerous pictures of his family were sprinkled along the remaining wall space. Behind Claude's gleaming walnut desk was a picture window overlooking Halifax Harbour, the body of water separating the twin cities of Halifax and Dartmouth. One of the two suspension bridges connecting the two cities could be seen from this window. Half of the arch disappeared into the sky. A few shafts of late afternoon sun fell on the thick blue rug covering the centre of the hardwood floor.

The message had been short and to the point. Claude knew the phone call was coming. In fact, he thought it should have come much sooner than this. But now that the event had moved from hypothesis to reality, his advance mental preparation seemed inadequate for the gravity of the situation.

Matthew Lane had been a thorn in his side for three years, three long suffering years. That had been when he first found himself deep in financial trouble. There were money problems before but not like this time.

As the cliché goes, desperate times called for desperate measures. That was true both at that time and currently. Until this exact moment though, he hadn't realized how desperate he had become. Perhaps his actions were too impulsive. A man's life had been extinguished, forever.

He replaced the buzzing receiver back into the cradle of the phone and slid the drawer shut. An empty bottle of Pepto Bismal lay on its side by the phone. This direct, private line from the outside bypassed the company switchboard. Business conducted on this line met the definition of "private and confidential" often seen stamped on envelopes. The very private business conducted on it wrought the desperate situation he was now confronted with.

Jackson's downfall was not caused by those common, but nevertheless expensive faults, which often overran successful business men like gambling or snorting coke. People involved in those disgusted him as being weak and failures. His downfall wasn't even caused by a fault in him. It was caused by a positive feature—ambition, the desire to improve his lot in life or at least he defined it as such. A neutral observer might not agree.

The light on his intercom flashed to life accompanied by a low buzz. The call originated in his brother's office. A glance at his Seiko indicated it was almost 6:30 p.m. If he ignored it, his brother would think he had left for the day. He pushed the button and reached for the phone.

"Yes, Neil," he said.

"Claude. Glad I caught you. Could you come over for a minute before you leave? I want to discuss a flyer order."

"Sure Neil, I'll be right in."

Neil Jackson was the president and CEO of Jackson Printers and Publishers, JP&P as it was known, and believed in a hands-on approach to running the operation. Their father had co-founded and co-owned the business. When Neil took over, he made a point of working in every department as well as carrying out his presidential duties.

He used to quote American president Dwight D. Eisenhower: "It is easy to be a farmer when you use a pencil as a plow and are over a thousand miles from the nearest corn field." Neil was a get your hands in the dirt kind of farmer.

To educate himself in the business, he started in the mail room, as corny as that may sound, and worked in every other department including a stint in the unionized press room.

There were some objections about that from the die-hard unionists but he paid his initiation fees and his dues every month and became a member of the GAIU. Granted, he didn't finish his four year apprenticeship. He did learn, however, what was involved in running the presses. After a few weeks of awkwardness, most people treated him as one of the guys. He carried his share of the load and more, expecting no special treatment and getting none. The relationships he developed during this period made his current job easier.

Now when he demanded the impossible from his staff, he knew he was doing it but also knew they would do their best to deliver. Usually they did. This gave the company a competitive edge in the cut throat printing business.

With the advent of desktop publishing, the company needed any edge it could get. A lot of their customers were meeting much of their own needs with an in-house printing system. This made the big orders even more important because that is all they were being left with.

It was just a matter of time before the bread and butter orders like business cards, letter heads and envelopes would come back. Quality would win out in the end.

Their presses were presses and not ink jet printers. They produced quality. Perhaps it was time to put together an ad campaign to recapture this lost business.

Doing it at a high level might be the best approach— president to president. Point out the savings they could generate by returning this work to the printing plant.

He would bring this up with Claude and get him working on it. Claude was vice-president in charge of sales and promotion. He never took any interest in the more mundane operations of the business. He was more the shirt, tie, and suit guy. He preferred to be at the local club rubbing shoulders with customers than in the back shop breathing ink fumes or standing over a paste-up table.

This was all right with Neil because Claude did bring in the customers and without customers there was no reason to be in business. Some of his expense claims seemed to be a little outrageous but he was a co-owner. Lately, however, his head didn't seem to be as much into the business as Neil thought it should have been.

The door to his office opened and Claude stepped in. Neil's office could only be described as utilitarian. The mandatory diplomas hung from the wall behind the big, blonde oak desk which looked like it had been picked up in an army surplus store. There was only one picture of his family hanging from a small area of exposed wall. The rest were covered with file cabinets and book cases. A chesterfield and chair took up the corner opposite the desk. Neil sat in the solid oak armchair behind the desk and greeted his brother.

"Claude, are you feeling okay? You look terrible."

"Greetings to you too, big brother." Claude forced a smile. He thought he had gotten himself together before he came in. "It must be too many late meetings taking their toll," he said as he made a point of looking at the gold wristwatch on his arm and then back at his brother sitting behind his desk. The move was wasted on Neil. Neil gave no thought to the amount of hours he put in. Like Mathew Lane, the business was his life.

"You look gray," Neil said as he came around his desk. "Maybe you are coming down with something. Your eyes seem to lack their usual sparkle. Not a good thing for a salesman to lose." He softened this remark with a smile as he guided Claude toward the blue leather chesterfield along the wall to the right of his desk.

"Relax Neil," Claude pushed away the arm with a gentle motion. "I'm just a little tired. I'll be fine tomorrow. What did you want to see me about?"

Neil walked back to his desk, picked up a sheaf of papers and returned to the couch to sit beside his brother. "I was looking at these figures on the Arenburg account. They look a little low. Not much of a profit margin if we run into any extra expenses."

Claude took the papers and perused them in silence for a minute. "This isn't the whole story," he said. "Everything is going to be supplied camera ready except for a couple of floorlines to list the addresses and I got a good deal on some older stock from Stora Paper that is good enough quality for this run."

He rubbed his temples. He was tired, more than he had realized. Then there was also an advance cheque. He had received it with the order. This, he didn't report or mention to his brother. He just seemed to be getting in deeper and deeper. With Lane dead, things could only get better.

Neil studied the figures a while longer, smiled, slapped Claude's knee and said "I knew there would be a logical explanation. It's just that profits for the first half of the year don't seem to be as high as I thought they would be."

"Must be inflation," Claude said in a weak voice. How much had he siphoned off? He hadn't thought it was enough to be noticeable. It appeared he was wrong.

"Perhaps," Neil said. "Drop over on the weekend. Sally is arranging a barbecue." He let the subject of finances drop.

Sally and Neil shared more than a matrimonial bed. Sally owned fifty percent of the printing plant compared to the twenty-five per cent owned by each of the two brothers. Her dad had been a cofounder of the company with the boys' father. She inherited her father's total share when he passed on.

It would be unfair to say the marriage between Neil and Sally was strictly a business arrangement. Sally was an attractive young lady. They did like each other. For Neil, that was a bonus. Over time, the liking developed into loving. Most importantly, ownership of the company was controlled.

Claude started to stand up. Neil put his hand on his arm and held him down.

"Claude, are you in some kind of trouble?" His green eyes stared right into Claude's. "I'm always here if you want to discuss it."

Claude looked down. Discuss it, he thought. What could he say? Neil, I've been ripping you and the company off for the last three years. I know how understanding you are, everyone says so, I'm sure you won't mind. Instead he looked back at Neil, staring into his chest and said "I'm having a few minor problems, but nothing I can't handle. In fact things are starting to come around quite nicely." He looked up into Neil's eyes and continued: "Thanks for the offer though, big brother."

"Good," Neil said, "I'm glad. But remember, if you need me—" He let his voice trail off.

"Sure," Claude said. This extra attention made him a little uneasy. What was it they said around the building—he can look right inside of you so don't try to bullshit him. Well, Claude had been succeeding for quite a while now. At least he thought he had, but as he looked at Neil now, his confidence faltered. This meeting suggested his deceptions weren't as successful as he thought they were. Neil's bullshit alarm seemed to be buzzing.

Neil had never questioned Claude's costing of a job before either. Did he know something? It didn't matter now, the deed was done. Claude's problems had been solved. Crosley's phone call had verified that. Claude pulled up his sleeve and looked at his watch. The seven o'clock news was about to begin. He needed to hear the details that the phone message had promised.

Chapter 4

As soon as Crosley finished his phone calls, he climbed into his rental car, a mid-sized blue Dodge, unassuming, unpretentious. He aimed towards Exit 7 and headed back to the city. Everything had gone as planned. Crosley expected nothing less. He followed the 7-P formula: proper previous planning prevents piss poor performance.

For three weeks he had followed Lane as Lane left his office in the hot, crowded city and drove the 50 kilometers out to his peaceful, elegant, country estate, leaving the heavy traffic behind him as he got farther from the city. There was little worry of there being a car in front of Lane to slow him down. He, habitually and without exception, passed every car on the road. He could not stand to have any one in front of him, Crosley observed. What now passed as modern full-sized cars, Lane seemed to consider mid-sized. To a car lover they were an abomination. He blew past them at every opportunity. There were very few cars which could fend off the challenge of the sleek, Caddy which had rumbling power to spare.

Crosley counted on this compulsive driving habit of Lane's when he formulated his own plan. Indeed, Crosley had pushed his rental car to its limit to get to his watching post before Lane made his final appearance.

Crosley had dogged Lane far beyond this daily trip from Halifax to Hubbards. For the last month, he had taken a first hand view of every aspect of the life of the rich and famous. What a joke. Lane's life consisted of a series of telephone calls and meetings followed by more calls and more meetings. The Cadillac even came equipped with a satellite phone and a wireless laptop connection for God's sake.

Expensive, but no dead zones. Lane could not afford to be out of touch with the outside world. He didn't leave the office at six; he packed it into his briefcase and took it home with him. All that money and no time to enjoy it. The thought made Crosley shake his head.

Crosley chose Wednesday night for this event because there had never been a variation in Lane's routine on Wednesday as there were on other nights. This tidbit came from a chat with Lane's chauffeur, James Nelson.

Crosley had "accidentally" run into the chauffeur several times in the past month at local restaurants and coffee shops. To follow Lane, all he had to do was keep an eye on Nelson. Tim Horton's coffee ran through everyone's veins it seemed.

Early in the surveillance, Crosley followed Nelson into a crowded coffee shop.

"Mind if I join you?" Crosley asked, coffee cup in hand.

Nelson absently looked at him. "No, pull up a chair."

"You got out of that Caddy parked in front, didn't you? Nice car. What is it a '76? What a cream puff."

Nelson's chest swelled a little. "I'm afraid I only get to drive it. I don't own it." Crosley now had Nelson's full interest.

"My father had one like that when I was a boy." Crosley looked lost in thought. "I loved that car. Haven't been in one like it since my Dad died back in eighty. The car went to my brother and he crashed it a month later. Complete write-off. I never forgave him." He turned from gazing dreamily at the car to look into Nelson's eyes as he made the last comment.

The simmering look that came into his eyes convinced Nelson that statement was still true today. "Want to have a closer look?" he asked.

The two men made their way out into the parking lot. Their coffee remained on the table unfinished.

"Nice stereo system," Crosley said as he slid into the passenger seat.

"Mr. Lane installed that for me," Nelson said. Pride was evident on his face. "He never uses it himself. He just sort of blocks out his mind to whatever kind of music I choose. Sometimes, I notice him tapping his fingers to the beat. He listens, he just won't admit it."

Crosley recalled that statement as the eureka moment in this assignment. He never came into a job with preconceived ideas of how to carry it out. A little study of the subject would give him a direction.

"You've got one hell of a job. You get to drive a cherry like this every day of the week."

"Not quite everyday," Nelson said. "Mr. Lane gives me Wednesday's off. He drives himself on those days. It's his one chance to take this baby out on the open road and open it up. I hear he drives like a maniac. I've seen the traffic tickets. But what the hell, he can afford them."

"Wednesday? That seems like a strange day to have off."

"It's his wife's idea. She entertains on Wednesday evening. Mr. Lane's presence is mandatory. He never lets her down, although sometimes on Thursday morning when we talk about what had happened the night before, he hasn't a clue. He has obviously tuned everyone out. His body was there but not his mind. Hates the hangers on who are just there to be seen with him, to touch the master's hem he calls it. But he loves his wife and puts up with the annoyance."

"Been there, done that," Crosley said. "Those social events can be killers."

"Well it's not just the social aspect. Mrs. Lane is trying to get him to slow down a little. To enjoy some of this money. Mr. Lane says the enjoyment is in making it, not spending it."

Crosley did check out the other days of the week as well, the 7-P's.

Mondays, Lane sometimes stayed late at the office to work on some idea he had come up with on the weekends. These ideas popped into his mind when he was supposed to be relaxing at home or while sailing his forty foot C&C class sailboat among the many small islands scattered like discarded debris off the coast of Nova Scotia.

Places with names like Oak Island where Captain Kidd was supposed to have buried a huge hoard of gold, silver and jeweled treasure. Lane wasn't interested in tales of pirate booty from bygone days. He was more interested in creating his own rewards in the present day.

Crosley had been sitting on the dock when the Lanes crawled out of their car one Sunday morning. He had watched them packing back at their estate and an educated guess on his part told him sailing was their day's activity. He was right. He arrived on the wharf first.

"Leave that damn laptop in the car," he heard Marilyn tell her husband as she started towards their boat.

"I just have a little work to do, maybe a half-hour. No more than an hour." Lane tucked the carrying case under his arm and reached for the picnic basket.

"Bring it on the boat and I'll throw it overboard." There was no doubting that she meant it. "This is your time to take a break. You don't want to have a nervous breakdown from overwork."

"There's no such thing," Lane said. Crosley barely heard that last remark. Marilyn hadn't. He noticed Lane scrunch up his face behind his wife's back and stick out his tongue. Very mature, he thought. The laptop went back into the car. Lane may have been the boss at work and several other places around the world but at home the magic words were still: "Yes, dear." Crosley noticed a small notebook sticking

27

from Lane's shirt pocket as he walked by. Lane would have to settle for old-fashioned, long hand notes for the afternoon.

Monday mornings would find him speeding into the office to start the ball rolling on these latest schemes. Crosley could picture all these little slips of paper spread on his desk and the money mill starting up one more time. This was Lane's life.

Thursdays and Fridays had no discernible pattern. Lane might stay late to clean up some pressing items before the weekend. He might travel out of town checking out some business opportunity first hand or he might spend long hours at the City Club in unofficial meetings with his cohorts. There was nothing Crosley could depend on.

Saturdays were like Thursday and Friday only with the possibility of golf thrown in for good measure. That had happened on one occasion and because the course was private, the best Crosley could do was watch from a distance. On the seventeenth, he noticed documents being signed. Not every one kept score the same way.

When all these factors were dissected, Wednesday night came up the winner. Lane's dependability was only guaranteed on that one occasion each week. Besides, Crosley decided he liked Nelson and would spare him. As a general rule, chauffeurs were expendable when Crosley's job required the removal of someone who was always driven in their private limo. That went with the auto jockey's job description as far as Crosley was concerned. Nelson lucked out. He would be spared, at least for a little while.

In a short time, Crosley took the friendship with Nelson to the next level where meetings were prearranged and not happenstance. He remembered the surprised look on Nelson's face when he presented him with a couple of CD's.

"I had a lot of those artists you mentioned," he told Nelson, "so I burned you a CD of your favorites." Nelson had hesitated before taking them.

"What's the catch?" he had asked. In the world he observed every day, nobody did anything for anybody without an underlying reason. "I'm not gay, you know. I just like to keep in shape."

"Come on man," Crosley said. "It's country music. It's made to share." His smile was so disarming that Nelson could only smile back. He read over the titles and the smile turned real.

"I've been trying for years to get some of these songs. Gee, thanks."

Nelson would never know that his amiable attitude had spared him the impending fate of his employer. He would never know how much he contributed to Lane's demise. At this time, while Crosley made his way back to the city, as Lane still sat cuddling up to the engine of his favorite toy, as Jim McDonald pondered the events of the accident that nearly included him and as the two Jackson brothers discussed low first half returns, Nelson prepared to check out the bar scene on Argyle Street in downtown Halifax, thirty miles and a lifetime away, oblivious of the changes about to take place in his life.

Chapter 5

Jim McDonald sighed and flexed his back muscles, tanned and compact from daily workouts. Even though he had reached the rank of sergeant, he still believed in keeping up his fitness level. As a detective, his work could be described as sedentary by a patrolman's standards more paper work than foot work. But on those occasions when bursts of energy were required, Jim had no intention of coming up short. His life could depend on it.

"Oh that feels good. Keep it up," he said.

Stell stopped rubbing his back with a kneading motion and started using her knuckles in a rapid up and down motion. Jim squirmed as the tension left his spine under Stell's loving ministrations. A big smile spread across his face as he arched his back a bit, leaning into the moving knuckles. A moan escaped from his lips.

"That feels really good," he said, "exactly what I need."

He lay on a cot on the balcony of his apartment overlooking the Bedford Basin. The early evening sun reflected off the silver label of a Moosehead Light beer through the drops of condensation running down the bottle. Stella knelt on the floor beside him wearing a thin SMU T-shirt and white shorts, stretched tight by the kneeling action.

She paused from her massage, reached for the beer, took a cool, refreshing drink and then set the bottle down on Jim's back. His reaction was what she expected and immediate. He let out a sharp little yell and leapt to his feet.

"Dirty trick," he said, a sparkle in his eye. "You'll pay."

He snatched the bottle from her hand with a lightning quick motion and stuck it up under her shirt sending goose bumps over her body. Laughing, she twisted out of his grip and bounced across the balcony disturbing a hornet sitting on the guard rail in the process. She made a wild swing with her hand.

"Get out of here," she said. The little insect flew up and circled her head. She ducked into the corner of the balcony with her hands held in front of her ready to ward off any attack. A small propane barbecue sat sheltered under a plastic covering next to the railing beside her.

The black and yellow bug lost interest and flew towards Jim. Jim stood his ground. He laughed at Stell cowering in the corner.

"It won't hurt you," he said. "As long as you don't bother it, it won't bother you." As if to demonstrate how unthreatening it could be, the hornet landed on Jim's bare shoulder and started walking towards his neck.

Jim drew back slightly. "But that's no reason to get intimate," he said and flicked the hornet away with a casual motion. "Come over here and let me relax you." He reached out his hand but Stella kept a wary eye on the insect as it floated over the edge of the balcony and was swept away on a rising current of air. She came over and sat down, twisting the cap off a beer of her own. She still kept a watch out for the return of the winged assailant. She envied Jim's casualness around the stinging insects.

"What did you find out about that accident?" she said with a more serious look on her face.

Jim sat beside her, slipped his hand under her T-shirt and rubbed her back, the smooth flesh leaning into his pressure and twisting slightly when he hit the right spots.

"It's a strange case," he said. "I told Scott Bowen, the responding officer, what we had seen so they ran some tests on the body and are conducting an autopsy before releasing it to the family. But the initial findings show no foreign substances in his blood."

He took another swallow from his Moose.

"There was none of this," indicating the bottle in his hand, "but I'm not surprised because I could smell no liquor on him or in the car. There were no signs of drugs, legal or illegal, either. It will take a couple of weeks for a full report."

He paused, looked right at her and went on.

"Did I only imagine the crazed look on his face as he whizzed by us? It all happened so fast."

Stell shook her head. The image was vivid in her mind. Eyes bugged out, waving his hand around, mouth going as if he were screaming. Crazed did not do justice to what she had observed. Deranged, unhinged, possessed by Satan himself, that was it.

"The man was possessed," she said. "Utterly possessed." A chill passed through her body as she made the comment.

Jim nodded his head in agreement but his mind rebelled against the idea. There had to be a more earthly reason.

"The accident reconstruction guys were there late into the night. Don Levy's our top guy in the field. Tracked him down and dragged him from a play at Neptune Theatre. This morning he told me tickets are a bitch to come by for this production. He wasn't happy. Still did the job right though. Held up traffic for hours." Jim gave his head a little shake. "Really pissed off the locals. They don't appreciate what our job is. When your second car is a BMW, you think the world revolves around you. Mere mortals should be skewered and quartered for delaying your busy schedule. Chief's phone was ringing off the hook all morning."

"Yeah, well I've been in some of those lines," Stell said. "It does seem to take forever and there doesn't always appear to be a reason for it. The accident happened. Nothing can change that. Clean it up and move on."

Jim scowled at her. "Those are fighting words. You could get forty lashes in some places for that sort of blasphemy." His face broke into a smile. "The process does serve a purpose. You only get one shot to gather evidence at the actual scene. Once the road is open again, everything is destroyed. Someone like Don can read the scene like he's reading from a book. He gathers a wealth of information that translates into the exact chronology of events leading up to the accident. I've heard he was instructed to be especially vigilant this time around."

Jim got up and leaned over the railing looking off into the distance. Sheets of light green corrugated fiberglass on both extremities provided a degree of privacy to the balcony which overlooked a band of trees, a luxurious green at this time of year. Beyond the trees, an uninterrupted view showed the blue waters of the Bedford Basin being churned up by a huge container ship navigating its way to the shipping terminal to unload its cargo from some exotic location on the other side of the world.

"This victim must have been important to have everything held up while they searched for Don. Other investigators were available." Jim took a long swallow of his beer before continuing. "The man may have been important yesterday but today he was as dead and as equal to any of the winos who died in the 'jungle' while hanging around Hope Cottage on Brunswick Street. The root side of the grass had no class system unlike the green side of the grass."

Jim wondered what the brass knew to change this from a routine accident to one requiring such special attention. It had to be more than him saying the dead man had a crazed look on his face before the accident. He would be flattered to think his words carried that much weight but he knew better.

He turned and looked back at Stell. She sure looked good in those tight shorts and little T-shirt. The SMU logo had never looked so good he thought as it stretched across her breasts, the M dipping into and highlighting the cleavage. He held out his hand and she joined him at the railing.

"The car has been impounded," Jim said. "The first thing they checked was the gas pedal. It is in perfect working order as near as they can tell considering the mess the passenger compartment was in. They have a lot more tests to run on it."

"I don't know how he made the corner off the exit ramp," Stell said, arching her back as Jim continued his massage and making the front of the T-shirt stand out even more prominently. "You'd have thought he would have rolled over at that point."

"That's another thing Don said. Nothing out of the ordinary took place on the off ramp. There is no indication of a panic stop. The shoulders were intact. It appeared that everything was cool until he started to pull away. That's where the rubber started. He was never in control after that point. The car had so much power that when we saw him he was flying low.

"They are checking for a heart attack or something but our description seems to rule that out. He was very much alive when he went by us. I think they suspect something questionable. He may have been involved in some shady doings although nothing appears on the record to indicate that.

Stell leaned up against him, wrapped her arms around his neck and gave him a big, wet kiss.

"Enough about wild, possessed drivers. That joker ruined last night for us," she said, her voice low and seductive. "Let's not let it happen again tonight."

It was true she was still upset when they got back to the city the night before and not in the mood for any thing but going to bed and trying to forget what she had seen. She didn't want to be alone. She lacked Jim's experience of putting these sights out of his mind. As a result Jim had been content just to be with her, consoling her as best he could.

She spent the night in the comfort of his arms and woke up this morning feeling refreshed.

Her hands ran down his back, across his buttocks and started working their way around to the front, with playful, little taps on him as they progressed.

"Right," Jim said. "There's no way we will let it do that."

His hands were already feeling the fabric of her shorts as they were stretched taut over her rounded bottom. Then with a massaging action the hands started working their way up, catching the back of her shirt on the way and bringing it up over her head in one quick motion. She gave a slight duck to allow easy passage and he let it slide down between them dropping off her arms to the balcony deck. He then snuggled in to take up the space left empty by the fabric of the shirt and let his hands drop back to those curvaceous buttocks, a slight lift brought her even closer.

The events of the previous day were momentarily forgotten. Jim would relish this moment for a long time to come when he thought back on it. Everything was about to change. The accident and the subsequent investigation would soon dominate his waking life in ways he didn't believe possible.

Chapter 6

"**S**ergeant, could you come in here please."

Jim had just entered the headquarters building in Halifax. He gave an involuntary glance at his watch, a reflex action almost. He was twenty minutes early. What was the old man doing here already?

"Yes sir," he answered as he put his briefcase on his own desk. He looked at the others in the squad room, most of whom were from the overnight shift, appearing busy with their own work and preparing to go home. A couple looked at him and shrugged as if to say "I don't know why he, the inspector, is here so early."

Inspector Garry Holland was seated behind his desk when Jim reached the door. Jim paused and went in when the inspector gave an invitational beckoning motion. The inspector noticed the concerned look on his face.

"Sit down Sergeant, and relax."

Jim took a seat in front of the desk as instructed but he did not relax. To be summoned this early in the morning was not a good way to start a Friday. Transfers rolled out of meetings like this. Friday morning in this office, Monday morning in some remote part of the country like northern Ontario or, heaven forbid, even Yellowknife.

Jim spent three years stationed outside Sudbury which he compared to living on a cold, barren rock pile. In the summer his yard was covered with wilted, brown grass. In the winter it was still covered with wilted, brown grass plus traces of wispy wind-blown snow. That was when the nickel mine was in full operation and the town was booming, a busy time for any police officer. He would not relax until the inspector made his intentions known.

"You saw an accident a couple of days ago," Holland said. He had a copy of Scott Bowen's report in his hand. "Tell me about it."

Jim looked up surprised. What interest did the head cop in Nova Scotia have in a single car accident?

"Not much to tell sir," he said. "I was turning off Route 3 heading towards the 103 interchange when this big, red Cadillac came barreling towards me. I evaded it and it continued on down the road and snapped off a power pole killing the driver in the process." The report was brief and concise.

He paused searching the other's eyes to see if that was the information he was seeking.

"Yesterday, I advised Sergeant Levy of my observations. He is making a detailed investigation of the site," Jim continued when there was no response from the inspector. "He will be making a full report I assume, if he hasn't already."

"Yes," Holland said as he separated a sheaf of papers from the document in his hand, "I've read his interim report and we've issued a press release saying a fatal accident took place, driving conditions were good, no alcohol was involved and the victim was not wearing a seat belt but the investigation is ongoing. He was well-known in the community and there were rumors of suicide. We wanted to put them to rest."

"You know, this has all the earmarks of a suicide, sir," Jim said. "Our examination shows that he never touched his brakes. He was still accelerating when he left the pavement, but –" He paused.

"Go on Sergeant, but what?"

"Did any of the reports you've read mention the crazed look on his face as he went by me? That look forces me to rule out the possibility of a self-inflicted death. He was fighting to live."

He hesitated, looking for the right words to continue. "He looked possessed, as if he was fleeing from someone, or, or something." These were not words guaranteed to bring career advancement, in fact just the opposite. He could only tell the truth though. It was ingrained in his psyche.

Jim grinned. "Not a very professional analysis, is it?"

"Not very, but I've been involved in too many weird cases to dismiss anything. Bowen accepted them enough to include in his report." The inspector smiled. "He did attribute them to you, however. Facts are facts even when they don't appear professional. But let's not include this in any news releases just yet." The smile got a little broader and Jim relaxed a little for the first time since entering the office.

He could picture the headline in one of those supermarket tabloids—Devil Grapples With Driver Reports Police Detective, complete with a suitable grainy photograph from God knows where. This was the kind of publicity to be avoided even if the facts were the facts.

"What is going on, Sir?" he asked, his curiosity getting the best of him. "Levy was dragged, off duty, from a Neptune play. There were extra patrols in the area at the time. I'm in your office giving an accounting. This lacks the feel of a routine accident investigation. Is it?"

"Well Sergeant, I guess that's why they call you a detective. You grasp all the little clues scattered around and put them together to come to a different conclusion from the general public." Holland gave him a fatherly grin. "Within five minutes of that press release airing, I had a call from the family lawyer demanding to know what was meant by an ongoing investigation. Without any prompting, he assured me Lane had not committed suicide and was not involved in anything shady. He ordered me to re-release the statement without any mention of a continuing investigation.

"He wasn't too flattered when I told him that by supper time his client wouldn't even make the *Live At Five* newscast. That he was yesterday's news so he should forget about any retractions or re-releases. But–" and now the Inspector hesitated.

"But, he protesteth too much," Jim said, finishing the sentence for him.

"Yes," Holland said. "But I think he's duped by the suicide theory too. Worried about insurance complications, no doubt. You know, pays double for accidents, nothing for suicides."

Jim pondered this angle for a moment. It hadn't occurred to him but that was because he knew in his heart that suicide was not an option in this case. He reached into his pocket and pulled out a package of Trident. At times like these, Jim missed his cigarettes the most.

"Mind if I chew?" he asked and offered some gum to his superior.

"Go ahead," the inspector said. He waved off the offer. "With all these stupid no smoking rules you have to do something. There's never a cop around when your rights are being trampled all over."

This time Holland's smile was forced. He had not joined the ranks of the nonsmoking majority. Bitterness was evident inasmuch as he couldn't even light up in his own office because of a bureaucratic ruling forbidding smoking in all federal buildings. He reached into his pocket and brought out his treasured pipe and fondled it. At least he could hold it in his hands and that provided some solace.

His demeanor took on a much more serious look.

He gave Jim an intent stare. "I have asked Staff Sergeant Kennedy to assign you to this case full time."

McDonald must have looked startled by this statement because Holland smiled.

"You are right," he said. "There is a lot more to this case than can be seen on the surface. About a month ago, June 14th to be exact, I received a call at home suggesting that Matthew Lane's life might be in danger."

Jim leaned forward a little in his chair. If this was homicide, it was now entering his area of expertise. He may have been less excited if he knew how much of a challenge this case would be. There would have been no excitement at all if he knew the final outcome, but for now he was pleased that his initial gut reactions had been right. This was not a routine accident. Now it was in his genre.

The inspector opened the centre drawer of his desk and took out a thin file. He passed it across to Jim.

"There's not much in it," he said. "It was a warning; I don't call it a threat. I believe the person who called me had somehow or other come across the information that Lane's life was in danger. He wanted me to pass this information along to Lane. He thought it would carry more weight coming from me. He was insistent that I warn Lane personally. I'm not sure what he expected Lane to do about it. The information was so vague. At first I thought about discounting it but then thought better of that. I have to admit I was a little curious. I had never received a call like this before."

He paused as if to reconsider that before he went on. "The warning came from a male, in his fifties I would guess although it's often hard to tell on the telephone. His voice was refined and very persuasive. He wouldn't tell me the source of his knowledge but insisted Lane was in danger. Some activity Lane was currently involved in had to stop. He could offer no additional details but Lane would understand. He then bid me a good evening and hung up."

The inspector paused as if trying to conjure up more details. "As I said, my first instinct was to ignore it. There was really nothing of substance in the message. I don't believe in passing on anonymous threats. Still, the man didn't sound like he was the one making the threat. So in the end I decided to contact Mr. Lane."

He pointed to the papers in Jim's hand. "That's all in the report here. I guess I don't travel in the right circles because I didn't even know who Matthew Lane was." Holland put his pipe in his mouth and started to draw on it. He withdrew it at the first bitter taste from the cold, empty bowl, looked at it with disgust and placed it on the desk in front of him.

"Damn silly mandarins in Ottawa," he said in a voice so low Jim almost missed it. He then got up and walked over to the window looking out over CFB Halifax. The RCMP property bordered that of the Canadian Armed Forces separated by a 6-foot wire fence. At this early morning hour, he could see the newest members of the army, drilling in the parade square, no hair visible below their caps, ears sticking out like elephants. They marched back and forth executing snappy right, left and about turns, all working as a single unit in their drab khaki, army fatigues. The first steps that would, in all likelihood, lead to a barren dessert in the Middle East.

Further up on Windsor Street he could see the morning rush hour traffic starting to build. The line of cars from the four way stop sign at the intersection disappeared from sight down the street even though the flow was pretty much in one direction. Most drivers stopped, yielded to no one, and continued. Others just slowed a bit, glanced left and right before accelerating though. The inspector shook his head. He knew familiarity with the situation fueled their attitude. One of these mornings, another car would be coming up the side street and there would be a collision.

The inspector turned back towards Jim and continued with his summary of events. "First, I checked the phone book," he said. "I didn't find anyone there under Matthew Lane because as we know now he lived in Hubbards. I checked the Halifax, Dartmouth, Bedford, and Sackville listings. Then I checked for middle initials being M still to no avail.

"It's funny how you can overlook the obvious while reading the small print. In larger type boxed in by two black lines was a listing for Lane Investments with a number for M.F. Lane included. My friends at the newspaper have told me how they find all the mistakes, well most of the mistakes, in the body of the story. Meanwhile, the headline, in big print, will have a bad misspelling which no one ever notices, at least don't until the paper is on the street. Then, even people who can't read will point it out to them.

"None of that is in the report." He looked back at Jim, a smile lighting up his face. "I don't want it in writing that the old man is losing it and can't even find a name in the phone book on the first try."

Jim chuckled but he knew what the inspector meant.

"Outside of the fact that he drove an older, red Cadillac that appeared to be in immaculate shape, I have to admit to knowing nothing about Lane myself," Jim said. "Scott Bowen, from the traffic division, told me Lane was filthy rich and he couldn't make speeding tickets stick to him. Who was he?"

Holland raised his eyebrows at that bit of news.

"I'll look into that aspect," he said. "But I doubt it has any bearing on what we are working on now." Privileged treatment always bothered Holland. He believed in the same rules for everyone. That was why his pipe sat unsmoked on his desk even though he was in the privacy of his own office and no one was going to report him if he decided to light up.

He reached out for the file and Jim returned it to him. The inspector flipped through a couple of pages and passed one of them back to the sergeant.

"Business investment consumed most of his time. He did financial counseling for a fee, a big fee; like a week of your wages wouldn't even get you an hour of Lane's time. He did research for companies looking to buy out or take over other companies. He had a knack for finding out what was behind the figures in the annual reports, what really was being said. His supporters, the few there were, referred to him as a very serendipitous person. Whatever his talent, he cashed in on it. Finally, he was a holding company."

"Was a holding company?" Jim raised his eyebrows.

"Yeah," the inspector said. "President, CEO, treasurer and sole stock holder of something called Maple Corp. It had a red maple leaf for its logo very similar to the Canadian flag. There was one big difference though. There was no red ink on its books. He could have gone a long way towards paying off the government deficit all by himself. He bought and sold companies like Wood Motors buys and sells cars.

"No wonder that lawyer was so upset when he phoned. It will take years just to figure out what the old codger owned let alone where everything is. Ah, the problems of the rich."

"Did you tell Lane about the call?" Jim asked when he realized the inspector was not going to continue.

"Yes, since the call had come to me personally, I thought perhaps I should deal with it myself." Holland seemed to be trying to justify his involvement in the case. "I went over to the offices of M. F. Lane Investments.

"When I told Lane about the call, he just laughed. He went to a filing cabinet and handed me a packet of papers which all contained death threats. Making enemies was one of the hazards of his trade. He thanked me for my concern and said he would take care of it himself.

"I suggested that was what we were there for and he sort of laughed at me. He then assured me that although he personally didn't take these threats seriously, there were a couple of people on staff whose job it was to check out all calls and letters of this nature. They had an understanding of what was happening in the business at any given time that the police would not comprehend, by that I assumed he meant wouldn't be told. This gave his investigators an advantage and saved police manpower for more important things but if anything was uncovered the appropriate authorities would be informed, if necessary. It kept him safe to date, he replied.

"Besides that, he took one of those executive defence courses. His Caddy was so old because it was built like a tank and it wasn't worth the hassle to rebuild a new one to those standards. The glass was bulletproof, the suspension was beefed up and he and his chauffeur both took a special driving course to learn to outmaneuver any attackers. There was an emergency alert button on the steering wheel which, when pushed, sounded with his own security people. This located where the car was at that time and tracked where it was going with some sort of GPS device.

"This signal wasn't tripped the other day. I checked with them when I became involved Thursday morning.

"We couldn't force our help on him but we did increase surveillance in the area. Well, that was a month ago and I sort of let it slide from my mind until I heard he died in a car accident. It could be a coincidence but your version of what happened seemed to take it out of the ordinary. Without your description I wouldn't have given it too much thought. The guy drove like an idiot ever since he took the driving course. He missed the point about being cautious. I guess he had to get his kicks somehow."

The inspector again sat back in the chair behind his desk and looked right at Jim. Jim smiled inwardly at the description by Scott Bowen of some desk jockey who never leaves his office deciding to monitor traffic in Hubbards. The next time he saw Scott, he would pass on the name of the idiot.

"Find out what was going on, Jim," the inspector said. "That lawyer may have been protesting a further investigation because he didn't want us nosing around the company. If this is a murder, they can't stop us. It's our case now."

"OK. I guess I can start with the handful of death threats he gave you."

The inspector shook his head. "Sorry, he showed them to me and then took them back before I even had a chance to read through them. I don't know if the tip I received has anything to do with them or not. Maybe whoever called had somehow acquired some sort of information about one of the threats. If the death proves to be more than accidental, someone out there knows something about it."

He put the two reports together and handed them to the sergeant. "Good luck, and keep me up to date."

An hour later, Jim was down in the motor pool. The Cadillac was still up on a hoist and three mechanics in white coveralls were hanging out of various holes in the car. Some were tapping with hammers. Some were taking parts off, examining them and reinstalling them after making notes on a clipboard. Jim waited until a big man with wavy, black hair crawled down from under the back wheel well. He stood on a metal step ladder.

"What do you think Chuck?" Jim asked the head mechanic.

Chuck Bezanson looked at the clipboard in his hand and shrugged at Jim. He came down to floor level.

"She's a wreck," he said. A look of admiration came into his eyes, "but she was well maintained. No, that does not describe it. Perfection. Babied.

"The gas petal worked, we can't make it stick. The brakes are working, the steering, everything. The thing weighs a couple of tons with all the extra plating. The power pole didn't stand a chance against it. To be honest Jim, the only thing that was even a little bit out of the norm was the right, rear tire. It was low on air. In most cases, this wouldn't even be worth mentioning except everything else was in such good order, a slack tire seems to be odd. The tires are self-sealing. Hard to lose air."

"Could that have happened during the accident?" Jim asked as he wrote the tidbit of information in his notebook.

"We don't think so," Chuck said. "The back end of the car is pretty much intact. Just a broken tail light. I think a sign post fell on it. There are no nicks or anything on the rims or tires. It was low enough that it could have affected steering at high speeds though."

Jim added that observation to his notes and looked to see if the mechanic had anything else to offer, the eyes asking the question.

Chuck consulted his clipboard once again and looked up at the car on the hoist about six feet in the air.

"The inside of the car was spotless, if you disregard the blood stains and engine." He forced a slight smile. "We did find one Styrofoam cup, a wooden wedge and a piece of plastic in the back. There was an empty Tim Horton's cup in the garbage container in the front along with a paper napkin. His last meal was an apple fritter. Coffee was black."

He pointed to the nearby workbench where five plastic bags held the items. Jim walked over, picked up the bags and looked at the Styrofoam cup. It appeared empty. There was no coffee or any other stains inside. The other cup had traces of dark brown which resembled a coffee stain.

"Send this over to the lab," he said "Let's see if it was really coffee in here."

He looked in the white Styrofoam container again.

"If that was the coffee, what was in here? Let's get this one checked out too."

He put the bags down and walked back to the car. He looked in the driver's door at the steering wheel. He located the emergency button Holland had told him about. It was accessible and would have been no problem to depress if that had been Lane's intention.

"Do you know if this is working?" he said.

"Yeah, we called his security company and then hit it about fifty times, easy, hard, glancing blow from the side, it never failed. He never tried to signal for help."

"Thanks Chuck," he said to the mechanic. "Send me a report when you finish, please. I've been assigned to investigate this case."

Chuck was taken aback.

"Listen Jim," he said, "we've checked it out with a fine tooth comb. Nothing was tampered with. There are no signs of homicide here. Unless the autopsy tells you different, this is a routine car wreck. Some clown driving too fast for conditions. It looks to be out of your jurisdiction unless you have changed departments."

"Yeah, well send me a report anyway," Jim said as he walked out of the garage into the morning sun. He wasn't sure what he had hoped to find but whatever it was had evaded him. Now, he would have to try a new direction.

Chapter 7

R obert Crosley was upset.
It was Tuesday morning and a light rain was falling. The damp weather wasn't the cause of Crosley's bad mood. He had just came out of the Bedford branch of the Royal Bank. On Friday, he had checked the dummy account set up for Claude Jackson and the money was not there. Then, he could give him the benefit of the doubt. Perhaps it was deposited but not credited to the account yet. Computers can't be rushed. Banks don't add money to your account put in after 3 p.m. Friday until Monday night but they sure take it out right away if you use your debit card on the weekend.

That was Friday. There was no doubt in his mind on Tuesday that the deposit had never been made. That meant trouble for one Claude Jackson.

In Crosley's business, there were no such things as outstanding debts. He didn't turn bad accounts over to a collection agency. *He* was the collection agency.

Crosley had an ingenious method of getting paid by his customers. Automatic banking machines were made for him. He would go to a bank and open up an account in the name of one of his many aliases, get a couple of deposit slips with the account number encoded on them and pass these along to the client. Deposit slips were the opposite of cheques. They allowed strangers to put money into your account without any assistance instead of taking it out. Everyone dreams of having strangers deposit money into their bank accounts. Crosley had it happening.

He would fill out the deposit slips, give the client instructions to deposit twenty-five per cent of the fee up front as a good faith move. It gave him walking around money. It also ensured the client understood the payment system. If there were going to be problems, let's find out early in the game. The other seventy-five per cent of the fee went into the account when the job was completed. Payments were to be made using the night deposit to avoid questions. This was more than acceptable by his clientele as they had as much at stake as Crosley did. Everyone wanted to remain anonymous.

A black line over the encoded number prevented anyone from reading and copying it. The deposit slip would be read by a machine at the bank. Simple black lines could not fool the machine because the number was magnetically encoded and read electronically.

The system was almost perfect. After the crime, he had no direct contact with the client, but received payment at once. He always had cash at his fingertips. There were machines with the *Plus+* sign on them everywhere, banks of course, but also corner gas stations, Seven-Elevens, even at McDonald's golden arches. Crosley preferred to deal with cash for most of his day to day operations. There was no paper trail to cross him up later. Every so often he would move the remaining funds in the account to an offshore bank for safe and private keeping, close that account and open a new one for the next incoming client.

As good as this bank plan was, there was one thing that could screw up the works: nonpayment. Only once had a client double-crossed him. The client had lost his nerve, turned over the deposit slips to the police and reached a plea bargain giving him very little jail time. Crosley had already solved his problems. The subject of the contract was dead. Nonpayment didn't allow even Crosley, Messenger of God, to bring these people back to life.

The police could read the coded number even if it was blacked out or at least the bank could. They put a warning on the account and when Crosley tried to access it, an internal alert was triggered. The machine gobbled up his card and a message flashed on the screen for Crosley to come inside the bank and see the manager about the problem. This little drama played out at a mall branch of the bank.

Crosley noted a security guard running past him into the bank. Here I am stupid, he thought. Another was standing guard at the door. These were rent-a-cops so Crosley wasn't too worried. Going into the bank was not an option. How naive did they think he was? Getting out the mall door undetected was his only concern. The real police would be on the way. Then, as luck would have it, he spotted a couple of African-Canadians. He loved these hyphenated names. They had the dreadlocks, clothing that screeched "Look at me", the full meal deal.

Crosley approached them, told them he was a freelance reporter, produced a business card he carried for this and similar occasions and asked for their help. He told them he was working on a story on racial profiling. They were more than willing to give him examples but Crosley stopped them. He didn't want anecdotal evidence, he wanted to see it for himself. Of course they would walk past the security guard at the door to see if he reacted, they said, and guaranteed a reaction.

Their walk to the door deserved an Oscar or at least an Emmy. They were loud. They slouched as they walked. They were obnoxious. The guard responded as expected. What kind of an attention span did he have? Crosley walked out holding the door open for the arriving policemen. The guard saw the arriving cops and rushed over to assure them no one had left the mall through his entrance. He did have some suspicious characters lined up along the wall though.

Crosley was not concerned about any video cameras that may be on the bank terminal. He wore a hat on these occasions, kept his head down and never stood directly in front of the keyboard. He took out the maximum amount each time to limit the number of times he visited these contraptions.

The delinquent client, by the way, received even less jail time than he had negotiated for. He didn't even manage to make the transfer from the local holding cells to the federal penitentiary. His death in custody was investigated but never solved. Unlike much of Crosley's body of work, this killing generated lots of attention in the media. Crosley encouraged it.

Despite the publicity, every so often it was necessary to remind the client to fulfill his part of the agreement. Crosley did not threaten to break legs or arms or to even kill the delinquent account holder. He was in the business for the money, not for the joy of killing. His principal interest was getting reimbursed for his services. So he would first of all encourage the overdue client to pay by threatening to knock off an acquaintance of that person and following through with the threat at the promised time. At this point most people realized how serious he was and paid at once. If this failed, and it seldom did, he took his losses and removed the non-payer from the face of the earth.

Most people who used his service were aware of his reputation for the quick resolution of payment failures. There were very few problems in this regard. He didn't discourage stories like the one about the squealer who had died in jail under the protection of the cops. There were even more wild stories circulating about his methods to handle delinquents. Crosley had no idea of their origin but he allowed the myth to grow. Jackson would just need to have a chat with his customer relations department. Jackson may have been out of the loop down here in the Maritimes and not heard these stories. He would now get the information first hand.

Crosley dropped a quarter into the phone and listened for the ring on the other end.

Jackson jumped as the ringing interrupted the soothing music playing in his office. For four days, he expected this call and thought he was prepared for it. This resolve faded with each ring of the private line.

Jackson was not a person who reneged on his debts with one glaring exception, Matthew Lane. But damn it, he wasn't going to pay for a service he hadn't been provided. There were going to be no windfall profits for Crosley. If he had done the deed, he'd have been paid. Only last Monday, Jackson had to make another payment to Lane. The task should have been completed by then. It was over a month since he made the initial installment on the contract.

Now Lane managed to kill himself in a car accident. He heard the police report on the radio Wednesday evening. He listened to the story on every newscast until the late TV news came on. He watched it on CBC at 10 o'clock and on CTV at 11. The death was accidental. Crosley was robbed by the grim reaper not by himself. Tough luck, my man, he would tell him but you were too slow.

Squaring himself in his seat, he slid open the desk drawer.

"Yeah, Jackson here," he said with a bravado he didn't feel.

Mr. Jackson," the voice almost sounded pleasant, "I will be in front of your building in ten minutes. Pick me up in your Mercedes. We are going to go for a little drive."

Chapter 8

Where had Claude first heard of this terrible person who was giving him orders? It was from Neil, wasn't it? That made no sense. His brother would not be associated with this type of person. But yes, it was Neil. He thought back to that day in late May. Spring had started early. Temperatures had been at midsummer values for several days already.

They were sitting around the pool at Neil's house. Sally wore a one-piece, tight fitting bathing suit that showed her figure at its best. Even in her fifties, she maintained her youthful beauty, although as Sally would tell you, it wasn't without a lot of hard work on her part. She worked out at Nubody's Fitness Centre three times a week.

The two men wore long, loose fitting boxer type suits. Neil's was a light blue, Claude's a blazing red. Only Claude was showing a few extra pounds packed on around his waist. Claude's wife, Becky, was swimming laps in the pool.

Neil was drinking beer and passing on some of the stories he picked up from the Graphic Arts International Union representative. The two men had finished a successful round of negotiations with the pressman's union and Neil and the rep had gone out on the town together. Neither saw this as a conflict once the contract was settled.

Claude remembered Sally was kidding Neil about the contract negotiations.

"What did the big city boy take us for this time?" she asked. As the major share holder in the company, she had already passed carte blanche power to Neil to handle all negotiations.

Neil laughed at the suggestion. "Don't underestimate this small town pup," he said. "I can run with the big dogs."

"Great," Sally said, "but what all did you give them this time. They don't bring in the big guns for nothing. Did you ever think about hiring a labour lawyer to help you?"

"You've got it wrong, my dear. The question is: What did they give up? As you know we acquired those new, modern presses last year. It takes a lot less manpower to run them. Instead of one man per unit, under the new contract there would be one man for every three units."

"Oh, I am impressed," Sally said. "How did you pull that off?"

"He gave them an outlandish raise," Claude said. "Those guys make as much as our top salesmen. The sales staff is on commission. They at least earn what they make."

"I gave them exactly what I planned to give them before negotiations started," Neil said. "As for your salesmen, you guys can get as many contracts as you want but someone has to actually do the printing. The printing has to be up to a high standard or it doesn't matter how good you think the sales force is. The contracts won't be renewed. I believe our standards are higher than most in this country. Those high standards should be rewarded. I believe in sharing the profits with everyone who does the work."

Neil took a huge drink from the bottle of beer in his hand, finishing it off. He set the bottle down with the five others on the table in front of him.

"As long as you think you did a good job," Sally said, "that's what counts." She grabbed her towel and went inside.

Neil snapped the top off another beer. "He was telling me some stories about negotiations in some of the big cities in the industrial centers. Now those dogs take the whole game seriously."

"And you don't?" Claude said. He knew how much work Neil put into the contract before negotiations even started.

"The rep said it would be nothing out of the ordinary to have one of the negotiating committee members die under suspicious circumstances during the talks. Let me tell you I found that a hard pill to swallow. I told him as much."

"Yeah, what did he say?" Suddenly Claude was more interested in what had transpired between the two men.

"He said: 'I bet you think Jimmy Hoffa is off on a tropical island with Jim Morrison and Elvis.' Then he turned serious. 'People I know have died or disappeared. Not someone I know who knows someone. People *I* know. This is no urban legend.' By the look on his face, I believed him."

Neil leaned in a little closer to Claude. The smell of the beer assaulted Claude's nose. "You're really pouring back the beers tonight. That's not like you," Claude said as he pulled back a little.

Neil looked at the one in his hand and drained the bottle. "It's lite beer," he said and continued his story. "The deceased could be from either side if he had been effective for that team. The rep knew the man who arranged these deaths. Let me tell you that little bit of knowledge scared me. It makes you wonder why he knows him. I wouldn't want to be on his wrong side. He said the hit man was from down this way. Bob Crosby or something like that."

Not Bob Crosby, Robert Crosley. Neil would have been shocked to find out that Claude was now involved with this individual himself.

Chapter 9

Meet Robert Crosley out front and go for a drive. That was never going to happen. Even in his current state of false bravado, Claude wasn't that stupid.

"I don't think that will be necessary," Claude said into the phone. "The subject met an accident. I see no reason for you to profit from his misfortune."

Crosley laughed. The laugh sent shivers through Claude. "Ten minutes. Out front. Your car. Be there."

Crosley again broke the connection without waiting for an answer.

"Damn him." Jackson threw the receiver into the drawer and kicked it shut. Then he opened it again and withdrew the Pepto Bismal bottle, removed the cap and tipped it up. Nothing came out. He lowered it and studied the pink sides of the bottle and realized it was empty. He threw it into the garbage can beside his desk. The loud clang resounded around the room. Again he kicked the drawer shut and slumped down in his seat.

Twelve minutes later they were both sitting in Claude's office. It wasn't that Claude stood up to Crosley showing a brave front and insisting that things be done this way. It was just that he was too afraid to meet with him. For one obtuse moment he hoped Crosley would disappear if he didn't go out front. Crosley had not hesitated for a second. When Claude failed to be out front at the appointed time, Crosley walked right into Claude's office as if he had a scheduled appointment. An appointment arranged in a proper and legitimate manner sometime in the past longer than twelve minutes ago.

"Mr. Jackson is expecting me," he said to Jean as he breezed by. He was through the office door before she could even look up and get a good view of him.

"Don't take the Mercedes out in the rain?" he asked.

Claude half raised himself from his chair ready to protest the invasion of his private office and then resignedly sat back down as he recognized the voice as the one from the phone. He turned and watched the rain streaming down his large picture window. He started to answer and then realized Crosley was being sarcastic.

Crosley grabbed an armchair and set it in front of Claude's desk. "Nice music," he said as Beethoven's Sixth came from the corners of the room. "Do you have an extensive collection?"

"Not really," Claude said. "That's the one I play most often. I guess I can't bother to change the tape. Maybe I should get one of those programmable CD players that choose from five different CDs. I don't really listen to the music that close anyway. It's like white noise."

It seemed incredulous that he was there discussing classical music with an assassin, a hired gun. However, he wasn't anxious to change the subject. What was the quote? Music calms the savage beast.

"It appears we have a misunderstanding," Crosley said, the contented look still on his face as he appeared to be keeping time to the music. "Perhaps it was I who didn't quite follow what you desired," he went on. "You see, I thought that you just wanted this package delivered to the other side with no questions being raised. I didn't think you were trying to make a statement. If I had known you wanted fanfare and fireworks that could have been arranged. It could have been done at high noon in downtown Halifax at the parade square with a thousand witnesses." He had done things similar to that in the past.

He paused, then continued.

"But you didn't want that. You ordered a quiet, sure delivery. Do you understand what I'm saying? A problem can be disposed of quietly or a problem can be used as an example to others.

"I thought you just wanted a quiet, no questions asked, disposition. Am I getting through to you or should I be blunter?" Crosley's gray eyes darkened. The stare burned into Claude.

Claude studied the other man before averting his eyes down to his desk top. He was confused. Was Crosley trying to suggest that he caused the accident? That couldn't be true. The police report said Lane lost control, was not been wearing his seat belt and died. No, he wasn't going to be fooled. Crosley was trying to bilk him out of some easy money without earning it.

"This package was delivered by the post office. You had nothing to do with it." He could use the same analogy as the killer. "When I pay a courier, he has to deliver himself, not just drop the package in the mail box and let nature take its course."

He was starting to relax. This language made it all seem like one big game. With a little effort he could dismiss the fact that Lane was dead, possibly murdered, from his mind. Well maybe not easily, but he could dismiss the thought.

Three years ago Lane seemed to be his savior. That changed last May.

He thought back to how things had gone so bad. He was coming out of the City Club one night when a stretch limo pulled up and one of his former customers, Steve Wilcox, got out. "Did you win the 649 lotto?" he asked as a joke. Better, Steve told him, and that was Claude's introduction to the wonderful world of the commodities market.

They went back inside. Steve gave Claude a quick overview of how to make money in commodities futures.

The commodities market was nothing more than buying raw materials from the producers and reselling them to the manufacturers without ever taking actual delivery. Instead you bought and sold a contract for so many bushels, feet, ounces, pounds or tons depending on the product.

In its infancy the mercantile exchange had been designed to allow producers, grain farmers, cotton growers and the like to get some of their upfront costs in advance of producing the final product. It paid for things like seeds before they went into the ground and fertilizer before it was spread. It worked well for a while.

Then people with no interest in the actual crops got involved, speculators with risk capital. They would buy the contract for a product, they didn't care what, with the hope of reselling it later at a profit. These paper products would be bought and sold several times before the food ended up on your table or the cotton arrived at the mill.

Depending on the vagaries of the market place—good weather, bad weather, wars, peace—the price went up and down on a near daily basis. Money was made or lost. These traders soon lost sight of the actual products they were dealing with. For them, it was simply a piece of paper, a promise that something would be sold sometime, somewhere. Claude didn't understand the underlying principles. He knew there was money to be made. What else mattered?

Like all investing the secret was simple—buy low, sell high. A man in Toronto put $5000 into sugar futures at nine cents. Prices started to rise. He kept pyramiding his profits until he finally sold out at twenty-eight cents a pound with a profit of six million dollars! If he had hung on to the end, the price rose to over sixty cents. The profit would have been over one hundred million dollars. No one ever held on that long and, of course, this was not a typical example. Still, there was money to be made, lots of it.

Claude checked Steve's stories out, made inquiries among people he trusted. The most damning thing anyone had to say about Steve was that he "has friends he still hasn't used yet." But then, who hasn't? Claude lived in the business world as a salesman. He understood what it took to close a deal, so did his friends, both the used and the waiting to be used.

Claude tried to interest Neil, but Neil had no sense of adventure. Neil told him to stay away from commodities. The downside was too great. The subject was never discussed again.

The first couple of times out, Claude made quick profits. He put in the private phone line. Decisions had to be made at a moments notice, Steve assured him. Steve called at all hours of the day with hot tips. It seemed Claude was making lots of money although in retrospect, it was his broker who was cleaning up. The broker took his commissions every time Claude bought or sold, regardless of whether it was at a profit or a loss.

Then came Claude's downfall. He committed the fatal sin in the commodities game — selling short. He had three big scores in a row. One on winter wheat, one on alfalfa and one on pork bellies, whatever they were. How could three big hits be the start of his downfall?

On the commodities exchange, it wasn't necessary to put up all the cash to buy a contract. Only a small percentage was required to show your good faith to pay the rest in the future. This was buying on margin. The margin could be called at any time and when it was you had to pay at once. The object was to turn the item over before the margin was called.

With three major wins, he had a lot of money to put on the line for his fourth hit.

A friend, just returning from Bogotá, Columbia, told him about visiting a coffee plantation. Coffee would be produced in record amounts this year. Juan Valdaz himself whispered that in his ear. His friend had personally viewed the sweeping, green coffee plantations with waves of red berries hanging in thick bunches. Coffee bean prices would soon drop. Claude and Steve decided to go short on coffee.

They sold contracts which they didn't own yet at $1.50 a pound. Each contract was for 37,500 pounds and they sold five each. For every cent the price per pound dropped, they stood to make $1,875. They would just buy contracts later at the lower price to fulfill their commitment. Claude failed to ask if this was legal. The price fell as predicted. Profits were rising, on paper anyway. Claude was in his glory. He was on his way to the big time. Watch me Neil.

With twenty-twenty hindsight, some called it greed. To Claude and Steve it was smart business. They sold five more contracts short. How could anyone predict a hurricane would wipe out acres and acres of coffee plantations?

Smart money would have purchased a call to cover these contracts in case they were wrong. Calls give you the option to purchase shares under agreed-upon conditions such as price. You pay for a call whether you exercise it or not. This little insurance would have saved the two men hundreds of thousands of dollars. Steve was so sure the coffee price would drop that he passed on the opportunity and decided to make the maximum profit. Claude didn't even know what a call was. He could only rely on Steve's street smarts and Steve said this deal was a lay-up. Lay-ups were street talk for a gamble that was sure to succeed.

The night of the disaster, Claude slept in peace. Many nights would pass before he enjoyed that luxury again. The private phone conveyed the bad news to him early the next morning. The call came too late, by far. All was lost.

CNN news cameras captured some of the flooding and damage along the shore. The country was so devastated no pictures came from the interior. There was no communication, no access. Coffee production was halted in these fields for years to come. The paper and the product had come together. Claude tried to immediately buy 10 replacement contracts. No one was selling. The fortunate few who owned contacts hung on for the huge profits to follow. Claude could only put in a standing order to buy whenever any became available, and then wait and watch the price rise. Money was being made, money was being lost. Claude was on the wrong side of the table.

The price per pound percolated up to $2.90 before he managed to replace his contracts. He owed over one half million dollars. From boom to bust in less than eight hours. Claude slept through it.

On the day following the hurricane, Steve was found in his leased, stretch limo with a bullet through his brain. Steve was aware of the perils of selling short. Perhaps that was the wisest way out but it was not Steve's lucky day. He lived.

He could no longer function for himself. He had to be fed, dressed, diapered, but he lived. There was one strange thing though. Whenever he was given coffee to drink, he would spit it back at whoever served it. That was the only time his otherwise dull, lifeless eyes showed any awareness.

Unlike Steve, it took Claude a while to find out how much trouble he was in. His loss totaled $515,625 when the dust from the big wind settled. Was that a lot of money? Not to someone like Matthew Lane. That was spare change. But to Claude it was a fortune. It could have been a manageable amount with a great deal of sacrifice if he was open about it. He could sell his house; sell his car; sell just about everything he owned. However, pride reared its ugly head and he didn't want to admit his stupidity to anyone, especially to Neil. This was to have been his way to show that he was every bit as shrewd as his older brother. Now look at him.

At that point, his savior Matthew Lane entered the scene. One afternoon Claude ran into him while having lunch at the sedate City Club. Lane beckoned him over to his table and before he knew what happened, he arranged a loan to cover his losses. Claude never found out how Lane knew about his difficulties. At the time he didn't care. The repayment terms were a little steep but in five years he would have been clear of the debt. No formal papers were ever signed. They weren't required. No one tried to jerk Matthew Lane around.

Claude started cheating his own brother. He didn't want to, but had no choice. He cut back his personal lifestyle but it was never enough. He fell behind on the payments. The amount of his debt seemed to be rising instead of falling and before he realized what was happening, Lane was threatening to take over his share of Jackson Printing and Publishing. That could never happen.

Claude was past the point in life where he could start over. He was living well beyond his means before his current problems began. Lane assured Claude he would have a job with the company, but would be on commission. A salesman's commission wouldn't even pay the mortgage on his exclusive Eaglewood house, home of the nouveau riche, overlooking his mortgaged sailboat in Bedford Basin. He tried the market once more, but without Steve to guide him, had lost his nerve. It was indeed a desperate situation but now it was taken care of. His benefactor was dead. There was no paper work.

"Crosley," he said, "Lane died in an accident. You had nothing to do with it, so get out."

Crosley smiled but remained seated. He leaned back in the chair and placed his right elbow on the top of the chair back, the other on the left arm rest. He looked perfectly relaxed. "Whatever are you talking about?"

Crosley was too smart to make confessions on hidden tape recorders. The language about parcels may have been a little silly but it prevented future blackmail or arrest.

"Perhaps," Crosley said, "if I were to make another delivery, you would realize the error of your ways. Let's say Monday at 2 in the afternoon.

"There will be an additional charge plus an extra week's expenses. Pay up now if you want to avoid that charge, or, be prepared to pay next Monday." The smile turned cold. "The choice is yours."

Jackson's face drained of colour. Was Crosley talking of killing someone just to prove it could be done to look like an accident? Who was he talking about?

"Wait a minute," he said. "Don't try to threaten me because I'm not buying it."

Crosley got to his feet. "There is only one additional demonstration of the service," he said. "The delivery after that will be a very personal package, if you know what I mean."

He turned, walked towards the door, looked back at Jackson and pointed his forefinger at him with the thumb pointing towards the ceiling. He closed one eye, slowly the thumb dropped to the top of the finger like the hammer of a gun falling. At the same time he made a soft "choo" sound. There was no doubting the message. "That delivery will be the afternoon of the 28th. Expenses are a thousand a day until you pay up."

He eased the door shut behind him. That was the first and only time Jackson got to meet Crosley in person.

Chapter 10

As Crosley left Jackson's office, he slipped on the sports coat he was carrying. The built-in padding added an extra thirty pounds to his appearance unless you looked real close. His chiseled chin denied the presence of an overweight person.

He reached into his pocket for a pair of glasses. They had black wire frames, the kind most people currently wore, nothing out of the ordinary. He put them on as he walked down the hall and stepped into the men's washroom. Two minutes later he emerged wearing a pencil-thin, black mustache. This was the man who set up the bank accounts, the one the tellers would remember if they remembered anyone at all.

He appeared very familiar with the offices of JP&P. He turned the corner in the corridor and entered the sales area. Rows of desks in little cubicles lined the floor. A 20 inch computer terminal sat on each desk with advertisements in various degrees of completion showing on them. Most areas were cluttered with stacks of papers, coloured flyers or marked up correction proofs. Everyone at least looked busy. Cooper looked up from his desk.

"Mr. Burke." Dan was surprised to see the client in his office. "Is there a problem with your order?"

Crosley reached out and shook Cooper's hand.

"No, Dan," he said, "no problem. I was in the Park and thought I'd drop in and get a few more envelopes printed. Small peanuts for a salesman of your status but I figured you'd take care of it for me."

"Sure thing." He appeared relieved. Last Thursday they sealed up a big order for catalogues. Full colour, thirty-two pages, great help to his commission cheque. Negotiations were tough and he didn't want any hitches. After the deal was signed at the local pub, they had supper there. It was after midnight when Dan got home.

Friday morning he found the signed contract in his briefcase. Burke talked him into a good deal for a new customer but the company wouldn't lose on the agreement either. Dan just hoped he hadn't made any more concessions as the night wore on. From eight o'clock on everything was pretty fuzzy.

Burke had bought into a franchise for a mail order catalogue business. The costs of printing were shared between himself and the home company. Cooper got the impression the home company was paying its full share while Burke would enjoy any savings he negotiated. But what the hell, why shouldn't he?

The home company would also supply much of the catalogue material. This would keep costs down all the way around and also increase his profit margin.

"Have you had lunch yet?" Crosley, a.k.a. Burke, asked. "Let's go over to Bud's Pub and wrap up the final details."

"Great idea," Cooper said as he straightened up the few papers on his desk. "It's too muggy to be in here on a day like this."

Cooper had once been a top salesman but now he had developed a taste for the suds especially if someone else was buying. Neil Jackson, among others, observed this new found habit. He didn't like to lean on employees. Often the problems were temporary and worked themselves out without any interference which might cause additional stress on the worker. Neil liked to wait and watch before stepping in. Cooper was under the watch.

Having employees under the watch was one of Neil's less pleasant duties but one he took seriously. His and Sally's fathers had conceived the business when Neil and Claude were just children but Neil was the one who delivered it from a small local company to one competing on the national scene. It was his baby. To paraphrase Vince Lombardi, the company wasn't everything, it was the only thing. Nothing or no one stood in his way to ensure its success.

He did his best to keep his employees happy but it was a two-way street. Everyone was expected to carry their share of the load. Not everyone agreed with his management style. That explained the presence of the pressman's union. Still he treated his employees the way you would treat a friend unless they took advantage. Then, like a friend gone bad, they were dropped.

One disgruntled employee who met that fate was quoted as saying about Neil: "I thought he was reaching out to shake my hand but he was just balancing himself while he reached down and pulled the rug out from beneath my feet." When told about the quote, Neil laughed and said if the man had displayed that creativity in his job, he would still be employed.

Others in the company knew no one was fired indiscriminately. They knew the departed person would be replaced by someone willing to share the workload. Competition was too keen to allow for deadbeats. They backed Neil in his decisions.

Like many people in their late forties, Dan's problems were centered at home. He had two teenage daughters and one teenage son. Where had he gone wrong, he often asked himself.

One of his daughters had orange hair. Her clothes were so tight that if she had a pimple on her ass, the whole world would know about it. She spoke a language he didn't understand. She was the good one.

The other had her head shaved except for a long tassel that hung in a braid from the top. The scalp was painted white. She wore four studs in her nose, two on each side, one in her tongue that made him shudder every time she opened her mouth and who knows what other body parts were pierced. He didn't even want to speculate about that. She always dressed in black. Her bookshelves were filled with books on Satanism. Every day was just like Halloween.

His wife told him it was just a phase they were going through and for him not to worry. For God's sake, how could he not worry about this.

Early in his sales career, he brought customers to his house for barbecues or a few beers on the patio. This made them feel like friends and even if he was out of the office when they came in, they always insisted on dealing with him. They recommended him to their friends. Those days were gone. He was ashamed to bring anyone near his house.

His son was his only hope. He was clean cut, had short hair, shorter than Dan's in fact, and was an above average athlete. During the winter he played midget hockey in the A division.

At first, this was something to be proud of. Now, as he went through the age groups, the game seemed to be rougher and his son became harder. No longer did discussions centre around goals and assists. The highlights were the high sticks, elbows and fights, who could beat up whom. The point was reached where Dan no longer enjoyed going to the games. The hockey arena appeared more like a Roman coliseum with helmeted gladiators battling for their lives. It was only a matter of time before his son would receive a serious injury or would deal grave harm to someone else. Which would be worse? Dan wasn't sure.

Dan chose the extreme move of relocating his family to another community in hopes of changing his children's friends. Another failure. Teens will be teens wherever they are. The Halifax hockey community was tight. His son's reputation preceded him. If anything, the games got more violent as his son tried to live up to the preconceived expectations of his play. His wife initially agreed to the move but grew sullen at being so far from the city centre.

Dan found some new friends to replace his family—Jim Beam, Jack Daniels, Captain Morgan. They didn't talk back, or bring home punks that made him afraid to enter his own living room.

But it was the familiar story. Soon, people became aware of his drinking. They no longer considered him a friend. They didn't want to be associated with him. This is bad news for a commission salesman. So when Burke came in and specifically asked for him, he was thrilled. Burke said he came highly recommended. Dan never questioned by whom.

Cooper realized Burke had him jumping through hoops like a trained dog. He needed the sale and they both came out winners. Cooper may have lost some of his edge through drinking but he did know the printing and advertising business. He made several suggestions which Burke agreed to. Cooper found himself thinking that this could be the turning point. Maybe he could get back on track.

They drove to the pub in Dan's car. Burke showed a great interest in his stereo system and even gave him a couple of new tapes—*Greatest Hits From the Sixties and Seventies*. These are from the new catalogue, Burke told him. Enjoy them.

Dan looked at these tapes with misty eyes. The world was a better place in those days he said. Peace and Love.

Slowly, in an almost eerie fashion, he ran the fingers of his non driving hand over the list of titles before his eyes focused on one particular title—*Where Have All the Flowers Gone*. He hummed, poorly and not quite the right tune, that song for the rest of the trip. The windshield wipers added the necessary rhythm to the tune.

Now they were having steak and fries for their lunch washed down with lots of beer.

"Listen," Burke said, "I have my staff getting all the final copy and camera-ready material for the catalogue assembled. Why don't I make a reservation for the House of Mei Mei in Rockingham for lunch next Monday? They have a buffet. You can pick up the stuff then and get the ball rolling at your end. I'll have a cheque for a deposit on the work."

He caught the eye of the waiter and signaled for two more Labatt Blues.

"I've got to run Dan," he said. "Have a couple more on me. Till next Monday."

Dan looked at him.

"Peace brother." He held up his first two fingers in a V shape. He was in another place and another time.

"Sure man, peace," Burke said and then went out and hailed a Yellow Cab to take him back to his own car.

Chapter 11

Jim McDonald leaned forward and flipped the cassette out of his stereo.

"Why don't you get rid of that broken tape?" Stella asked him. "At least break down and spend $9.98 and buy another version that works. In fact you could find that old thing in the $1.98 bin somewhere."

Jim scowled at the cassette in his hand.

"Show some respect woman," he said. "This is the original Capital recording of the Beatles *Let It Be*," he said. "My father bought it the day it was released. I danced along with it every time he played it. I was about two or three at the time so he gave it to me. I've owned it all these years."

"Maybe so," she said, "but now it's worn out. Get rid of it or frame it and put it on your mantle if it carries so much sentimental value."

"It's not broken," he said. "It just sticks a little."

He reached into his pocket, removed his pen, inserted it into the gears and wound the tape a little ways. A smile spread across his face as he popped it back into the slot in the dash of his car. Paul McCartney's voice filled the interior with a plaintiff plea from Mother Mary to "let it be."

"There you go," he said. "Good as new."

He settled back to listen to the rest of the tune. His right arm went behind the seat and rested lightly on Stella's shoulder. His fingers keeping time.

"I could use some words of wisdom," he said as the song died away. They were parked outside Tim Horton's. Two cups of coffee sat on the dash. Stella looked over at him and asked: "Case not going as well as you would like?"

71

He brought his hand back down from the seat and reached for his coffee.

"Case?" he said. "I'm not sure a crime has even been committed."

He held up the cup without taking a drink and looked Stell right in the eyes.

"Be a sounding board for me while I go over everything I've done in the last week." She nodded in agreement.

He put the cup back on the dash and held up his first finger.

"One," he said. "The autopsy showed Lane was in perfect health, nice pink lungs, no scarring to the heart, no cholesterol build up in his arteries. He didn't even have any cavities in his teeth.

"There were no foreign substances found in his blood. He hadn't been drinking, doing drugs, or even taking prescription medicine. In short, nothing was wrong with him."

He paused, reached for his cup again and this time took a drink.

"Oh damn." He spit the brown liquid back into the cup. "The coffee is cold. How long have we been sitting here anyway? I guess I'm getting too absorbed in this one. But I've got to get it solved so let's go on."

He held up his second finger after replacing the cup.

"Two, the car was gone over by experts. It was mechanically sound. The brakes, steering, accelerator, all the things that would cause an accident like that, worked. In fact the mechanic commented on the high level of maintenance on the car. One tire was low on air. One slack tire is clutching at straws when you're looking for some concrete clues but all things considered, it is strange," he slowly shook his head, "but hardly a murder weapon."

"The car was built like a tank. When he creamed his head against the windshield, that's what killed him incidentally, the inside of the glass shattered while the outside remained intact. It was bullet proof glass.

"Anyone who went to that much trouble with a car must have enemies." That conclusion seemed obvious to him.

His third finger unfolded. "The inside of the car was empty except for his briefcase, a Styrofoam cup, a piece of wood, a little sheet of stiff plastic and some residue of a trip to Tim Horton's in the garbage bag. Examination of the Styrofoam cup showed nothing. The lab boys concluded it had never been used for anything. This was strange in itself. There were no canisters containing gas or anything of that nature. Detailed checking of the interior showed no foreign substances. The seats were Scotch guarded but revealed nothing else."

His little finger stared blankly at him.

"Number four. Nothing at the scene would indicate Lane made any effort to avoid the accident. He appears to have just gunned her into the pole as fast as the car could go. Never touched the brakes. With his erratic steering, it's hard to tell if he even tried to turn onto Route 3.

"That seems to be linked to number five." He extended his thumb. "The call to the radio station came from a man claiming to be Marilyn Lane's husband. There was a cellular phone in the car but it wasn't used. We traced the call to a pay phone outside that little store up the road. The owner of the store denies making the call. He claims to have been having his supper at the time doesn't remember anyone else in the area.

"He's an older gentleman and a little hard of hearing. Claims to have not even heard the crash. Didn't know anything about the accident until after his supper when he saw all the flashing lights. So, who placed that call?

"The timing of the accident and the timing of the call to the radio station, are so close it's hard to say which came first. They seem to have been simultaneous. Whoever called it in had to be there. I didn't see anyone else and neither did you.

"If it wasn't for one small detail, it would appear to be an open and shut case of suicide. People use cars for taking their own lives more often then we realize. They just drive into a concrete post, an oncoming tractor trailer or, as in this case, a power pole. His lawyers will see to it that it is never more than an accident. Suicide won't be an option to them. Family pride won't allow it."

Stella had been listening as he ticked off the facts. She often was able to give him some insight. Sometimes he explained that he got too close to a case and was overwhelmed by all the information. An outsider could pick up something obvious which was right at the end of his nose, too close to focus on. This was the reason for these little review sessions. Often just laying the facts out to someone else brought things into perspective for himself. Things he missed would jump out at him. But not this time.

"That was no suicide," Stella said. The determination in her voice was evident. "I still see that look on his face in my dreams, my nightmares."

Jim nodded in agreement. "That is the one small detail I referred to. We were there and saw his face just before he died. Definitely not suicide, but," and here he smiled, "I don't think either Inspector Holland or Lane's family will accept 'possessed by the devil' as the official cause of death.

"Deep down the family believes it was suicide. As a result when I try to question them about his lifestyle or anything that might give me a clue, they clam up. All they say is it was an accident and why don't I let him rest in peace and leave them alone in their grief.

"Inspector Holland suspected there might be an insurance policy that paid double for accidental death. I checked, but there was no insurance at all. He was richer than most insurance companies, self-insured it's called.

"No one stood to gain from his death. All of the family members reaped the rewards of his wealth. Now they are still wealthy but Lane was the source of their money, the engine that made it all run, and everyone seemed to realize that. He wasn't one of those millionaires who bought all his clothes at Frenchies discount stores and made his wife steal from the grocery money to afford to go to Bingo. Money was for spending. He was not a selfish man. Their grief seems to be genuine.

"Making money was a game to him, it appears. If he wasn't the Wayne Gretzky of the business world, that would be Warren Buffet, he had what it took to play on the same line with him. He was very, very good at it. He could make it faster than his family could spend it. He didn't object if they tried. Everyone was happy.

"Well almost everyone. Someone phoned Holland a month ago and warned him about Lane's impending death."

Jim took a package of Trident from his pocket and popped a piece in his mouth. He offered the package to Stella. She declined, still sifting clues in her mind.

"Lane had his own file of death threats and a staff to investigate them. They are not cooperating with us either. Their knowledge is tied to ongoing business practices which may have been a little shady if not outright illegal. They are remaining loyal.

"As popular as he was with his family, it was a different story in the business community. His public persona was that of a snowy white ermine but many of those he had dealings with knew that most of the time he was just a sneaky weasel.

"It was said he often would bail out a failing company with a loan, but when the loan wasn't repaid on time, he just took over. That could be just malicious gossip. He wasn't well liked. He was ruthless, powerful and successful. So there could be a jealousy factor involved when you talk to his competitors. The company itself is still in operation so his associates and employees aren't talking to anyone.

"If Lane saw a company that he wanted, he went after it and always got it. Hostile takeovers were a way of life for him. Once he had the company, as often as not, he broke it up into its components, sold off the profitable ones and dumped the rest. Most of his competitors I talked to said 'Good riddance.' Lots of people are glad that he's dead but no one believes he committed suicide. Not the type. Also they don't think he was murdered. They think he was too smart for that. That leaves accidental and you and I are the main, if not the only, doubters of that."

"Is anyone too smart to be murdered?" Stella asked.

Jim shook his head. "Not to my knowledge. If someone wants you dead, they can usually get you. The problem here is that nothing indicates murder, not even a remote indication."

He drained the cold coffee from his cup out the car window and watched the rain wash it away. "Want another cup?" he said. "And maybe one more doughnut? I am a cop after all."

Chapter 12

Crosley looked through the rain streaked windshield of the taxi taking him back to pick up his car at JP&P. Two motorcycle cops, red lights flashing, yellow slickers trying to keep them dry, stopped in the intersection ahead of him. One looped around in a U-turn and halted on the opposite side of the road. The other stopped his bike in front of them and balanced it on the toe of one boot. His flat, upraised hand indicated they were to stop and wait.

"What's this," the driver said. He leaned forward in his seat to check the intersecting street. "Oh hell," he said and crossed himself. "It's a funeral. Rotten day to be buried."

Crosley noticed the face of a small boy up against the glass of the limousine following the hearse, staring out at the waiting traffic. Tears were supplied by the falling rain. The look was more of confusion than of sorrow.

"Poor kid," he said, "Hasn't got a clue what's going on."

A man in a dark suit sat beside the boy staring solemnly ahead.

"Probably lost his mother and no one has even told him about it yet," Crosley said.

The cabbie nodded. "Too young to understand," he said.

"Yeah, too young."

Crosley's thoughts went back to another eight-year-old boy. Everyone, his aunts and uncles, grandparents and a bunch of strangers gathered in a big room decorated in dark wood and lots of flowers. One end of the long, narrow room contained a large, wooden box with ornate trim. Everyone who came in went up and stood by this box for a minute or two. Some knelt at a kneeler provided for that purpose. Then they walked away and never went back to that end of the room. The boy was curious but too short to see into the fancy box. No one offered to lift him up for a look. He sensed it was wrong to ask.

His father was there but not his mother. The first day of the gathering, everyone was sad. There were lots of tears. On the second day, only the new arrivals were sad when they stood by the box. By the third day only his father exhibited any signs of grief. He never saw his mother again after that.

Then the following year, the whole thing was repeated. This time his father failed to show up to the gathering of family and friends. By now the boy was a year taller. On the second day, when no one was paying any attention to him, he snuck to the end of the room and stood on his tip toes. To his surprise, his father lay in the box, apparently asleep. An aunt saw him and rushed forward and led him back out of the room to a reception area. She gave him some cookies and a drink of juice. She never mentioned his sleeping father.

By the third day, the boy ceased grieving. He was confused but accepted the fact that another someone he loved had disappeared from his life.

This was the boy's early introduction to death. The lesson he learned was dying is no big deal to those left behind. Be sad for a day and after that life goes on. This hard-learned lesson would serve him well in his future occupation.

The taxi driver noticed a tear running down Crosley's face. "I hate funerals too," he said.

Crosley looked at him, wiped the tear away and said. "No big deal, death is just a part of life. You've got to accept it. The sooner the better."

Chapter 13

Herb Clattenburg stood on the river bank, looking, listening. Plop. A half circle of ripples wafted towards the edge of the pond. A rush of adrenaline shot through his body. This was the big one—Walter from Golden Pond. He leaned out as far as he could, straining to catch a glimpse of the hungry Rainbows lurking around the corner. A bank of trees blocked his vision.

The river turned sharply just below him and then, according to his map, turned back to a good sized pool. So far, he could only see the ever expanding ring of tiny wavelets. It wasn't waves he sought, but fish, big fish.

He fed some line into a little loop in his hand, flipped back the rod, paused, and then snapped it forward. His *Mickey Finn* fly whisked by his ear and settled on the water, its red and yellow colours in sharp contrast to the dark, murky surface.

"Not quite the right spot," he said. He waited a full twenty seconds before reeling it back in, just in case.

He studied the thick growth to his left. Tight, dark green spruce, interwoven with lighter coloured firs, produced a solid fence of trees. No passage there. He looked back. The scrub stretched several hundred feet. Going around was not in the cards. Hungry Rainbows were feeding right now.

He eyed the swirling river water, the colour of country tea steeped on the back of the stove all day long. It was high from the recent rains and the current swift, but he was wearing chest waders. *If I hang on to an overhead branch,* he plotted the course in his mind, *I should be able to cross safely.* That would place him at the pool's edge, a wide open shot at these beauties.

Another fish jumped. This time it was a splash not a plop. He looked back up at the coursing river. He hesitated.

Another splash. More ripples.

Herb slid down the muddy bank into the cold, rushing water. His waders collapsed tightly around his legs. He eased out into the deeper water. The rocks under his feet felt solid. He took two more steps before exceeding the reach of the supporting branch. He let go and watched it spring away. The surging waves slapped at his crotch. Ten feet of open water lay between him and fishing heaven. He could almost reach the opposite shore with his fishing rod. So close.

He edged forward. Something seemed to tug at his right foot, keeping it down. He slid sideways slightly up river. The push of the water increased. He struggled to maintain his balance.

Again, he tried to lift his right foot. Again, he had to settle for sliding it along the smooth rock surface. He looked down for the restriction. Green slime, evidence the water was much higher than usual, covered the rocks. Cautiously, he lifted his foot. The wavering, ever changing image showed nothing impeding its passage, but the foot still didn't want to come up.

Another leaping trout grabbed his attention. From this new vantage point, he could see his quarry. The overhead sun highlighted the glistening red, yellow and blue colours running down its back. His eye measured it at fifteen, sixteen inches, hell, maybe even twenty. Excitement overtook him and he lurched forward. His right foot stayed anchored. His centre of gravity shifted beyond the balance point and Herb toppled into the swift, flowing current of the river.

No problem, he told himself. He just had to secure a foothold. He thrashed forward and tried to get his hands and knees into position so he could push up. His feet seemed tangled somehow. His hands searched unsuccessfully for the rocky bottom just beyond his reach. The rushing water dragged him towards the center of the river. He strained to keep his head above the surface and coughed out a mouthful of water.

I'm sinking? The first signs of fear flashed in his mind.

Then it registered. His waders were filling up. The fasteners at the waist must have released. Instead of rubber hugging his body, he could feel cold water seeping down around his legs.

Arms and legs thrashed as he battled anew to regain his footing. He tumbled backwards still carried by the current. Now it was all out combat.

Another uninvited thought popped into his mind. *I'm going to die.*

His head went under and his lungs gulped in another huge drink. This time he didn't come up.

Instead the flow plunged him downstream, kicking and flailing but still sinking deeper. He could feel the bottom rocks pummeling against his back as he bumped and skidded along. Each gasp bringing more liquid death into his lungs.

Keep calm. Keep calm. He recited this mantra in his head. *You'll float ashore if you keep calm.* He forced himself to stop struggling and went with the flow for a few feet.

Suddenly, his progress snapped to an abrupt halt. Currents of water rushed by him. His head pointed downstream, his body fully extended. He seemed, somehow, to be stuck by one foot. He gave a hard, twisting kick. His leg sprung free. Immediately, he picked up speed again, but he was still glued to the bottom, bouncing from rock to rock like a pinball.

He summoned all his strength to make one last heroic effort to pull himself to the surface. That valiant attempt also ended in failure. Out of air, battered and bruised, he was no match for the weight of the water in his waders.

Little whirlpools eddied above him where the river spread out to become the pond. Herb peered through what seemed like an endless tunnel to the distorted light at the surface, a mere six feet overhead.

His thoughts turned to his wife. She had begged him to stay home today. It was their anniversary. His stubbornness had come to the fore. He insisted on going fishing.

I'm sorry, Marilyn. I should have listened. I'm so sorry.

The shimmering spot of sunlight faded. Herb's limp body became a tumbling rag doll. The pull of the current lessened in the deeper water of the pool, but for Herb, it no longer mattered.

As the flotsam from the struggle settled, the upper reaches of the pond became calm again. Another large trout broke the surface as it snapped an unsuspecting fly out of the air. The ripples from the splash extended uninterrupted to the tree-lined bank. Nature was at peace again.

Chapter 14

Jim McDonald swung his stark, black, unmarked cruiser into the narrow lane. Once more he was searching for new leads in the unexplained death of Matthew Lane. His conversation with Stella the day before had helped him line up what he knew in his mind. It also pointed out how little progress he was making. It was a Saturday morning, but he had to keep on plugging.

Trees lining both sides of the street were now a lush green. Their leaves formed a canopy; the shade creating a sanctuary from the bright sun. He consulted the top sheet of paper on the clipboard hanging from the dash. This was the right street. According to the number on the corner house his destination was four more down, a yellow, one-storey with an older Chevy in the driveway.

Most of the houses on the street were in need of painting. The lawns were cut, not manicured, and most had a few flowers growing out front. The flowers of choice were orange and yellow marigolds. These things, he noted, showed a certain pride in ownership, but a definite lack of money. Most nurseries sold them for a couple of bucks a dozen just to get you inside where you could feel the need for the really expensive plants

This would be a good area for a neighbourhood improvement project. The government money would be well spent on this street. Oh no, there's an oxymoron if ever there was one. Government money and well spent in the same sentence. Working on Saturday was muddling his thinking.

Jim pulled into the driveway of the yellow house and turned off his engine. Before he could get out of the car, a middle-aged man came around the corner from the backyard. He gave the car and the stranger in it a suspicious once over. His face remained stoic. Jim slid out from behind the wheel and slipped the leather case containing his identification from his pocket.

"I'm Detective-Sergeant McDonald," he said. "Are you Ronald Welton?"

The plaid-shirted man studied the proffered ID card and nodded in the affirmative. He wiped his hands on his green work pants and examined the lawman in his driveway. He waited without making any comments.

Jim noticed the concerned look on the man's face and hesitated before continuing. Jim's record check indicated Welton had never broken the law in his life. He wanted to put the man at ease but not right away. Let him contemplate what it meant to have a lawman in his driveway for a couple of minutes.

Welton worked for Matthew Lane as a janitor. To date, Jim had received no cooperation from anyone connected with M. F. Lane Investments. As the Chief Inspector pointed out, they had circled the wagons. Keeping this fellow on edge might work to his advantage. Unlike the lawyers and investigators Jim interviewed, Welton was outside his comfort zone dealing with a law officer.

"You work for the maintenance department of M. F. Lane Investments?" Jim said, consulting a notebook he had taken from his pocket as he returned his ID. The plan was to have Welton thinking Jim had already gathered information about him.

Welton shook his head in the negative. "No, I don't. I work for Lane Cleaners," he said. "That's a completely separate company. We look after the Lane Building among others that Mr. Lane owns." Welton lowered his head and his voice. "Or at least he used to own them."

Jim smiled. Lane Cleaners, every little department was set up as a separate company thus generating lots of tax loopholes. All the angles were covered.

"I've been told Mr. Lane was pleased with your work," Jim said. "You did all the cleaning in the executive suites?"

"That's right," Welton said with obvious pride. "I even have my own key to his private office. Mr. Lane and I were good friends. He called me Ron."

Yeah, sure, Jim thought and you called him Matt.

"That's what I was told," he said instead. "I wonder if we could go inside and talk a bit.'

Welton's eyes clouded again. "I've nothing to say to the police. Mr. Lane died in an accident. That's all it was."

As Jim expected, everyone in the company was warned the police might want to talk to them. They were advised to avoid making any statements.

"Look, Ron," Jim said ignoring the previous comment, "I'm with major crimes working on a homicide. There are some rumors floating around that Mr. Lane committed suicide. I don't think he did and I'm trying to prove that. You could be a big help."

Welton looked confused. No doubt he had heard the suicide story but Jim noticed a slight shaking of the head. Like the family, Welton didn't want to accept the Lane killed himself theory. He waited for Welton to respond.

"We're supposed to call one of those company lawyers if the police try to question us. They are all a bunch of stuffed shirts and don't have the time of day for me otherwise. They even told me to stay out of Mr. Lane's office." Welton gave a snort of disgust. "Overpaid assholes. Mr. Lane treated me like a real person."

"Lawyers," Jim said. "I know what you mean. I think they are trained to act like jerks at law school." He wanted to create an us against them relationship.

Welton nodded. He was coming onside with Jim.

"I don't know anything anyway. What can it hurt if I talk to you? No fancy mouthpiece is going to tell me who I can talk to. Besides, it's the weekend. They're probably not available anyway."

"Probably not," Jim said, thinking of the lawyers he knew and their 80-90 hour workweeks. "Let's go inside."

Jim didn't want to conduct his interview standing on the street. He had to get Welton more comfortable before he would be able to get him to talk freely.

Welton gestured towards the back of his house with his head. "I've got some lawn chairs out back. Let's talk back there. It's a lot cooler under the trees." He looked up and down the street to see if any of his neighbours were watching.

Jim could see the hesitation in Welton's eyes. Jim wasn't in uniform and not driving a marked police car. Any nosy neighbour might think he was an insurance salesman or perhaps a Jo Ho pushing the word of God and saving the world.

Jim made a move towards the back yard. Welton scrambled to catch up.

Although it was still only morning, this was developing into another hot, summer day. Yesterday's heavy rains had cleared the air of excess humidity. The sky overhead was dark blue with only the odd wisp of cloud high and off to the east over the ocean. The backyard was shaded and would be more comfortable than the poorly insulated house.

"Could I get you something to drink," Welton asked, then rushed to add "lemonade or water or something."

Not alcohol, Jim concluded was the message. "Water will be fine."

Welton slipped in the back door of the house and returned with a condensation covered pitcher of ice water. He poured two glasses before sitting down.

Jim had agreed to the water to be polite, but now he swallowed a large mouthful. He let out a contented sigh. "Thanks," he said. "Nectar of the gods. That really hit the spot."

Welton's face lit up from the simple gesture.

"I work mostly in the night time Sergeant. I don't know how I can be of any help," he said as he settled in.

Jim consulted his notebook. "I know that Ron. That's why I think you can be of help."

Jim looked around the backyard in an obvious manner. "Ron," he said, leaning forward as if they were fellow conspirators in on a secret plot. "What I'm about to tell you is not common knowledge. I trust you to keep it that way."

Welton puffed up and also checked out the empty yard. "Shoot," he said. "I hear all kinds of confidential stuff. Keeping my mouth shut is part of my job description."

That was what McDonald was hoping to find out about, the confidential stuff.

"I know I can depend on that," Jim said. He flipped back a page of the notebook, took one more quick look around and continued. "On June 14, we received a death threat against your boss." He paused to let those words sink in before continuing. "We informed him, but he laughed it off. Now it appears he should have taken it a little more seriously. Well actually, a lot more seriously."

The shocked look on Welton's face showed he was not privy to any former death threats. Welton squirmed in his chair.

"Death threats? It's a company of paper shufflers. Who would want to kill them? I sure don't know anything about that kind of activity. No wonder we were warned not to talk."

Jim nodded. Now was the time to crack through the corporate shield of silence that had been established.

"I guess they kept these things to themselves. No wonder. The lawyers said they could handle it, but–" his voice trailed off. A shrug of his shoulders finished the sentence.

"Those guys can't find their ass in the dark using both hands," Welton said. "I sure as hell wouldn't want my life depending on them."

Jim continued to nod. He and Welton were in complete agreement. "Did Mr. Lane meet anyone after hours during the first part of June or did you ever hear any arguments?"

Again, Jim could see Welton struggling with the question of loyalty. Jim had taken him into his confidence. They were on the same side. Jim pushed another button. "Your allegiance was to Mr. Lane, not these smart asses running around the office now. You don't owe them anything. As you said, they don't even give you the time of day."

Now Welton was nodding his head. His decision was in favor of the police. "There was one time, but I don't know much about it. I don't even know who was with him."

McDonald brightened. "Take your time," he said. "What were they arguing about? Anything you might have heard could be a help no matter how remote it may seem."

"Well," Welton began, "the other man was saying something about no more advance information. He had client confidentiality to consider. Then Mr. Lane said something about how the man had more pressing things to be concerned about.

"I realized this was something I shouldn't be hearing so I cleared out. But as I was leaving I heard the other man say this was the last time. His business would be ruined if word of the leaks ever got out. I don't know what he meant but the guy was sure upset."

Welton took a sip of his water. "Mr. Lane assured him he would do nothing to harm his business. He might even be interested in investing in a piece of it. Mr. Lane was like that. He often helped out other businessmen when they were in trouble."

Helped out, no pun intended, McDonald thought but didn't interrupt.

Welton paused. "I guess that's not what you're looking for, is it? I never heard any death threats or real arguments. This guy sure didn't sound like he was going to kill anybody. His voice had more of a pleading whine to it than a threat. Do you know what I mean?" Welton struggled for the right description. "You know, fingernails on a chalk board."

Jim winced. He heard that tone often while interrogating criminals who thought the police were treating them badly. Most of the time, it grated on his nerves as well. "I know exactly the tone you mean."

"It was just unusual to hear anyone argue with Mr. Lane at all," Welton said. "Nobody in the office did."

Jim scribbled this information down in his notebook. Someone who whined so much might not be a killer but they could be capable of hiring one.

"In this business you never know what is important, Ron," he said. "Is there anything else, anything at all?"

"No sir. This was the only time." After a slight hesitation he added, "I know Mr. Lane didn't kill himself. He wasn't that kind of man."

The statement was made with such feeling that it caught Jim off guard. Even though he agreed, his was only a hunch. Welton knew Lane. Welton's eyes became moist as he struggled to keep the tremor from his voice. The man really considered Lane to be his friend. Jim placed his hand on Weldon's shoulder and lowered his eyes.

"I know he didn't," he said in a low voice. A few minutes of silence passed before Jim looked up again.

"Here is my card," he said handing a business card to the janitor. "If you think of anything else, call this number and ask for me. Anything, no matter how trivial."

Welton hesitated, staring at the outstretched hand. He reached out and took the card as if it would burn him if he touched it. Jim could see him second guessing himself about talking to the police.

"We're both looking for the truth, Ron," he said. "I appreciate your help."

Jim rose and walked back along the path and into the bright sunshine to his car. Ron Welton followed along behind him. As Jim was sliding behind the wheel, Welton said, "There was one other strange thing."

McDonald looked up at the man standing outside his car and waited for him to go on.

"Forget it. It's nothing," Welton said after a while.

"Nothing is too trivial," Jim said. "Let me decide."

"A couple of times I found grocery ads in the garbage can in Mr. Lane's office." Welton looked a little embarrassed. "See, I knew it was nothing. It just struck me strange that someone that rich would be reading grocery ads to try and save a couple of pennies here and there. For sure, I could never picture Mr. Lane pushing a grocery cart up and down the aisles of Sobeys."

Both men smiled at this image.

"Good, it's little things like that that often break a case wide open for us," Jim said in an encouraging fashion. He took his notebook out of his pocket and recorded the information. Welton watched him write. Now Welton was really trying to help. Jim didn't think this information was of any importance but he wanted to make Welton think it could be. This attitude could lead to something. "Call me if you think of anything else."

Welton continued standing there.

"Is there anything else?" the detective asked when it appeared Welton wasn't going to move.

"These were newspaper ads." Welton started slowly choosing his words carefully. "I saw them in the Herald myself, but they were different. The backs of the pages contained no stories. It was just plain paper."

"You mean they were advance proofs?" Jim was writing again. Now he thought this might have some significance.

"I don't know about that but there were no stories on the back," Welton said.

"Did you see these before or after you saw the same ads in the paper?"

Welton struck a thoughtful pose, one hand massaging his chin. "Late at night I emptied the garbage cans and I read the same ads in the paper over breakfast. Same day, next day, it gets kind of confusing when you're on night shift. I saw the ads before the paper was on the street."

"All right," McDonald said. "This is the kind of thing we are looking for. Is there anything you can add?"

"No," Welton said. "That just sort of came to me."

"You have my card. Call me. It doesn't matter how trivial it seems." Jim emphasized this last point. Often two unrelated and unimportant points merged to break a case open.

He started his car and backed out of the driveway. Even the rich and famous have to eat, he thought, trying to envision a Cadillac version of a grocery cart. But advance copies of the ads, now that made no sense. What was going on there? Lane was into investments. He wasn't involved in day to day business operations of any companies he might have owned. Word was he looked at the big picture. He didn't micro manage. He didn't have time for that with all the irons he had in the fire.

Down the road, Jim saw a brown and yellow Tim Horton sign. He stopped in for a coffee and tried to make some sense out of this new information.

Chapter 15

Corporal Scott Bowen raised the fork full of rhubarb pie to his mouth and slowly slipped it in, savoring the tart taste. Kate's Kafe served the best rhubarb pie in the county, flaky pastry, real cream topping, generous portion and not loaded with sugar to overwhelm the true flavor. He smiled at Kate as she wiped down the counter with a wet cloth

"More coffee?" she asked and reached for the nearby pot. She knew the answer was yes. Sunday mornings were a quiet time in the community and Scott often stopped in just to relax.

Most people on the roads were making their way to one church or the other. They were thinking of atoning for their sins, not committing new ones. She was about to refill Scott's cup when his two-way radio barked to life.

"Any car in the vicinity of Shad Bay."

"Back on duty, Corporal," Kate said. Her smile flashed even, white teeth. She held back on refreshing his coffee cup.

A reciprocating smile spread across Scott's well-tanned face. When not patrolling the highways, he was out in the fresh air hunting or fishing.

"Guess so," he said, then touched the answer button on his neck mike. "Twenty-four."

"Acknowledged 24. We have a reported drowning victim at Basil Gate near Shad Bay Lake. The local volunteer fire department is aware of this location. They will wait for your arrival."

Scott looked through the plate glass window of Kate's Kafe. The fire station stood directly across the road. Two cars squealed to a stop. Two men exited each vehicle and rushed inside.

"10-4," Scott said. "I will meet the firemen at their station."

In two quick bites he shoveled in the rest of his pie and washed it down with a mouthful of coffee. He fished a five dollar bill from his wallet and laid it beside the plate. "I'll be back for more. Save me another piece."

"Anything for you, cowboy," Kate said. "Next coffee will be on the house."

Scott grabbed his hat and ran across the street to join his fellow body searchers.

The four men Scott had seen arriving crowded around the open office door. Brad Johnson, the paid fireman, sat at the desk with a phone in his hand. "Calm down," Scott heard him say. "Are you sure he's dead? Did you try CPR?" He paused and listened. "Swollen and bloated. OK, you're right. He sounds dead." Again he listened. "Right where the water gets shallow as it comes out of the pond. I know where you mean? Wait for us. We'll be there soon."

Brad hung up and looked at his audience. "I guess you heard? Body at Basil's Gate."

The others nodded. "Anyone we know?" Gerald Turple asked.

Brad shook his head. "Bill Mack found him. Doesn't know who it is? Says he looks like he's been in the water awhile. Bill's got his boy with him. He's going to send the boy to meet us at the bridge and make sure we stop at the right place. Wants to get the kid away from the scene I think."

The men exchanged knowing glances. They had all seen drowning victims before. None looked forward to repeating it today. They would do their duty.

"We'll take the rescue truck," Brad said. "We'll need a rigid stretcher to maneuver the body out of the woods."

"Three of the men climbed aboard the fire truck, Brad driving. Gerald Turple jumped into the police cruiser with

Scott. One man stayed at the fire hall to field incoming calls from other firemen who would soon be getting out of church. Lights flashing, but no sirens, they made their way up the steep hill to Basils Gate.

Basils Gate was a narrow ribbon of river joining Helman Marsh Lake to Shad Bay Lake. The area above the Gate was known as The Funnel. The Funnel emptied its waters into a prime pool for fly fishing before squeezing through the Gate. After a heavy rain, the water rushed through this gap with a vengeance. A small tributary, more of a brook that a river, drained excess water from the lower end of the pool during the wet season. This brook meandered down to meet the road, crossing under a small bridge on the approach road. Bill's son, Danny, was to meet them there.

A heavy silence marked the trip. Both men's thoughts concentrated on the identity of the victim. Would it be someone they knew? Scott frequently fished in this area and had met several people who populated the edge of the pool when the trout were biting.

Near the top of the hill, they spotted Bill's truck parked at the edge of the bridge. A young boy stood behind it waving his arms over his head. He took his assigned task seriously. Nobody was going to get by him.

"Looks like Bill was content to just catch the little brookies," Gerald said breaking the silence with some small talk. "Gotta go further up the road to catch the big rainbows."

"He had his boy with him," Scott said. "Probably bait fishing. Guaranteed to catch something. The Rainbows can be elusive unless you are using the right fly."

"You got that right," Gerald said. "We caught our limit a couple of days ago on a *Lioness*. Only thing they'd look at."

Scott visualized the black fly with the yellow and red streamers and white mane. "That should work. I had some luck with a *Mickey Finn* my last time out."

Both vehicles pulled in behind the truck. Scott rolled down his window and listened to the boy's explanation of events. He withdrew his cell phone and looked back at Brad who had exited his truck and approached the boy. "555-1739," Brad said. The 9-1-1 operator had given the fireman all the details she had received from Bill Mack.

"Good thing there's a tower on the top of this hill. Bill would have had to walk all the way out to report this."

"Yeah," Gerald said, "and we would have had to wait for him to catch his quota first."

The others laughed.

"Dead is dead," Gerald continued; "but fishin' is fishin'."

Scott dialed Bill's number and waited for the call to go through. A shaky voice answered.

"Corporal Scott Bowen, RCMP, here Bill. How's it going? Baby sitting a corpse is not much fun?"

"Damn sure isn't. You found Danny all right? Is there someone with you who could maybe look after him? I don't want him to see any more of this."

"Good idea," Scott said. "I'll get one of the firemen to give him a tour of the fire truck or maybe they can fish off the bridge if we're too long. What's our best bet? Coming in from your truck or going further up the hill and taking the path above the pool?"

"Water's too high. Path'll put you on the wrong side unless you're prepared to swim. Best just follow the river up." He hesitated. "And Corporal, could you hurry along. This thing is giving me the creeps. It keeps staring up at me."

Scott grabbed his new digital camera from the seat. "I guess we'd better document what we find." The three men headed into the woods along the river's edge.

The fourth, with a look of relief on his face, started opening hatches on the truck. Danny scampered up on the back to look in. He picked up one of the helmets. "Wow. Can

96

I try it on?" he was saying as the others disappeared out of hearing range.

Both Brad and Scott were in the river up to their waists. The body just didn't want to float ashore like it should.

"There's a fishing line tangled around one of his feet," Scott said. "It must be snagged on something up river."

Brad pulled a Swiss Army knife from his pocket. "I'll just cut it. Give me a sec."

Scott watched the fireman make his way towards the feet. "Wait," he said. "That might not be a good idea. You never know, it might be evidence."

Brad hesitated. "Give me a break. What evidence do you need? He got tangled in his line, fell in, filled his waders and drowned. Happens all the time. You know that."

"Sure. You're right, but just in case, let's see if we can untangle it."

"Did you ever hear the expression, 'When you hear hoof beats on the plains of Arizona, think horses, not zebras.'"

Scott smiled. "I'll dive in and see where the line's caught up. I'm not going to get any wetter. You just hold the body steady. Take the pressure off the line."

Scott had already discarded his gun belt, wallet and other assorted paraphernalia on shore. Now he emptied his shirt pockets as well. He placed one hand on the fishing line and gave a kick with his feet, disappearing under the water. Ten feet out he surfaced, holding a three-foot stick in his hand. The line was tightly wrapped around it. Suddenly the body became active again and surged downstream pulling the wet stick from Scott's hands.

"Whoa. Don't let him get away."

Brad made a lunge at the retreating form. His hand found no grip on the slippery rubber of the waders and he landed face first in the water, splashing and kicking.

Gerald reacted from the shore. He sloshed into the river up to his knees and grabbed a foot as the body floated by, picking up speed in the current of the river. Bill Mack waded in and secured a grip on the top of the waders. Together the two men managed to wrestle the body into the shoreline where they hung on to it like a trophy fish trying to escape back into its watery home.

Soon all four men were soaking wet as they fought the body out of the water and onto the waiting stretcher. They sat down around it to catch their collective breaths.

"Guess you coulda taken the upper path," Bill said. "Wouldn't be any wetter."

Scott pulled his shirt from his pants and wrung out some of the water. "Guess not," he said. "Anyone recognize him?"

Gerald leaned closer and studied the bloated corpse. Gerald sold real estate in the village and surrounding area. The face was cut and swollen. "Can't swear to it, but I think I sold this guy a place in that new subdivision back towards the city, Shady Acres Estates. Four, five months ago."

Brad took a closer look and shook his head. "Don't recognize him but those people haven't accepted Shad Bay as home. They still do all their business in the city."

Scott leaned over the body and undid the Velcro pocket at the top of the waders. His fingers slipped inside and extracted a sealed Baggie with a piece of paper inside.

"His fishing license," Scott said. "Herb Clattenburg." He looked from face to face. No one showed any recognition except Gerald.

"Yeah, that's the name. Lives in the new subdivision."

The men fell silent again.

Scott absently wound the fishing line trailing from the stick into a loop in his hand.

"Pretty heavy line for fishing in these waters," he said. "Must be at least 20-pound test."

The others looked over. "Guess that's why the branch broke instead of the line," Brad said. He reached out and took the stick from Scott. "It's an old stick. Wouldn't take much to break it."

He held up the fly fastened to the other end. "*Orange Cosseboom*. That's a salmon fly."

"Wouldn't have much luck with that in these waters," Gerald said. The others nodded in agreement. "Water's too murky for a fly like that."

Scott retrieved the stick. He grasped the fly in one hand and the line in the other and pulled. Slowly, one by one, a series of overhand knots untied themselves. Soon the two items separated, one in each of Scott's hands. He looked at the others to see if they realized the significance of what had just happened. No one was paying attention to what he had done. They were too busy discussing what kind of fly should be used at this time of year. Scott stood up.

"I don't like the way this is playing out," he said. "Don't disturb anything else. I think I'll call in the big guns to have a look at this place. You can never be too careful."

Chapter 16

Jim was enjoying the quiet solitude of his office when the phone startled him. His mind was grappling with what had caused Matthew Lane to drive his car through a telephone pole with no thought of stopping. He had been assigned the case the previous Friday. A weeks worth of investigation had turned up no concrete evidence of murder. All his notes and reports were spread across his desk as he struggled to find the missing link. He had read and reread everything before him but no flash of inspiration had struck him.

He pushed the papers aside and took another long sip from his coffee mug. The ringing phone was almost a relief from the frustrating task. He pulled an empty notepad from the drawer in his desk.

"Major Crimes, Detective-Sergeant Jim McDonald," he said into the phone. He had drawn weekend duty. New Sunday morning calls were unusual for the detective branch. Cleaning up paper work was the usual Sunday task.

"Sergeant McDonald, Scott Bowen here. I've got a suspicious drowning you should have a look at." There were no preliminaries. Scott got right to the meat of the matter. Jim recorded all the details Scott had to date and headed for the site. First, he stopped at his apartment and changed. A suit, tie and leather shoes were not the uniform of the day when tromping through the forest along a river bank.

When he arrived, Scott took him aside. "There's nothing definitive here, Sergeant. I've just got a bad feeling about this." He showed Jim the salmon fly. "No fisherman worth his salt would try using a fly like this in these waters. It would be a waste of time. And this line is way too heavy for any kind of fish in this pool. This is a saltwater line." Scott explained the knot holding the fly to the line didn't meet basic fishing standards. Special knots were needed for securely tying nylon. All fishermen quickly learned that fact after losing one or two expensive lures.

Jim didn't fish enough to know what Scott was talking about. Still, he respected the corporal's hunches. After all, his other case was based on a lot less. "Should we bring in the crime scene guys?"

Scott shook his head. "This isn't the scene of the crime. The body was just washing down the river and got caught up on an underwater branch where it narrows at the Gate. Lucky thing. Otherwise, it would have ended up at the bottom of the lake. Might never have been found."

Scott looked back towards the small pool. "Whatever happened took place up river, probably on the other end of this pond." Scott pointed to where the river widened out and made a turn. Another path comes in up there. Both are good fishing spots but fly fishermen prefer the upper location. After this week's heavy rain the Funnel might be flowing too fast to cross. That's its one drawback."

The sergeant followed Scott's gaze. "Guess we'd better check it out then. Should we cross here?"

"I'd say so. The path comes in on the other side." Scott turned to Brad. "Can the three of you handle the body? The sergeant and I will go check the path above the pool. There should be some gear someplace."

Brad stood up and flexed his 230 pounds of solid muscle. "No problem," he said. "You two go play. We'll alert the coroner. May as well ruin his Sunday as well."

The two policemen waded across the river and set off through the woods skirting the edge of the pond. Scott looked back. "Don't wait for us. We'll follow the upper path out; see if we can find his vehicle."

Scott and Jim crawled up the slight incline of the bank and ran into the band of tight, closely growing coniferous trees. Scott forced his way into the brush.

"Wouldn't want to try to get through here with any fishing gear," Jim said as he caught a branch snapping back from where Scott had disappeared into the growth. Scott didn't answer. Jim protected his face and followed at a safe distance.

"The upper path is right up ahead. I can see the clearing," Scott said after a couple of minutes fighting through the seven foot hedge of trees.

He gave a final push and was standing in the clear. Jim popped out behind him and they turned left towards the river searching for evidence that Herb Clattenburg had started his adventure here and not farther up the river.

"Looks like the spot," Scott said after a few seconds. "Here's his lunch and tackle box."

Jim pointed out into the overhanging trees. "There's a fly rod suspended up there."

Scott looked up. "That sort of suggests he slipped and fell. Rod went flying when his arms shot out to catch his balance."

"Maybe, but why did he slip? His line is still intact on his rod. I can see his fly."

"Mickey Finn," Scott said. "At least he knew what he was doing." He studied the bank along the river side. He still carried the stick retrieved from under the water with the line attached.

"See down there, right at water level." He pointed ten feet downstream. "Looks like a fresh break." He held up his branch. "Same thickness."

He worked his way along the edge to the broken stick. The two pieces mated exactly. He snapped a couple of pictures before breaking off the matching length of stick. He passed them both to Jim as he scrambled back up the embankment.

"Someone from the other side may have gotten caught up here," Jim said. Getting tangled in the trees was his principle memory of fishing. He looked across to the clearing on the opposite side.

Scott gave him a skeptical look. "Could have." He held up the line. "But have a look at this."

The portion of the line that should have come from the reel displayed two overhand loops. Scott examined them more closely. "Looks like they held a rock at one time."

Jim leaned in for a closer look. "You think the line had a rock attached to it and was thrown out into the water." He looked out into the fast churning river.

"That's exactly what I think. Then, the other end was wrapped around this stick. If you happened to see the fly dangling there, you'd think someone got caught up in the brush and broke their line. Nothing suspicious." He inserted his hand into the centre of the loops. "About an eight or nine inch rock at this end. With the slope of the bank, it would catch you just above the ankles and below the knees. Great trip line. I sure wouldn't want to stagger over something with the water running this fast. You wouldn't stand a chance. Don't call this area The Funnel for nothing."

Jim considered the surging current. The fresh image of what could happen was all too vivid in his mind. A bloated drowning victim was not a pretty sight.

"When I die," he said, "I want to go quietly in my sleep like my grandmother did." Jim paused. "Not screaming in terror like all the passengers in the car she was driving." He held back on his smile while he waited for Scott's reaction.

It took a couple of seconds for the punch line to sink in; then, Scott gave a harsh grunt of a laugh. "I can imagine this guy's terror, but it would be hard to scream underwater."

"If he opened his mouth at all, that would speed up his inevitable death."

Scott nodded. "Drowning is rumored to be peaceful, but not tangled in a piece of fishing line. Some jerk created a cruel, diabolical trap."

Jim nodded in agreement. His attempt at levity was short lived.

Scott snapped a few more pictures of the scene. He placed the broken sticks carefully into an evidence bag along with the line and the fly.

"Now the really gruesome part," Jim said. "We go and inform the family. The body's been here at least overnight. Any missing person reports?"

Scott shook his head. "Not a peep."

They stood on the front porch of the baby-split waiting for someone to answer the door. The house sat on a quiet cul-de-sac with 100 feet of road frontage. All the houses on the street looked like the same builder was responsible for their creation. The only difference was the colour of the doors and the curtains in the windows. The double driveway stood empty except for Scott's official vehicle. Jim left his parked at the lot by the fire station.

Scott tried to look through the white, lace curtain covering the sidelight windows. There was no movement from inside. Even though he could hear the doorbell when it rang, he knocked, a loud frame rattling knock.

A man appeared on the newly sodded lawn next door.

"I don't think anyone's home. Can I help you?" He slurred his words. When Scott turned, the man noticed his uniform. He stepped back a step. "Sorry, officer. They're all away."

Scott stepped down on to the walk. "Do you know how I can reach them?"

The man shook his head. "I think Marilyn has gone to visit her folks for a few days. Herb went fishing yesterday. I haven't seen him around today. Might be out again. That man loves to fish."

Despite his gruesome mission, that statement drew a smile from Scott. He also loved to fish. "And your name is?" Scott asked.

The man crossed the lawn and extended his hand.

"Dan Cooper. Just moved in a year ago myself. Herb and Marilyn have only lived here for about six months. Lovely people."

"Scott Bowen." Scott shook the man's hand. He turned to Jim. "Detective-sergeant Jim McDonald. You don't know how I could reach Mrs. Clattenburg?"

"Sorry, I don't. Her Mom's first name is Sue, but I don't know the last name. Is there a problem?" Dan stumbled a little.

The two cops noticed but said nothing. "I'd just like to talk to her."

"Herb should be home soon. He's fishing locally. Some place called Basils Gates or The Funnel or something like that. I have a map if you're interested. Don't participate myself. Catch my fish at the super market. Never been shut out." He laughed at his own little joke. Scott forced a smile.

"Herb's business partner was up here a couple of days ago for a barbecue. They spent all evening talking about fishing. Seemed pretty tight. He might know Marilyn's folks or maybe know for sure where Herb is fishing. He suggested the place."

"Do you know his name?"

Dan reached into his shirt pocket and produced a thick pen. The company name, number and slogan were printed on the side. "He told me to use this to keep track of my expenditures and assets. I gather he's the company accountant." He passed the pen to Scott. "Here, keep it."

Scott glanced at the pen. "Clattenburg & Gallant, Office Products. Let us keep your shelves stocked." Both office and cell numbers were included.

"You say you have a map?"

"Somewhere. Joel drew it in case I wanted to try my luck. I took it in case I want to take a client there sometime. I'm a salesman, you know. Whatever works to close a sale."

Jim looked at the empty house once more and withdrew a business card from his shirt pocket. "Could you have Mrs. Clattenburg call me when she gets home. It's important."

Dan took the card. "Sure thing. I'll keep an eye out for both of them. Herb's all right, isn't he?"

"You keep an eye out for them," Jim said, ignoring the question. "That would be a good idea because I don't think you want to be getting too far from home. You especially don't want to be getting behind the wheel of your car."

"Nope," Dan said. "No place to go. I'll just sit out on the lawn and watch for the Clattenburgs. Do my civic duty and maybe have a little drinkie."

Again the two cops looked at each other. Jim pointedly looked at his watch. "You've got an early start on the little drinkies, haven't you?"

Dan laughed. "I'm of British descent. I do my drinking on Greenwich Mean Time. Just relaxing a little. Got a big, big meeting tomorrow. I'll watch for Marilyn."

Chapter 17

"**Y**ou've got to be able to reach him," Claude Jackson pleaded into the phone. "This is a life and death situation here."

"I'm sorry, Mr. Jackson, but as I told you the last five times you called, Mr. Christie is unavailable. He's on an executive retreat on Mt. Whitney in California. There is no way to reach him or any other member of the party."

"Dammit woman, you don't understand. Someone is going to die if I don't reach Christie right away."

An exasperated sigh came across the phone. Wayne Christie spent his days as a union negotiator for the Graphic Arts International Union. Everyone who called for him thought the situation was life or death. Long hours on a picket line with no pay cheque coming in distorted people's views of what life and death really meant. She sympathized with these people but when you came right down to it, the decision to strike was theirs, not Wayne's. Claude Jackson was one of three people trying desperately to reach her boss. She was Wayne's last line of defense for maintaining his sanity. She took this position seriously.

"I've left several messages at the retreat's head office in Modesto. As soon as Mr. Christie comes off the mountain, he will get your message. I'm sorry, Mr. Jackson, but that is the best I can do." She hung up.

Claude snapped the phone away from his ear when he heard the dial tone. Another hang up. He threw the receiver on the desk. This stupid woman didn't realize what a mess he was in. The first couple of times he called on Saturday, he had been polite. That was a mistake. She interrupted that to mean the calls were unimportant. The next time he called he was more insistent. This was his third call today. Time was running out. He could not accept that in this day of electronic communication, Wayne Christie and all those with him did not have at least one cell phone or one pager among them. He'd bet they all carried Blackberries.

He picked up the phone again. This time he would tell the woman the whole story. Then she would understand the importance and would put his call through to Christie. He dialed. The phone rang and rang and rang. After thirty rings the connection was broken. Someone had lifted the receiver and replaced it. She was no longer taking his calls.

Chapter 18

Joel Gallant sat outside the viewing area at the city morgue, head down, fighting off the feeling of nausea that was overtaking him. Jim patiently stood in front of him waiting for the man to compose himself. He held a glass of water in his hand.

Some colour crept back into Joel's ashen face. He looked up.

"Herb loved to fish. The bottom line is that if he had to die, this is the way he would want to go." He took a white handkerchief from his pocket and wiped his brow. Jim offered him the water. Joel accepted the offering and drank it down.

"Poor Marilyn. Yesterday was their anniversary. They had a real spat the day before, Friday that is. Herb insisted he was going fishing for a while on Saturday before they went out. Marilyn told him that if he did, he may as well fish all night. She wouldn't be there when he got home. It's not like Herb to be so stubborn." Joel paused, lost in thought. He gave his head a shake and looked up at Jim again. "It looks like he went fishing."

Jim nodded. "Looks like. Do you know how to reach Marilyn?"

"They've fought like this before. She never stays mad long. She should be home soon. I can call her mother to see if she is there with her. Her mother planted the idea that Marilyn not hang around if Herb went fishing. She can be one old battleaxe. Always causing problems. I'm sure Herb would have stayed home if it hadn't been for his mother-in-law nagging him. It was like she was baiting him to defy her.

She grates on Herb's nerves. I'm sure he went just to spite her."

Joel pulled out his cell phone and punched in a number from memory. "I knew her family before I knew Herb. Marilyn and I used to date. That was a long time ago."

His focus shifted to his phone. "Dr. Thornton, Joel Gallant here. Marilyn doesn't happen to be there?"

Jim watched as Joel listened. Joel was nodding his head. "Right, right," he said. "He can be an ass but you might want to save that criticism. Herb has been in an accident. It might be a good idea if you drive on out to Shad Bay to be with Marilyn for a bit."

Again Joel listened. Jim could see he was trying to impose himself back into the conversation but not having any luck. "Well Dr. Thornton, Sue, we don't like to speak unkindly of the dead..." He flushed. "Oh, I'm so sorry. That just slipped out. Yes, Herb is dead. I'm here with the police. We're on our way to tell Marilyn now. We'll meet you at her house."

He gave Jim a sheepish look. "Sorry, but she was saying some pretty nasty things about Herb. Never forgave me for introducing him to Marilyn."

"So Herb wasn't a well-liked person?"

"Herb, everyone loved him, except his in-laws. That wasn't Herb's fault. They thought Marilyn should have done better. You know, doctor, lawyer, Indian Chief. Not a salesman, even if he did co-own the company."

"Marilyn's mother is a doctor?"

"Psychologist. She teaches at the university."

By now the two men had reached the door of the hospital building. "I'll take my own car and meet you out there," Joel said. "I'd like to be there when we break the news to Marilyn."

Scott's police car pulled into the Clattenburg driveway just as Marilyn was disembarking from hers. Joel followed Scott, parking behind him. Dan Cooper stood at the edge of his property about to call out to Marilyn. The earlier visit of the two policemen had piqued his interest. He had been watching for her to return as promised.

Marilyn had a couple of grocery bags in her hands. She had obviously stopped at a convenience store on the way home for bread and milk. She set the bags down on the seat and turned to face the policeman in her driveway. Then she spotted Joel. Female intuition kicked in.

"Where's Herb?" she said. "Joel, what's going on?"

Joel reached out his arms in a consoling manner. Marilyn pushed them away.

"What has happened to Herb? Is he hurt?"

A dark, green BMW squealed into the driveway behind Marilyn's car. Her mother leapt out.

"I knew he would amount to nothing," she said before anyone had a chance to say anything. "Now look what he's done."

Marilyn looked from her mother to Joel to Scott.

"Somebody tell me what's going on."

Jim stepped to the forefront. "Mrs. Clattenburg, I'm sorry to inform you that your husband appears to have been in a drowning accident." He hated being so blunt, but he was sure someone was about to blurt it out.

Sue Thornton turned on the policeman.

"What do you mean, appears? He's dead isn't he?"

Marilyn's face lost all colour. Her eyes lost focus. "Dead? Herb, dead?" She put a hand on Joel's outstretched arm. "He can't be dead."

"I'm sorry for your loss," Jim said. He was following the script learned at police academy. "We found him earlier today at Basils Gate floating in the river. I'm afraid he drowned."

Marilyn sank to the black asphalt of the driveway. Joel controlled her descent. Then he knelt down to face her. "The only consolation is that he died doing what he loved. That's the bottom line here."

"Bottom line?" Marilyn's eyes came back to life. "The bottom line is a 35-year-old man is dead. He was in the prime of his life. He had a wife and responsibilities. What the hell was he doing at that goddamn river. He should have been home with me. It was our anniversary."

Her mother reached down and pulled her to her feet, crowding between Marilyn and Joel. "Come inside dear. Let me get you some tea."

Marilyn's faded blue eyes lost even more colour, turning to a robin's egg blue. She looked at her mother.

"Is Daddy here? Does Daddy know?"

"No dear. He's fishing in the Annapolis River. I haven't been able to reach him."

Joel took Marilyn's other arm and then looked behind her at Sue. "Still trying to catch the record breaking striped bass is he?"

Sue shot him a look of contempt but said nothing.

Dan had worked his way across the lawn to the driveway. He displayed Jim's business card like an invitation. "Is there anything I can do to help? I've got some tea already made. I'll bring over the pot."

Jim looked at the man. He looked like he was sobering up. Was he being a helpful neighbour or just making sure he didn't miss anything? How many pots of tea had he made in the last couple of hours to guarantee him access to the Clattenburg house?

Jim turned to go up the four steps leading to the front door.

"Where do you think you're going?" Sue Thornton blocked his passage. "You've done what you had to do. You've informed us that Herb is dead, now leave us alone to grieve in peace."

Jim was taken aback by the attack. "There are still a few questions, I have to ask, Ma'am," he said continuing up the steps.

The older woman held her ground. "Is there something you're not telling us?"

Jim stopped. "We consider the death of anyone this age suspicious until we know different. I'll try to be brief but there are some things I have to ask."

By now Dan was back with the teapot. He stood on the bottom step beside Scott.

"Let them in, Mother," Marilyn said. "I want the details anyway."

The little procession paraded in through the front door and up the steps to the living room. Marilyn detoured into the kitchen. Cupboard doors could be heard opening and closing.

"What are you doing out there?" her mother said. "Come in and sit down. Let's get this over with."

"I'm getting some cups and saucers for the tea," Marilyn said. "I don't know which ones are appropriate. The good ones I guess."

Sue went to the kitchen and tried to herd her daughter back into the living-room. "Let me take care of this. You go sit down."

"It's my house, Mother. I can do it."

Then the floodgates burst and the tears started to flow. "How am I going to be able to take care of anything without Herb around? We just bought this house. Can I even afford to live here now? What am I going to live on?"

113

Joel rushed to the kitchen. "Come on Mar. Herb wouldn't leave you without two nickels to rub together. The mortgage is insured and the company had life insurance. You'll be all right financially."

She struggled to control her tears. "And there's still the business. That will be a source of some income." She snuffed back some mucus dripping from the end of her nose.

Joel offered her the sweat stained handkerchief he had used at the morgue.

"Yeah, the business," he said. Slowly he shook his head. "Herb is going to be a hard man to replace. He had the gift of gab. Everyone loved him." Tears could be seen forming at the corner of his eyes.

Marilyn passed him back his handkerchief and gave him a hug. "We'll get through this together," she said.

Jim noticed the intimacy between the two but said nothing. They had dated at one point Joel had told them. How deeply buried were those feelings for each other. Jim returned to his place in the living-room. Sue made sure each of them had a cup and saucer. Dan poured the tea.

"It's nice of you to be so helpful," Jim said to Dan. "Have you known the Clattenburgs long?"

"Ever since they moved in. Herb and I were in the same line of business, so to speak. Everyone in the subdivision is new so we have formed friendships quickly. Besides, this is what one does when a neighbour dies." He held up the teapot.

"Yes, it is," Jim said. "Did you see Herb before he went fishing yesterday?"

Dan stopped to think. "Yeah, I did. I was just getting back from my morning walk. Herb was loading the car with his gear. Said he'd be back as soon as he had a couple of trout for Sunday supper. He didn't like to be skunked."

Dan was quiet for moment. "I went in the house to change my boots. When I came back out, he was gone and Marilyn was leaving for her mother's." He looked over at Marilyn for confirmation. She nodded. "She looked pretty upset."

"Walking where?" Jim asked.

Again Dan hesitated. "No place in particular. I just walk for exercise. No set destination."

Joel studied Dan's mannerisms as he sat explaining his whereabouts to Jim.

"Didn't we once do business together? I thought you looked familiar Friday night but can't quite place from where."

"No," Dan said without hesitation. "I never forget a face."

Joel shrugged. "That's what Herb used to say. Me, I never forget an account number. Good thing Herb was the one meeting the clients."

Jim turned his attention to Joel. "I understand you're a bit of a fisherman as well."

Joel was surprised at Jim's statement. "I am. Used to fish down this way quite a bit, as a matter of fact. When Herb moved here, I was quite excited about going out with him."

"But you didn't go yesterday?"

"No. Year-end audit. An accountant's busiest time of the year."

"The year ends in July?"

"Ours does. Corporate years vary from company to company. Summer's our slack time. Good chance to do inventory, wrap up the books."

Scott took advantage of the lull in the conversation. "Some fish are being caught around here, but the water is a little high from all the rain. Did you tell Herb about any of your favorite spots."

"As a matter of fact, I drew him a map to Basils Gate. You can always catch your limit there. That's where he was supposed to be yesterday. I can't understand how a seasoned fisherman like Herb could drown. I warned him about the force of the water coming down The Funnel and into the pond when the water is high. Even suggested he put the trip off until next week when the water would be lower and I could go with him. He promised me he'd be careful."

Scott pondered how much information to give out. He looked at Jim who nodded for him to continue with his questions. "Herb's chest waders filled with water when he fell in. The buckles at the sides didn't stay tight. Looked like they were broken or something. Anyway, they didn't hold back the water like they should. Weight of the water dragged him under. Didn't have a chance."

Marilyn let out another loud sob and covered her face.

"Damn unlucky break." Joel said. "If I had been there, this never would have happened."

"When Herb decided he was going fishing, there was no stopping him," Marilyn said as she struggled to compose herself again. "It was our anniversary and he still insisted on going out for a few hours. I told him I wouldn't be here when he got home." She put her head down and started crying again.

"There, there, dear," her mother said, putting her arm around Marilyn's shoulders. "I feel as responsible as you do about your not being here. It was my idea for you to come to our place if he went fishing. I thought it would teach him a lesson. He's just like your father. Worse. Too stubborn for his own good."

"Jim's attention focused on the mother. "You knew Herb was going fishing as well?"

"Yes, I was here Friday night. We were having a barbeque. I heard their spat. I don't want to speak unkindly of the dead, but I never did like the man. Didn't have his priorities straight. I told him it was his duty to stay home."

"Mother."

The room became silent as Marilyn pushed her mother's arms from around her.

"I loved Herb. You know that."

Sue glared back at her daughter, refusing to back down. "Love. You weren't in love. You were taken in by his glib tongue. He had that same gift of gab that you father has." Sue's face flushed a little. She looked around the room at the others and then back to her daughter. "If he had loved you, he wouldn't have gone fishing and he wouldn't be dead now. It was his choice. I always told him life was about choices but he never listened to me."

The tears again flowed freely from Marilyn's eyes. "If you hadn't goaded him so much, he would have stayed home. He only went because you made such an issue of it."

Silence again pervaded the room. Jim looked around. "Let me get this straight. Everyone in this room knew Herb was going fishing and where."

More uncomfortable silence. Then Joel spoke up. "Of course I knew. I drew the map. Wish I hadn't now, that's for sure."

He looked over at Dan. "You took a copy. Said you never knew when it might come in handy to know the good fishing spots. Sue didn't have a copy but Mr. Thornton did. He fishes too. More than Herb, if you can believe that. He said he'd love to give the place a try." Joel smiled. "Told me it had better be as good as I claimed." No one shared his brief attempt at levity.

"What time did Herb leave on this trip?" The question was addressed by Jim to Marilyn.

"Somewhere around noon, just before lunch. I really thought he was going to stay home. We had plans for the evening. That's why everyone came up on Friday night. To celebrate early and give us Saturday night alone." She blushed at that statement. "Then the phone rang. He took the call in his den. When he came out he said he was going fishing. He said to stay home would be giving in to my mother." Again she glared at Sue. "It didn't make sense, but I couldn't change his mind. Did you call him?"

"Don't be silly. Why would I?"

Jim waited a few seconds before asking: "And everyone can account for where they were Saturday morning?"

"I've already said I was hiking," Dan said. "But not up there. That's too far away to walk." He looked around at the others for confirmation. Jim thought he looked like he needed a drink.

"Me and my audit," Joel said. "It's a one person job at this stage."

Jim looked at Sue.

"Me? I was shopping by myself, not that it's any of your business. Mr. Thornton left for the Annapolis River to bass fish before the sun was up. He had to catch the tides. So all I could do was go shopping, alone. I have receipts."

"I spent the morning with Herb," Marilyn said, "We were planning our night on the town. Then he insisted he go dip his line for an hour or so. We fought and I went to my mother's. She got back from her shopping trip shortly after I got there. I should have just agreed to go with him and watch. He did invite me along. Being together should have been the important thing." Again tears welled in her eyes.

Jim took some notes but said nothing. He looked at Scott to see if he had any questions. Scott shook his head and got to his feet. "We'll be in touch," he said.

Marilyn gave him an inquisitive look. "I don't understand all the questions. It was an accident, wasn't it?"

"These are just routine questions," Jim said. "We'll be in touch."

Once outside, Jim and Joel stood beside the police car in the driveway. Scott leaned across the roof from the driver's side, listening to the conversation. Joel had followed the two policemen when they left. His car blocked Scott's in the driveway. Joel had other things on his mind. Things to say that he wanted only the cops to hear.

"I don't remember a Dan Cooper," Joel said, "but I do remember a Darryl Cooper. He was our main competitor when we started our business. Looks a lot like Dan."

"Friendly competitors?"

"That's kind of oxymoronic. There was no out and out hostility but we didn't have lunch together. I think Darryl might have gone out of business. Not because of anything we did," Joel hastily added. "He lacked customer service skills. The bottom line is his failure didn't affect our business one way or the other, but our success may have hurt his."

Jim pondered this statement. "You think Dan might be a relative?"

"It's possible. There is an uncanny resemblance."

"And you think he might have held Herb responsible for his brother's business failure?"

"I can only speculate. Dan knew Herb was in sales. They obviously discussed business with each other. People seldom take blame for their own ineptitude. Darryl may have complained to his brother somewhere along the line and blamed Herb. Then as fate would have it, Dan and Herb ended up living next door to each other. I know Herb's death was an accident but sometimes you have to wonder. Herb wasn't the kind of person who would drown himself. He was too good a fisherman for that."

119

The two cops exchanged a glance but remained silent as Joel went on.

"I hate to jump to conclusions, but Dan was at the BBQ Friday night. Put back quite a few stiff drinks. Doesn't look like he let up much as the weekend progressed. It may have been a family trait. From my experience, drunks are always looking for a scapegoat. Who knows, he may have contacted his brother when he found out who Herb was. Then Saturday morning, Darryl may have been at Basil's gate when Herb got there."

Jim nodded at the observation. "Anything's possible," he said. "Answer another question for me Joel. Did Herb often go fishing with his father-in law?"

Joel snorted a sound of disgust. "Never. Despite the impression everyone is trying to give, Herb was a considerate husband. He always fished close to home, never for more that three or four hours at a time.

"The old man was a different kettle of fish. Always after the big one. Travelled all over the province after striped bass. Stayed away over night. Salmon fished in northern New Brunswick on his vacations. The two never went out together to my knowledge. You heard Sue's opinion of Herb. Old man Thornton's was even worse. Herb stole his little girl. Are you a father?"

"No, but I've met lots of them in the line of duty. Herb couldn't have been quite the white knight you describe. His wife did go home to her mother."

"That was Sue's doing. If she hadn't been here Friday night stirring up the pot, that would never have happened. Herb probably wouldn't have gone fishing except for her constant nagging. Even if he did, Sue wouldn't have gone to her mother's. She's blind to the control her mother exerts over her. That was another bone of contention between the two of them."

Joel fell momentarily silent. "Friday night was a mistake. Someone should have told Sue to butt out. I should have told Sue to butt out. She wouldn't let it rest. It was like she came to the party to cause trouble. If she had kept her yap shut, Marilyn and Herb would have celebrated their anniversary in the city Saturday night as planned. Everyone would have lived happily ever after." He shrugged at the simplicity of his conclusion.

"Interesting," was all Jim said. "Did you ever fish with the old man?"

Joel laughed. "Years ago, before Herb and I went into business together and I was dating Marilyn. He would always introduce me to his big shot friends as 'Joel, he's an accountant.' I would give them my card. As long as you had a string of letters after your name, you were qualified to see his daughter. That changed when we opened the business supply store. What I thought of as networking, he called taking advantage of his friendship. He never gave Herb that opportunity."

Scott had been listening silently. "How serious was your relationship with Marilyn?"

"Pretty serious until Herb came on the scene. The same charismatic qualities that led me into business with him led Marilyn down the aisle. My own fault. I introduced them to each other." Joel shrugged in resignation.

"You resented that?"

"A little, at first. But they were made for each other. I was just a place holder until Herb came along. Besides, no one in their right mind would want the Thornton's as in-laws. I warned Herb. That's why he finally moved to Shad Bay. To put some distance between himself and his in-laws. They were never going to let go of their daughter as long as they lived in the same neighbourhood. The old man was an arrogant bastard but Sue, Sue can only be described as a controlling bitch. Maybe that's why Mr. Thornton spent so much time fishing. She resented her husband's time away from home and took it out on everyone else she came in contact with." Joel shrugged. "I sound bitter, I know, but you've never met anyone like these two."

Jim shook Joel's hand. "Thanks for the info." He looked over at Scott. "Let's see if the coroner has found anything of interest."

Chapter 19

"**M**r. C. is in now," Neil Jackson's secretary reported to him. Neil looked at the clock over his office door. It was 10:39 on Monday morning. He was becoming concerned about his brother. The previous weekend he had shown up for the barbecue but only in body. His mind had been elsewhere. Neil cooked a steak the way Claude liked them, medium rare, but most of it went to his dog who had no complaints whatsoever about the way Claude was acting. All week Claude seemed to be distracted, somewhere else, Neil noted.

Neil approached him about the campaign to recapture some of the business lost to the in-house PC's. At first Claude was enthusiastic about the project. They discussed various approaches at length, decided on a course of action and Claude was to get the research in motion to come up with the final figures and put together a hard-hitting, comprehensive approach.

Later in the week, when Neil contacted him for a follow-up, nothing more was done. This was unlike his brother. He wasn't in charge of promotion because he was a member of the family. He had a special talent for getting to the heart of selling points. This project should have been a cakewalk for him. But he hadn't even offered a reason for not completing it.

Neil was aware of Claude's financial difficulties. He was under the impression that problem was taken care of. The time was here for an in-depth, heart to heart talk with his younger sibling.

He got up from his desk, flexed his shoulders, sighed and headed for the door adjoining the two executive suites. The sight he beheld upon opening the door set him back on his heels.

The always present Symphony No. 6 of Beethoven was coming from the speakers. It was in the midst of the fourth movement depicting the tempest and storm. Some musicologists considered Beethoven was writing more about the storm leading to the universal deluge, the end of the world and not a mere wind and rain storm. At the moment Claude appeared to be expecting the same thing.

"My God, Claude," Neil said. "What is the matter with you? You look an absolute mess."

Claude raised his hollow eyes to meet the piercing gaze of his brother. It was as if they didn't register what or who they saw. Then recognition seemed to manifest itself.

"Neil?" he said. "I'm sorry, were you speaking to me?"

Neil regained his composure. He entered the office and walked over to his brother. Claude looked bad at the barbecue but the changes since then were hard to comprehend. This man bore little resemblance to his brother. The light gray suit he wore looked like he had slept in it for a week. There were stains on his wrinkled, gray shirt and blue tie. They looked like they were booze stains.

Now that he was closer, Neil's nose detected the stale smell of alcohol. He was unsure if the scent came from Claude's rumpled clothing or if it was the breath of a man suffering an extreme hangover. Nonetheless, this was not a normal action for his fastidious brother, the man for whom, as Neil had commented at other times, appearance was more important than substance. If that were not true, Claude would say, why do we use glossy paper and coloured inks on our presses?

Neil pulled a chair up to the side of the walnut desk so that he could reach his brother. He sat down and placed one hand on Claude's left arm. It was then he noticed the tears. "My God, Claude, whatever has happened to you?"

"Oh, Neil, I've done something terrible. No, beyond terrible. It was disgusting."

This had been a familiar scene in their youth. The first time he could remember was when he was seven and Neil was ten. Claude had devastated a neighbour's flower garden with his tricycle. Afraid to go home, he had gone crying to Neil.

His big brother had advised him to face up to it. Pick a bouquet of flowers from the remaining good ones and go apologize to the neighbour. The ruse had worked. As upset as she was, Claude looked too cute to be yelled at. She patted him on the head and accepted his apology while trying to fight back the urge to laugh at the boy. Appearance over substance, it had started early. As Billy Crystal said: "The important thing is how you look and I look marvelous."

At nineteen, Claude's girlfriend became pregnant. Again he took his problem to Neil. "Do you love her?" Neil had asked point blank. When Claude answered in the affirmative, Neil simply said: "Then what's the problem, marry her." There had been a huge outcry from other family members on both sides but thirty-three years later they were still happily married.

These events paled in the light of his current indiscretion. To arrange a murder, how could he have ever contemplated it? Not just arrange it, but pay to have it carried out. Again he found himself being the humble supplicant to his father confessor.

"This is a new low, even for me," Claude said. His self esteem was rapidly fading. He jumped in with both feet. "I hired a hit man to kill Matthew Lane, a professional killer."

He expected to see a look of revulsion come into his brother's eyes. Hiring a killer was worse than murdering someone yourself. It was cold and calculated and in a way, the act of a coward. The look of disgust wasn't there, only compassion.

"Neil, do you understand what I said? I paid a man to kill that rotten bastard Matthew Lane."

Neil was familiar with Matthew Lane. Not too long ago Lane was retained by Jackson Printers and Publishers as a time and motion expert. It was Claude's idea. Lane promised to make the company much more productive without any major capital outlay, except of course for his fees. These fees would be more than covered by the savings.

His method of increasing productivity was to get rid of a third of the workforce, work the ass off all the remaining employees and at the same time pay them less for their efforts. The time was ripe he pointed out. The workers were aware of the business being lost to desktop computers. They should be willing to make a sacrifice. Scare them with the new technology that was sweeping the printing industry as well as other manufacturing concerns and leaving lost jobs in its wake. He guaranteed it would work.

The increased profits would go to Neil, Sally and Claude as sole proprietors.

Neil considered loyal employees one of the major assets in his company. He concluded they were more productive when they were paid a decent wage and allowed to make some of their own decisions regarding working conditions. If new technology was a threat, the solution was to adapt to it. Make it work for you, not against you. Keep his staff on the leading edge. They already understood printing, technology was just a change of tools. Sally supported this view as well. To date that method served JP&P well.

After watching Lane snoop around for a week making all kinds of notations on his clipboard, Neil decided Lane had other intentions which had nothing to do with increasing productivity. Neil personally escorted Lane from the premises. Lane found what he was looking for however, as Claude would soon discover.

Neil put his arm around his brother's shoulder and gave him a gentle hug. He stepped back when there was no response.

"No wonder you look so terrible. Carrying all this guilt around with you. It was a week or so ago Lane bought it, wasn't it?" No answer.

He took Claude by both shoulders and gave him a little shake. "It's over and done with Claude. You've got to put this behind you. Lane is dead. Everyone thinks it was an accident or suicide. Move on."

"No, Neil, you don't understand. The killer didn't do it. Lane killed himself before the assassin had a chance to get to him. He didn't deliver the package."

"What package? Claude what in the hell are you talking about?"

"The package. He was supposed to kill Lane. That's how they talk. Instead of killing someone they deliver a package." His voice lowered. "It doesn't matter anyway. He didn't do it."

Claude started to sob again. Big, salty tears flowed down his ruddy cheeks. "He's going to kill someone else if I don't pay him."

Now Neil did look shocked, stunned.

"What the hell are you saying? You hired a professional killer and then reneged on the payment. Claude, you're not that stupid."

This outburst caught Claude off guard. "But he didn't do it. Don't you understand? Lane killed himself, accidentally or otherwise. He didn't deliver the package."

The elder Jackson sat back in his chair and massaged his forehead with the fingers of his right hand for a few seconds. Then he looked up at his still sobbing brother and shook his head.

"That is why they are called professionals, Claude. They can make any death look like an accident... or suicide... or natural causes ... or anything else they damn well want it to look like." He paused between each method. His anger building. "They're professionals. They always deliver the fucking package."

Claude sat back in his chair. He had never seen Neil so angry. Again Neil leaned towards his brother. "Claude, you've got to pay him. These guys don't fool around. They don't send two or three notices in the mail saying if they don't receive your cheque they will turn your file over to a collection agency. Claude, they kill people. Do you understand? Kill. Dead. You must pay him today."

He reached for the phone receiver on the desk and passed it to Claude. "Call him right now and arrange to make the payment. Right now Claude. Don't fool around."

Claude looked crestfallen. He stared at the phone in his hand.

"I can't."

Neil grabbed his shoulders again. This time he shoved him back into his chair.

"What do you mean, you can't?" Neil almost screamed. "Don't be stupid. You must."

Then he relaxed his grip and lowered his voice. "Claude, you must," he said again. "If it's a question of money, how much do you need? I'll write you a cheque right now."

Claude looked at his brother. Not once had he asked why he hired the assassin, why he wanted Lane killed or what kind of trouble he was in. Now, still without question, he was volunteering to give him the money to pay Crosley off. If only it was just a question of money.

On Saturday, after a grueling week of worry and misery, he decided to pay Crosley. Then he made the anguishing discovery. He couldn't locate the deposit slips.

He racked his brain to remember where they could be hiding. He looked in his car, the office, his den, everywhere. All to no avail. He knew he had them somewhere safe where no one would find them, himself included as it turned out.

A hundred times he took every business card, credit card, piece of paper out of his wallet. Nothing.

He searched his closet. What had he been wearing that day? He couldn't remember. Every pocket of every outfit he owned was turned inside out. The elusive slips were never to be seen again.

At one point he even found himself reciting a verse from his youth at parochial school.

"St. Anthony, St. Anthony,
Please come around.
Something has been lost
And must be found."

The first time he could remember using this prayer had been in school when he was about twelve. He was to pass in a report to Sister Mary Michael. He looked all through his school bag. No report. All the time she was standing there, tapping her foot, ruler in hand, a penguin conductor.

The others in the class had laughed when he came out with the verse. Not Sister Mary Michael. One would have thought she would have been an advocate of prayer. Just as she reached out to grab him by the ear, he pulled the report out of his bag. The prayer had worked. It had worked.

What an opportunity for her to point out the power of prayer. What an opportunity for her to lecture the class about the advantage of having faith. What an opportunity to extol the virtues of being on familiar terms with the saints. But she passed on all these opportunities. Instead she snapped the paper from his hand and warned him that his smart mouth was going to get him in trouble in the future.

Well Sister, I'm in trouble now he thought. Real trouble.

"St. Anthony, St. Anthony,
Please come around.
Something has been lost
And must be found."

Claude missed the irony of the current situation. He was evoking the power of prayer, appealing to the saints, to help him pay off a hired killer. God always answers prayers. Sometimes he says no. This was one of those times. No, Claude, no.

Claude didn't have the foggiest idea of how to get in touch with Crosley. Crosley always contacted him.

When Claude first came up with this lunatic idea, he contacted the GAIU representative who had told Neil about Crosley. Claude suggested the company was publishing a book about professional killers and wanted to consult a known pro to verify some of the things in the book.

The rep sounded dubious of the story but within a week, Crosley contacted Claude. After some waltzing around the deal was struck.

All night Saturday and all day Sunday, Claude tried in vain to reach the rep again. With every unsuccessful phone call he took another drink. It is a toss up which will be bigger, his phone bill or his bar bill. Regardless, the rep was not to be reached.

Now within three hours, some innocent person was going to die. It was Claude's fault but he didn't even know who to warn. How could he warn anyone without sounding like an idiot himself or confessing what he had done?

"No, Neil, you don't understand. It's not the money. I just can't. I don't know how." Claude explained the method of payment and the frenzied weekend of searching to his brother. Then he explained what was destined to happen at two o'clock that afternoon.

Fear came into Neil's eye. The possible victims ran through his mind. Himself? His family? Claude's family? An acquaintance? The possibilities were endless. What would be the thought process of a professional killer? There was no way he could put himself inside that mind.

He settled back into his chair. He would have to think this through. They would have to alert and protect their families without alarming them. It went without saying, they could not be told of the exact problem.

What would his family be doing this afternoon around two o'clock? To be honest he had no idea. He put in long days working in the plant, frequently taking extra work home with him at night. Outside of the occasional weekend barbecue, he seldom saw them anymore with the exception of Sally.

"I'll call Sally and think of some pretense to get her over to your house, something to keep them inside. Make sure all the alarms are armed and the doors locked. That will keep the women safe," Neil said. "Both of my sons are away on vacation, I think. I have no idea where." The killer probably knew more about his family's whereabouts than he did, Neil thought. "What about yours?"

Claude shook his head. "I don't know. It's been over a week since I've talked to any of them. If he harms either of them or the grandchildren, I'll kill him myself."

Claude was starting to get a grip on himself, Neil noticed. A shaky grip but at least he was thinking again even if his thoughts weren't what you would call rational. A salesman against a hired gun, sorry Claude, you lose.

For the next hour they tossed around possible victims and plausible scenarios to warn them without arousing too much suspicion.

At last, Claude said: "I'll have to stay here in the office in case Crosley calls. Then I can put a stop to this insanity. Surely he'll call once more before he does anything rash." Claude was partly correct. Crosley checked the bank machine one final time before sending Cooper to his destiny. He had no way of knowing Claude would be stupid enough to lose the deposit slips.

"You go and keep a protective eye on the women. Nothing is going to happen before this afternoon anyway. As a safety precaution take the Mercedes and leave your Buick in the lot. The one thing we are certain of is that I'm not the intended victim, this time."

The cars each man drove reflected their lifestyles. Claude drove a big, shiny black Mercedes, a symbol of his climb up the social ladder and proclaiming the success he figured he'd achieved. Neil, on the other hand, drove a Buick, a fancy one mind you, with all the bells and whistles, but still just a Buick.

"If Crosley doesn't call so I can stop him or if, heaven forbid, no one else gets zapped, we'll have the mechanics take your car apart piece by piece and put it back together again without any flaws in it." Claude said. "He claims to have killed Lane in a car accident."

The tempest in the background music gave way to a single clarinet playing a shepherd's song. Now that a plan was formulated, like the symphony things seemed to be settling down.

"Good idea," Neil said. "I'll call you from the house." He got up, replaced the chair to where it belonged and exited into his own office with one backward glance at his troubled brother. He still looked terrible, but at least now he was thinking again.

After advising his secretary that he would be out for the rest of the day, he stepped into the hall and started towards the parking lot. Most of the vehicles there were less than four years old. This reflected the standard of living that his employees enjoyed and he felt a little bit of pride about that.

Dan Cooper was just leaving the sales department. Neil noted how good Dan looked for a Monday morning. Good, he thought. Dan has turned things around. No intervention was required.

Neil gave him a slap on the back as he caught up to him. "You're looking chipper this morning, Dan."

Cooper turned and looked at his boss. Closer inspection revealed slightly bloodshot eyes. "Thank you, Mr. Jackson," he said. "I don't feel so great. My neighbour died in a tragic fishing accident yesterday. I spend a good deal of the night consoling the family."

"I'm sorry to hear that," Neil said. "Did he leave any kids?"

"No, just a wife. I guess that's a good thing."

The expression of Cooper's face changed. He forced a smile. "Things are looking up here though. I'm on my way to meet a client right now. This catalogue deal is in the bag. Just a few last minute things to clear up and it's a done deal. I'll be back shortly with cheque in hand."

Neil smiled. He heard of the catalogue order and was hoping it would come off. Press time was booked, everything was ready at this end. Now it was up to the client to supply the product. At one point he had considered having Claude intervene to insure success. As events had turned out, the past week would have been poor timing for Claude. Dan, however, seemed to have it all together again.

"Good luck," Neil said as they parted at the doorway, each headed to their respective part of the lot. "Landing this account will make us both very happy." He emphasized the both which brought a broad smile to the face of Dan Cooper. That was how Neil would remember the man.

Chapter 20

B ob Burke, a.k.a. Robert Crosley, sat at a corner table at the House of Mei Mei Restaurant in Rockingham. Two glasses of amber liquid sat on the table. The pleasant smells of Chinese food from the buffet filled the room. Murals of lions and dragons, gold on red, lined the walls.

Bob looked down the line of shiny, silver serving dishes. There was sweet and sour chicken in a pale red sauce, garlic spare ribs, beef hiding amongst bright green broccoli flowers, bamboo shoots, various chow meins and dish after dish of fried rice with different specks of meat or fish in them along with little shards of green stuff.

He could tolerate Chinese food, but it wasn't his favorite. This place was chosen for its location more that its cuisine. The Bedford Highway ran past its door and straight into the city without any major turns until you reached the traffic lights at Kempt Road. From there a hard left took you onto the approach to the A. Murray MacKay Bridge across the harbour to Dartmouth. This was the combination of roads he needed for his plan to succeed. Once again The Messenger of God chose the time and place. Once again he had followed the 7-Ps.

It was also right next door to the Royal Bank. Crosley made one final check on the account. The money was still not there. The time for talking had ended.

"Dan," he waved at the figure coming in the door of the dimly lit restaurant.

Dan Cooper looked in his direction, smiled and headed to the table.

Burke stood extending his hand which Cooper pumped, a salesman's hand shake. At last this deal was coming together for him. The commission was committed to time payments long ago when sales were better. This order would give him a chance to catch up on his back debts.

Plastic money allowed a person to appear to maintain his standard of living but even VISA expected to be paid some time. The tone of their letters changed from "buy, buy, buy" to "pay, pay, pay, or else" after a couple of missed payments.

The threatening notices were arriving in the mail of late. "We don't want to have to turn your account over to a collection agency but if we don't hear from you soon, we will have no choice. This," the letter went on "will have an adverse effect on your credit rating and we don't wish to do this. We have only your best interests at heart. Blah, blah, blah." Yeah, right. It was a form letter.

Now, finally, he could keep some corporate computer happy, as well as himself.

"I took the liberty of ordering a couple of drinks," Burke said as they slid into their green leather chairs which looked out over the restaurant. He pointed to the glass at Cooper's place, then took his own, raised it and as the ice cubes clinked together he said: "To a successful business relationship."

"I'll drink to that," Cooper said. He noticed his drink was neat but that was all right. He took a slug, gasped. Water came to his eyes as he inhaled a deep breath.

"Wow," he said when he could speak. "That's what I call a strong drink. I think they forgot the mix."

Burke tipped his own glass, downing it in one swallow and licked his lips.

"A strong drink for a strong partnership," he said. He caught the waitress's eye and held up two fingers. "Two more of the same over here, please." He gave her his best Tom Cruise-like smile then looked back at Cooper.

"Drink up," he said.

"Right." Cooper didn't want to do anything to upset his client. Down went the rest of his drink. His face flushed a bright red as the liquid roiled around in his stomach but he managed to force a smile. "Let's make the next one on the rocks."

The perky, young waitress arrived in her starched red and white uniform, set the drinks on the table after holding them up in front of her as she studied them in the dim light.

"I hope I got them right," she said. "Are you ready to order?"

Burke shot a quick glance at Cooper. He hadn't attached any significance to the waitress's remark about the drinks.

"What do you think?" Burke asked. "Eat first or business first?"

Cooper didn't want to appear anxious but he did want to get this deal cemented. He shrugged leaving the decision to Burke.

Burke looked past the server to the steaming table of food at the front of the restaurant.

"If we are just going to have the buffet, we can just help ourselves at anytime?" He took note of her name tag—Shirley—and added her name to the question.

The mention of her name produced a smile. "Sure, help yourself," she said, taking the two empty glasses. She wheeled and swished away, looking as good leaving as she had coming.

Burke brought his briefcase up to table level.

"Let's get this out of the way and then enjoy our lunch," he said.

Cooper nodded. He was eager to wrap up the business end of things. Burke reached up and pulled the heavy shroud of a curtain open to allow a little extra light to shine on the table and illuminate the papers required to wrap up the deal.

The waitress delivered another round of drinks while they put the finishing touches on the printing order. Burke had most of the material in camera-ready form, Cooper was pleased to see. The entire centre section was already offset negatives supplied by the franchiser to prevent any quality or typographical errors Burke explained. Yeah, thought Cooper, at least the mistakes that are there will be yours. He could remember one cook book they had made. One of the recipes was for date squares. Everything looked fine except they forgot to include the dates in the list of ingredients and then tried to renege on payment even though the mistake was theirs. Supplied negatives were perfect with him.

This would reduce the cost even more and would probably mean a bonus for him. He sipped his third drink. They seemed to be going down much easier now.

Burke gathered all the papers together and placed them in two large manila envelopes. Then he reached into his inside jacket pocket and produced a cheque. "I guess you'll need this to start the presses rolling."

Dan looked at the numbers and calculated his percentage.

"That is what greases the wheels," he said. He reached out to take the money.

Burke held back the cheque. "I'll just toss it in this envelope with the other papers," he said. "Keep it all together."

Dan looked at his outstretched hand for a second and then dropped it to the table. "Makes sense. We don't want to soil our hands on the grease."

Burke laughed and reached out his own hand to Dan. "Give me your keys and I'll get this stuff out of the way. I'll drop it off in your car while you get some food. Maybe I'll get the little lady to make you up a plate so you can just sit here and relax. I'll be right back."

That sounded good to Dan. He didn't feel up to walking around. Some food in his stomach would fix him right up though.

"Shirley," Burke put his hand on her soft shoulder as he walked up behind her. It held a five dollar bill. "Fix up a plate for my friend over there please. Just give him a little of everything."

He slipped out the door while she was still looking where he pointed. Cooper smiled at her and gave a slight wave.

When the food arrived, he noticed she prepared him a small plate, sticking to the vegetables, with nothing too heavy or greasy. She must have been thinking about the number of drinks the two men had consumed as well. Cooper was thankful for that. He did not want to get sick inside the restaurant.

Burke stepped into the bright afternoon sunshine and shielded his eyes. Overhead a few wispy clouds cluttered the blue of the July sky. He looked around and spotted Cooper's car parked next to his own rental. It was a two year old Chrysler purchased when Cooper was at the top of his game, four-doors, white on red.

Great, he thought. This makes everything a lot easier.

He threw the briefcase and envelope into his own trunk and took out a duplicate envelope and transferred it to Cooper's car. As he was putting it in he noticed a cell phone lying on the front seat. A grin crossed his face as he picked up the phone and dropped it into his pocket. This could come in handy later on in the game.

A few minutes later, Burke returned empty handed. He gave Cooper his keys and filled himself a plate. He felt hungry. Everything was ready to go.

"Be prepared for major changes," Cooper read his fortune cookie message at the end of his meal. "I'm ready for some changes for the better." His speech was only slightly slurred. Three martini lunches wouldn't be a problem for this guy, Burke thought. He holds his liquor well. The autopsy readings will be the same, however, whether he is stone sober or stoned out of his mind. In fact, he will just be stone dead.

"I hope we have a long and prosperous working relationship," Cooper said to Burke. "There are not many people who can drink like you do and not show any effects."

Burke laughed. "It just takes lots of practice. Serious, dedicated practice." The truth of the matter was that while Cooper was drinking his triples to please his client, the client was drinking flattened ginger ale, Canada Dry against Canadian Club. There was no contest.

He had made arrangements with the bartender beforehand. He explained that Cooper was his boss and looked on drinking as a machismo thing, a desired quality, mainly because he enjoyed it so much himself. For ten bucks, the bartender agreed to help make him look good. A few good shakes of the bottle flattened the ginger ale. A dollar a shake the bartender figured. He enjoyed being part of the little deception. Some bosses deserved to be fooled.

Burke looked at his watch.

"It's ten to two, Dan," he said. "I hate to rush off but I have another meeting with a buyer. I'll pick up the tab on the way out and we'll get together when we have the page proofs ready. I'd like to check over the few changes we made before they go to press." This was standard practice. Dan suspected nothing out of the ordinary.

Burke stood up, looked over at the food and added: "This is an all you can eat buffet so feel free to keep on eating. Would you like another drink before I tally the bill?"

Cooper seemed to think about that for a minute but must have decided that he had too much to drink already. He declined. He eased back his chair and came to his feet, testing how steady he was.

"You're right Bob. I'd better get back to the office too and get the ball rolling on this."

Together they walked to the front of the restaurant. Burke turned towards the cashier to pay the bill. Sixty dollars for drinks plus tip, fifteen for food, a little over eleven for the tax, you mustn't forget to pay Caesar his due. Total: a hundred dollar bill counting the tip to Shirley covered it. His job did have its expenses but at a thousand a day from Jackson, he would come out ahead. Further refusal on Jackson's part was inconceivable. That option would prove fatal.

"Shirley, could you call a taxi for my friend?" Burke said to the waitress as he walked by.

"No problem," she said, evidently relieved that this particular patron wasn't driving his own car. "It should only take about a minute. There's a stand just down the road."

Cooper made a pit stop at the bathroom on the way out and was now waiting for him at the door. He joined him and they walked outside in the bright afternoon sun.

"I'll be seeing you, Dan," he shook his hand once again. "I just have to make a phone call before my cab comes."

"No need for a cab buddy. I'll be glad to drop you off anyplace."

"Thanks, but the taxi is already on its way. Besides I'm going in the opposite direction to you." He steered Cooper towards his car and then headed for the phone booth down by the highway just as his ride pulled into the parking lot. Oh great, he thought. What a time for them to be super efficient. He waved the car over to the phone booth and asked the guy to wait while he made a phone call.

Cooper fumbled with his car keys, after some difficulty inserted them into the ignition, started his car, coasted back out of the parking spot almost hitting the cab, gave Burke a sheepish smile, then eased out into afternoon traffic and on to his meeting with destiny.

The cab driver was looking at him with disgust when he noticed Burke back at his door. He had a five dollar bill in his hand. He rolled down the window, letting the air-conditioned air escape into the heat of the day.

"Sorry man," Crosley was saying. "My next appointment is going to meet me here instead of at his office. Take this for your troubles." He offered the bill to the cabby.

"No problem," he said. No ride, no fare on the meter. This would be all his. He had only driven about 200 meters. "Thanks."

Crosley checked his watch again. It was one-fifty-four. The bridge was six minutes away. Everything was on schedule. He took Cooper's cell phone out and checked his watch again. Five minutes to wait.

Chapter 21

While Dan Cooper and Bob Burke were enjoying lunch at the Chinese restaurant, Jim McDonald was still tracking down leads in Matthew Lane's death. It was agreed that Scott Bowen would handle the early stages of the Clattenburg case alone. His knowledge of fishing gave him an advantage over Jim. They would divide and conquer. Solve both cases.

While driving around the day before, Scott had brought Jim up to speed on the Lane accident scene reconstruction. It pretty much proved what Jim had known from personal experience. An examination of the filament from the broken brake light confirmed that the brakes had never been touched. Dan Levy could tell that from the colour of the wire. Black indicated the wire was cool when broken; gray would have meant it was hot and the light on. The filament was black. The piled up rubber from the tires indicated the car was still accelerating when it hit the first sign. Suicide was the obvious conclusion. On this point, Jim wavered from the official explanation.

"You're still from the 'possessed by the devil' school of thought," Scott had said.

Jim laughed and told Scott that the desk jockey who ordered the police to be on the lookout for strange cars was none other than Inspector Holland.

Scott conceded that the Inspector may have had other things on his mind.

Jim had a few more of Matthew Lane's former employees to interview. Next on his list was a chat with the chauffeur, James Nelson.

143

McDonald had only recently found out about the chauffeur. At first, it had not occurred to him that Lane would have someone else to do his driving. In retrospect, knowing how wealthy Lane was, Jim realized it should have been obvious to him. The big question now was: Why wasn't the chauffeur driving the car on that fateful day? The explanation had better be good. He would keep an open mind but this might be his first real break in the case. At last a suspect with a name and not just an overheard voice in a meeting.

Jim checked his watch as he pulled into the underground garage at Lane Investments. He was early. This would give him some time to look around and see who else might know anything about the events leading up to Lane's demise.

He noted that he wasn't in the main part of the parking complex but in a smaller walled off section. This was the entrance he was told to take, however, when he arranged to meet James Nelson. He glanced around at the few cars parked in here—a Cadillac, a Mercedes, a Lincoln, two foreign sport jobs. He could never tell them apart. There were no compacts here. This place had never heard of an impending gas shortage. More than likely it shared in the rewards from spreading that myth.

He parked his car and started to get out. A uniformed man held the door shut.

"Sorry sir," the man said in a polite but firm voice. "This is private parking."

McDonald looked up at the muscular, blond headed man in his early twenties, who appeared from nowhere. He wore a tailored, white shirt with black tie under a dark blue sports coat and matching dress pants. He produced his badge.

"Thought so. You must be here to see me. I'm James Nelson." The man opened the car door and stepped back.

Jim took in his broad shoulders, narrow waist and powerful looking legs. Nelson did more than just drive the car for Lane. You didn't have to be a detective to figure that out.

McDonald had suspected as much. After arranging the meeting, he did some checking on Nelson's background. Among the things he discovered was Nelson was licensed to carry a gun. No bulges were noticeable in the well-tailored uniform. That could have been just part of the tailoring. This interview was not with a chauffeur but with Lane's body guard. If this were true, the question bared repeating, where had he been on that fatal Wednesday night? Not guarding the body it seems.

"There is an office over here where we can talk." Nelson indicated a doorway across the garage floor. He then stepped back and let McDonald lead the way.

"Nice place," Jim said as his gaze took in furnishings after he entered the office. One wall had a chesterfield running the length of it. There was a small desk in the corner with a fridge beside it and a microwave oven tucked neatly between them. Along the back was some nautilus equipment. Unlike most purchases of this type, this machinery looked as though it was used, a lot.

A bookcase covered the entire length of the opposite wall. Jim noticed there was an interesting mix of both hard covers and paperbacks. Some of the tomes looked like textbooks. He looked closer and discovered this to be fact. They also appeared to be well used. Others were popular novels of the day—Stephen King, Scott Grisham, Steve Martini, heavy on the lawyer stories.

Nelson noticed where he was looking. "I'm taking some correspondence courses from the local university," he said. This job consists of a lot of time spent just waiting. It seemed like a worthwhile way to fill it."

145

Jim nodded in agreement. "Philosophy?" he asked, judging his guess from the titles of the books.

Nelson smiled. "A healthy mind in a healthy body."

Jim took his notebook from his inside jacket and flipped the book open, rifled back and forth through the pages and found what he was looking for.

"The day Mr. Lane died," he began, "you weren't driving him. Was that unusual?" He may as well get right to the heart of the matter before Nelson got too comfortable talking to him.

The chauffeur leaned against the desk, sitting on the corner.

"It was my day off." He did not elaborate. He was following the corporate dictum of not volunteering any information.

"Who knew you would be off that day?" McDonald said when no additional information was forthcoming.

Nelson looked surprised at the question. "I'm off every Wednesday. What is the point of these questions? The boss died in a car accident."

"Right. The accident part is still to be determined. Unfortunate for Mr. Lane that it was your day off. How good a driver was your boss?"

Nelson laughed. "My boss could drive circles around almost anybody. He had a chauffeur because he did as much work in his car as he did in his office. Unused time was wasted time. That's why he paid for these college courses I'm taking. He didn't want me wasting my time either."

The policeman made a notation in his book. "How do you explain such a good driver having an accident?"

Nelson looked off in the distance as if this were not the first time he had pondered that question but as of yet he had not come up with an answer. After careful consideration, he said: "Why does anyone have an accident? The boss liked to drive fast. I think his secret ambition was to be a race car driver or something like that. You know, like Paul Newman. He liked speed. I figure he was trying to see how fast he could take the corner and lost it."

Judging from what McDonald heard about Lane this sounded like a plausible theory. Jim could have believed it if he hadn't witnessed the accident himself. There was no attempt made to try to make the corner. Lane was not enjoying the speed on this occasion, not one bit. Jim kept this information to himself.

"Who has access to the car besides yourself?"

The chauffeur shook his head.

"No one." He sounded emphatic. "Only two people ever drove that car. The boss and me. I looked after the car. If it wasn't locked up here or in his own garage, I was with it."

"There must have been other people in the car sometimes. Mechanics, cleaners, gofers getting papers, somebody?"

"When the car required mechanical work, which wasn't very often, I stayed with it. I did all the cleaning and polishing myself and there were no gofers. If Mr. Lane required something from the car, he would call me on my cell phone."

"And you would leave the car unattended while you delivered it?" Jim's eyebrows rose as he finished the question.

"Only for a couple of minutes and that didn't happen often," Nelson said. "Mr. Lane was well organized. He didn't forget things in the car."

"There was a Tim Horton's cup in the garbage bag. Yours?"

"No, the car was spotless, inside and out, Wednesday morning. Anything you found would have been added by Mr. Lane. Like everyone else, he liked his Tim's," Nelson smiled.

147

"Stopped in every morning, every evening. Went inside himself and picked out the freshest looking pastry. No favorites. Just wanted it fresh. I'd vacuum out the car Thursday morning first thing."

"You say it was locked in this garage. I just drove right in."

"No, I let you in. I saw you coming on the monitor." Nelson indicated a small television on his desk with a fixed picture of the parking lot entrance. "Car that plain had to be a cop car. There's a retractable steel bar that blocks the entrance."

"So you would know if anyone unauthorized was in here."

"Doesn't happen. There's a security booth at the entrance of the public lot. They keep people who don't belong out of here. I was expecting you so I let you in. Otherwise, it's just company executives."

Jim nodded. This would bear looking into. He made a note to talk to the security guards. If Nelson was telling the truth about being off on Wednesdays, he wouldn't know for sure what had taken place here.

"Who fills in as chauffeur on Wednesdays? Someone must take your place."

"Only me and the boss drive that car. If he needed a lift on a Wednesday, there was always someone around to drive him in their vehicle. He didn't have to ask twice for a volunteer." Nelson gave Jim a little smirk, "or he could afford to take a cab if he had to. That Caddy, it was his baby. No one else touched it."

Of course, Nelson thought, there was the odd girl that he had taken out. Fancy Cadillacs could be a great way of meeting and picking up women. The boss was a man. He didn't object to this use as long as Nelson remembered the back seat wasn't a motel room.

And then there was his new friend with whom he traded CDs. Had he been around the day of the accident? Nelson was off so he wouldn't know but come to think of it he hadn't seen either him or those CDs since the accident. There was one CD in particular that had all his favorites on it. He gave a list to the guy and he produced him a CD of extremely high quality. It was in the stereo machine constantly from that time. It might have been lost at the accident site. He would look into it.

At any rate, neither of these incidences was worth mentioning. They had nothing to do with Matthew Lane and Nelson didn't want to give the cop any wrong impressions about his having men friends who gave him gifts. He wasn't gay.

McDonald returned his notebook to his pocket and brought out a business card. He handed it to Nelson.

"If you think of anything that might be of help, give me a call." He got up and started for the door then turned back.

"I notice you carry a gun," he said. "Why is that?"

Nelson felt behind his back for the weight in his belt. He realized the cop was bluffing and he had fallen for it.

"I have a license," he said. "I'm a bonded carrier. Sometimes I'm required to carry large amounts of cash or bearer bonds. It goes with the job."

McDonald looked interested. "Cash?" he asked.

Nelson shifted from one foot to the other.

"Yeah, cash. Some people still do use it," he said. "You don't understand big business..." He hesitated and looked down at the card for a name. "...Sergeant. There are two main reasons for cash over other methods of payments.

"There are transactions where people want to remain anonymous. To do this they use cash instead of cheques. No paper trail. Harder to trace." Nelson's voice took on a patronizing tone as he explained. He rubbed shoulders with the moneyed people, understood their thinking, unlike this simple policeman.

"Were there many of these deals?" McDonald tried to give the impression that he considered this a learning process rather than advancing his investigation. As long as subjects talked, he didn't care why.

"Enough that I considered it important enough to carry a gun."

"Who were these deals with?"

"I don't know. That's what makes them anonymous, Sergeant." There was a touch of sarcasm in his voice.

McDonald thought he might be on to something.

"Your memory might improve if we take you downtown," he said. "This is a murder investigation."

"We are downtown. I don't know anything here and I won't know anymore at police headquarters. Don't try to hassle me, man.

"If I thought the boss was murdered and I knew anything that would help you catch the son of a bitch that did it, I would be overjoyed to pass it on. As it is I don't know. If what you say is true, that bastard did me out of a fantastic job. It's not the same around here now that the place is run by lawyers instead of Mr. Lane." Sincerity replaced the sarcasm in his voice. "So don't worry, if I think of anything useful, you'll be the first to know."

This sincerity convinced Jim not to pursue the matter any further for now. The chauffeur had not considered murder before. Now that the seed was planted, he would give it time to grow and flourish before he pushed for more information.

"You said there were two reasons for using cash," McDonald said as he changed the subject and hoped to keep Nelson in a cooperative mood. "What is the other?"

Nelson laughed a short harsh laugh.

"It lacks the compressive ability of cheques which allows them to spring back and make them bounce. Those guys trust each other less than we simple folk do. They, after all, know how they got to the top of the heap. You know, anything goes as long as it works for you.

"And, a cheque is merely a promise to pay at a later date. It doesn't mean a damn thing until it is successfully cashed. Successfully is the operative word here. With cash, there is no waiting period. It clears at once. No one can call the bank and cancel cold, hard cash."

The policeman nodded. Nelson enjoyed being close to the rich and powerful but he wasn't blinded by their way of life. He could be depended on to pass on any information which he might stumble across.

"Right. Were there any people who paid cash on a regular basis?" He was fishing but it might pay off. People were killed for less. Lane may have been shaking someone down. He had the power.

"There was one guy," Nelson said.

The sergeant hadn't expected a reply this fast. "Who?"

Nelson looked thoughtful and continued. "'He used to pay around sixteen thousand a month. Came in regularly for the last couple of years. Out of my league as a monthly payment, hell, out of my league as a yearly payment unless it was on a mortgage, but pocket change for these guys, I guess."

Now the sergeant was really interested.

"Who was he?" he asked.

Nelson shook his head. "I'm only the chauffeur. Drove the car; made some deposits; minded my own business. Kept my job for a long time." He looked as though he were still searching his subconscious for something so McDonald remained silent.

Nelson continued. "He may have been connected with advertising or printing. A couple of times they were talking about upcoming ad campaigns. Mr. Lane was involved in a lot of different companies. He took an active interest in their operations."

"What printing companies did Mr. Lane own?" McDonald asked. He was looking through the list of company names in his file but couldn't recognize any as printers. He was thinking about the page proofs Welton had told him about. There might be a connection.

Nelson thought for a minute before answering. "I don't know," he said. "I took him to one in Burnside a few times but I don't think he owned it. Not yet anyway. You have to realize there are so many layers of ownership with these guys that it's a wonder anyone knows who owns what."

McDonald again nodded in agreement. "Which one in Burnside?"

"Big one, just up from the bridge. Johnson, Jackson, something like that."

McDonald noted this in his book and waited. But there was no more information coming. Nelson didn't pay much attention to what was being said in the car and was never in the plant. He wasn't sure the two were even connected in any way. That would be for McDonald to find out himself. That was why they paid him the big bucks. Right?

He thanked Nelson for his help, told him to call if he thought of anything else and left the office. He was heading towards the security booth when the chauffeur called out to him. He waved a sheet of paper.

"The guards who were working the day the boss died are off today. They work a sliding four days on four days off shift. You'll have to come back tomorrow."

McDonald turned back and took the copy of the schedule. Nelson took a pen from his pocket and underlined the needed names. He was trying to help.

"Thanks," McDonald said.

He decided to head for the offices of the Dartmouth printing plant. This was a shot in the dark but at least he had the faint outline of a target. Two people had suggested there might be some sort of connection between Lane and the printers. It was worth a try.

Chapter 22

The phone jangled bringing the semi dozing Claude Jackson awake with a start. He knocked over the remains of the third drink he had poured for himself since Neil called saying he was safely at his house. The liquid soaked into the papers lying on the desk blurring the type. He grabbed them, gave them a shake, and then threw them into the black plastic garbage pail beside his desk without even looking to see what they were.

Neil had reported no problems, told Claude he could relax now. One more drink to help him relax led to another and that to another. The sleepless weekend caught up to him and he fell into a fitful sleep at his desk.

In his dreams he was walking down a street. At every corner an over coated man stepped out in front of him, pointed his fore finger and made a trigger pulling motion. Then beside him on the street there would be the screaming of tires followed by a tremendous crash. A wrecked car would go skidding by on its roof. Sometimes it was a Cadillac, sometimes it was a Mercedes, his Mercedes. The over coated stranger would let out a blood curdling laugh causing Claude to wake slightly. Then it would start all over again.

The ringing of the phone coincided with one of those laughs. It took four rings to bring him fully awake. His shirt was soaked with sweat. It was time to get this mess straightened out.

The printout on his phone indicated the call was from a Jackson Printing and Publishing phone. How did Neil get this private number he wondered. He grabbed the phone receiver and brought it up to his ear fumbling it in the rush.

"I haven't heard anything yet Neil –" he started but was startled to hear Crosley's voice interrupt.

"Well, listen and you'll hear it now," the calm voice said.

Claude fought past his confusion. "Crosley, there's been a problem getting the payment–" he started to explain.

Crosley didn't listen.

"Can you see the MacKay Bridge from your window?" he asked, knowing the answer. Crosley had observed the view himself the last time he was in the office. That had been a decisive factor in his choice of location. The messenger of God had again decided time and place.

"Damn it, Crosley, I have the money," Jackson said. "I've lost the deposit slips."

"Do you notice anything strange about the bridge traffic?" Crosley continued as if he were the only one talking.

Jackson spun his stuffed office chair around and gazed out the window at the ribbon of steel arching over the harbour connecting the two cities. Everything looked normal to him. Cars and trucks were travelling back and forth at a steady pace.

But while he watched a change was taking place. The stream of traffic from Halifax was dwindling to a few straggling cars and then to wide open barren highway. The line from Dartmouth was slowing and starting to build. It became two solid, unmoving lines of red brake lights disappearing into nothingness over the arch, a parking lot in the sky.

"You think about what you're seeing," Crosley said. "I'll get back to you when I've made alternate plans to collect the money. This time let's do it without any further complications. Shit man, no one has ever lost the deposit slips." Crosley had been listening. He had simply chosen to ignore Claude.

For the third time he left Jackson holding the phone without giving him a chance to reply. The steady tone indicated the other party had hung up. His watch gave two shrill beeps. Two o'clock. He needed no reminder of the time.

Jackson sat for a long time staring at the traffic congestion. There was little doubt in his mind what caused it. He had seen it many times before. The timing was exactly as promised. Deadly and precise. That was what he paid for, or at least was supposed to have paid for.

As he sat there, a resolve started to form in his mind. There was no way on God's green earth that he would pay a penny to this demented killer. Being paid to kill someone, although not justifiable, was one thing, but this was just a random killing.

My God, he thought. How random was it? Who was the cause of all this traffic tie-up? The reality of what was happening smacked him between the eyes and brought him back to the real world.

The phone display indicated it was a company phone. Was Crosley in this building? Was he at his house? No, those phones did not display who was calling. The display was blocked.

He still had the phone in his hand. He pushed the disconnect button without even realizing that was not required. Crosley had already disconnected from him. He dialed his home number. Neil had called to assure him he was there and safe, but Claude wanted confirmation.

"Mrs. Jackson went shopping with your brother and his wife," the housekeeper said when he inquired of their whereabouts. "I believe they've gone into Halifax. Your brother was quite mysterious about it when he arrived."

Claude hung up the phone. Gone shopping. Damn it. Why couldn't they have just stayed put? He crossed the room, turned off the stereo and tuned in a radio station. One thing about an accident on the bridge, the media were always giving reports on it because the traffic problems it created reverberated throughout the twin cities. The news cast was just ending. If there was any news he missed it.

He would call the police and get some information about the accident from them, he decided. He returned to his desk and was reaching for the phone when it rang causing him a start.

This was his desk phone not the drawer phone. Crosley never used this number so it wouldn't be him again but if it was Crosley, Claude wouldn't permit him to interrupt. He would tell him in no uncertain terms that there would be no money coming his way. If he thought he could kill him, let him try. Unlike his other unsuspecting victims, Claude would be aware of the dangers and would take measures to prevent it.

"Claude Jackson," he said from force of habit.

"Claude, this is Neil. Have you heard from Crosley?"

Tears of relief started to flow down Claude's cheeks. He sat down on the edge of the desk.

"Oh, Neil, thank God you're all right. I called home and you weren't there. You were shopping? Good God man, I was going out of my mind with fear that something happened to all of you."

Neil lowered his voice to a whisper. "I'm sorry Claude. I just thought it better to do something out of the ordinary. That would disrupt any plans Crosley might have made. Did he call?"

Claude again let his gaze drift to the window and the view of the bridge. Traffic was not flowing any better, wouldn't be for a while to come. The question of who had died came back to his mind. Neil and their wives were okay. The kids and their children were all out of town. Was this accident just another convenient coincidence? Not even Claude believed that. Who was the victim?

In the background he could hear the radio announcer warning people to stay away from the A. Murray MacKay Bridge.

"Hold on a second Neil, they are saying something on the radio."

He crossed the room again and turned up the volume on the set. He still carried the receiver in his hand. In this way Neil could also hear the report.

"Claude, what is going on?" The voice came from the phone but Claude was listening to the radio.

"... traffic is backed up in both directions. There appears to be only one car involved. It has rolled on to the entrance of the bridge. Pieces of metal are everywhere effectively blocking all four lanes. Fire department officials are on the scene trying to remove someone from the car. I can hear the hum of a small motor. They must be using the Jaws of Life to extricate whoever is in the car. As I understand it, there is only one person in the car and initial reports indicate there is no movement being seen inside. I don't want to jump to any conclusions, Frank, but it doesn't look good." A brief period of silence followed before the voice returned.

"I am trying to get closer but there are car parts strewn all along the approach from the Halifax side. It will take a while to clean up this mess so if you're heading to Dartmouth you will want to take the McDonald Bridge or perhaps even drive around the Basin. It will be a while before traffic is flowing here again."

"Is there any indication of what caused the accident?" the announcer at the station asked his man on the scene.

"We can only speculate at this time, Frank. I've talked to a couple of witnesses who say excessive speed was a major factor. The car passed everyone on the approach, careened

158

off the guard rail, flipped and rolled up the ramp to where it is resting now.

"Wait a minute Frank. Firemen have just peeled back the roof of the car." There was a short period of dead air. "The ambulance attendants are removing the body and are putting it into the back of an ambulance."

There was another pause as the reporter watched the events unfold on the bridge. More dead air. "Brian, Brian, tell us what's happening," Frank said. "This is radio, not TV." Dead air was a no-no this rookie reporter would soon discover.

Brian then continued.

"The ambulance is leaving towards Dartmouth without any sirens. That would seem to indicate that our initial prognosis was correct. The man is indeed dead."

Frank cut in. "We don't know that for sure Brian."

"It looks pretty certain ... No, I guess we don't. I'll be stuck here for awhile Frank so I'll keep you up-to-date on how fast the congestion clears. But as a guess, I would say rush hour will be a real mess. This won't be cleared away for quite some time.

"Police are getting out their measuring tapes and starting their investigation. You can hear the horns starting to honk in the background. Now that the body is gone everyone's patience is wearing thin in a real hurry. Back to you Frank."

"Thanks for the report, Brian. For now let's just say there was a single car accident on the bridge. Condition of the lone occupant appears serious but the status is unknown. Stay tuned for further details."

Claude reached up and flipped the radio off and the stereo back on. He then returned the receiver to his ear.

"He's done it again Neil," he said.

"Claude, what is going on?" Neil repeated his question. "Did Crosley call? What did he say?"

"I'm not going to pay him a red cent," Claude said. "Not a red cent. This was just a brutal, senseless killing. Not a cent." His voice faded a little at the end.

"Don't be hasty, Claude. Take some time to think this over. I'll take the ladies home and come back into the office. Don't do anything until I get there."

Claude shook his head. "I'm not going to change my mind on this one Neil. This was a senseless murder. I'm not going to pay him. I'm not going to be intimidated. So if you are coming in to try and convince me to do otherwise, save your time and your breath."

"OK Claude. Let's try and find out who was killed and we'll take it from there. I'll be in as soon as I can. But don't do anything rash until I get there."

"No, nothing rash." Claude hung up the phone and sat behind his desk. The strength drained from his body. He needed time to think. Events had spiraled out of control and left him in the wake of deaths and threats of death. He needed another drink. Pulling open the bottom drawer of his desk required no thought, no effort. It was becoming habit. He slowly nursed this drink allowing time to flow over him, waiting for Neil to come back to the office and take over thinking for him. In the meantime, as instructed, he would do nothing rash. Again, he dozed.

Another light lit up on his telephone console followed by a soft buzz. Claude opened his eyes.

"Yes, Jean?" Claude said, exasperation evident in his voice. He was in no mood to think about mundane things like business. Neil could take care of business affairs when he arrived. Nothing came ahead of the business in Neil's eyes, not even Claude's dilemma. That was not quite true. Neil would multitask. He would take care of both the business and Claude's concerns, seeming to devote all his attention to each task.

"There's a policeman here to see either Mr. Neil or you, sir." Jean's voice had a quizzical tone to it. The cop told her nothing about his reasons for being there and her curiosity showed through. "Mr. Neil is out of the office for the rest of the day."

A slight bead of perspiration formed across Claude's forehead. Why did the law want to talk to him? He could imagine the worst but there was no way for him to be connected to Lane's death. That is, no way unless Crosley was trying another tactic.

Wait. This could be information about who had just been killed. Of course, it would be someone Claude knew. That was the point of it, to scare Claude into cooperating. Claude leaned back into his office chair and watched as the door opened. He waited with fear and apprehension. Wanting to know on the one hand, but afraid of what he was about to discover, on the other.

Chapter 23

"**T**his is the same kind of luck we had yesterday," Scott Bowen told Cynthia Roberts, the force chaplain. "Believe it or not, Dan Cooper's neighbour died Saturday in a drowning incident. We had problems catching the wife home on our first call."

"A drowning? I wasn't informed." Proper procedure called for a chaplain to be present when informing the family of an accidental death. She looked at Scott for an explanation.

"We should have called you but we're investigating it as homicide instead of an accident."

"You're lucky I'm in the forgiveness business. Next time call me."

The two were sitting in Kate's Kafe planning their next move. Kate appeared beside them with a coffee pot in her hand. Scott held out his for a refill. Cynthia passed.

"I wasn't listening," Kate said, "but did I hear you mention Dan Cooper's name? Is he all right?"

"You know Dan Cooper?" Scott asked.

"Yes. He's a regular. Black, two sugars."

The cops exchanged glances. Cynthia spoke first. "You don't know where we can contact his wife in the daytime?"

"Sorry, never met the woman. What has happened to Dan?"

"When did you last see Dan?" Scott asked.

"Corporal Bowen, you're pissing me off." Kate noticed the white Roman collar at Cynthia's neck and stopped short. "Opps, sorry..." She hesitated. "...Father? Mother?"

"Chaplain will do," Cynthia said. "Dan's been in an accident and we're trying to contact his family. Do you know the children?"

Again Kate shook her head. "Not really. I've seen them around. Danny stops in every night on the way home. Has a coffee and slice of pie. His motto is 'Life is short. Eat dessert first.' How badly hurt is he?"

"So you haven't seen him since Friday?" Scott was taking advantage of this opportunity to pursue his investigation of the Herb Clattenburg case. He still had a murder to clear and Cooper, dead or alive, was a suspect. To him, the accident and subsequent reporting of the death was Cynthia's responsibility. He was just along for the ride.

Dan Cooper ending up dead in a car accident came as no surprise to Scott. The Sunday morning show declared the man to be a prime candidate for that kind of ending. Scott had witnessed too many dead drunks to be surprised by another one. Robert Crosley had chosen his victim well. Just another DUI.

"He was in here Saturday morning." Kate looked around and lowered her voice. "Waiting for the liquor store to open. Don't know why he wanted more. He was pretty hung over."

"What time was this?"

"Came in around 9:30. Picked up his booze at 10:00 and came back for another coffee and more pie. Stayed until about 11:00, 11:30. Didn't seem to be in a hurry to go home. I don't blame him. Have you seen his girls?"

Scott wrote this information in his notebook. He looked up at Cynthia. "According to his alibi, he was out hiking. Short hike."

"What about his girls?" Cynthia wanted to know.

Again Kate looked around the cafe. "I'm not one to judge but his home life must have been like a freak show. One's a

Goth, the other's a rainbow of colours. I felt sorry for the man."

"Yeah, well kids will be kids."

Kate looked back at Scott. "That poor Herb Clattenburg. You never did come back for that second cup of coffee. Not that I blame you. I've heard some of the firemen talking. That must have been horrible."

"It was. Do you still have my second slice of pie, as well?"

"Even better. One that I made fresh this morning." Kate looked at Scott's companion. "Chaplain?"

Cynthia shook her head. "I think I'll pass. I'm still on duty and I've heard your pies are sinful."

They all shared a laugh.

Chapter 24

Constable Larry Reyno stepped into Claude Jackson's office. He looked a little uneasy. This was the worst part of his job, much worse than confronting dangerous criminals. While doing that, you had an adrenaline rush to carry you along. There was no rush with this task. He was here to advise that someone had been killed, an employee of the man before him and more than likely a friend. Usually a chaplain accompanied officers on these kinds of calls. Cynthia, the on call chaplain was in Shad Bay trying to track down Dan Cooper's family. Reyno was on his own. He wasn't prepared for what happened next.

"Who's dead?" Claude said. "Who has been killed?"

Sweat was glistening across Jackson's forehead. There was a smell of alcohol in the office. He looked disheveled, not what one would expect for a vice-president of a company of this size in the middle of the afternoon. The officer's investigative senses were alerted.

"There was an accident on the bridge a short time ago."

"Yes, yes," Claude said. "I know." He made a sweeping gesture towards his office window where the traffic could still be seen to be slowed to a crawl. "Who was it?" It was almost a demand.

"Well, we don't have a positive identification yet," the officer said. This was a partially true statement. The police had a very good idea who the victim was; they just needed someone to actually view the beat up human remains and say without question: Yes, that is my husband, father, son, whatever. First they had to track down someone to take on that gruesome task. He continued: "But indications are that

165

it was an employee of your company. Do you have a Daniel Cooper working here?"

Jackson's face went through a variety of expressions. Relief, disbelief, shock, followed by despair.

"Dan, Dan Cooper. Yes, Dan is one of our senior salesmen. What makes you think it's him? No, it can't be Dan."

The policeman tried to keep his suspicions in check. A routine motor vehicle accident was being investigated, right?

"The identification in his wallet indicates that it is Dan Cooper and his business cards name this as his place of employment. We sent a car around to his house but there is no one there," Reyno said. "Tell me, does Mr. Cooper make a habit of drinking during the day?" Is this a company-wide practice trickling down from the top, he was wondering.

"Drinking?" Claude said. "No, maybe the odd beer at lunch but not what you would call drinking. Why do you ask that?"

"We are just investigating all possibilities. There was a smell of alcohol in the car. It's too soon to know anything yet so you might want to keep that confidential. But if there is anything you can tell us, it could speed things up." Reyno looked at the spilt drink on the desk. Jackson covered the liquid with a sheet of paper. It was a reflex action. The paper absorbed the alcohol making the spill more obvious as the ink started to blotch.

"Do you have any idea how to get in contact with his family during the day?" Reyno asked. Jackson might be in shock or he might be too stoned to talk. It became obvious that he had no further information to offer the policeman. The constable prodded him. "Mr. Jackson, are you all right?"

"Yes, just a moment. This is such a shock."

Claude had Jean call the Human Resources Department and got the information the policeman was seeking before seeing him out of his office. His mind was in a whirl. There was no doubt that this "accident" was arranged by the assassin.

Claude's headache suddenly felt worse. Cooper and Crosley. What possible connection did they share? He racked his brain to remember what projects Cooper was currently working on. Nothing came to mind. The past week for Claude remained a fuzzy blur.

Claude slid open the desk drawer and withdrew the bottle of Captain Morgan. He wanted, no needed, a fifth drink while he contemplated what to do next. Little did he realize how quickly events were going to spiral out of his control.

Chapter 25

As Jim McDonald pulled into the parking lot at Jackson Printers and Publishers he noticed the familiar colours of a city patrol car parked by the front door. He wheeled his own unmarked vehicle towards it and got out just as Larry Reyno came through the door. They played together in a pickup hockey league that the police and firefighters in the city had formed and recognized each other at once.

"Hey, Leaky," Jim said to the team goal tender. "What brings you over here?"

"There was a fatality on the bridge and the victim worked here," Larry said.

"What a screw-up that caused." Jim said. "I got caught in the traffic when it overflowed to the other bridge. It made for a long trip to get here."

"I was already on this side of the harbour so I drew the short straw. I get to pass the news on to the guy's employer. I was trying to get a line on his family but it was a strange meeting."

McDonald's ears perked up.

"Strange, how so?"

"The victim is a suspected DUI from initial reports but his boss looked to be three sheets to the wind as well. May be a great place to work for an alkie." Reyno looked back towards the building and then back to Jim. "It was like he knew what I was there for before I even opened my mouth. He demanded to know who was dead. Knock on someone's door at three in the morning, that's an obvious conclusion to jump to. Three in the afternoon in the workplace, someone being dead would not be my first suspicion."

"The dead man worked here?" Jim asked.

"So it seems. Daniel Cooper. He's a long time employee."

Surprise registered on Jim's face. "Dan Cooper? I met him yesterday. He was drinking then, too. What's the address?"

Reyno flipped open his notebook and showed it to Jim.

"Same guy," Jim said. "How'd he die?"

"Totaled his car on the approach to the bridge. Besides being drunk, witnesses say he was driving erratically in the moments before his death. He was all over the road with the petal to the metal."

A feeling of déjà vu passed over Jim. "Can you get me the names of those witnesses?"

Reyno gave the homicide detective a strange look.

"Let's get in your car and go over some of the details of the case I'm working on," Jim said. "This is too coincidental to be a coincidence."

Jim laid out the case he was working on, going over the particulars of the accident that took the life of Matthew Lane. Having been present at the event, he was able to bring depth to the last wild moments of Lane's life. Larry agreed the description was in line with what witnesses on the bridge told the investigators.

In fact, after listening to McDonald those descriptions made more sense. Prior to meeting Jim, he thought the reports were exaggerated. Tying multimillionaire Matthew Lane and drunken, salesman Daniel Cooper together however, was a bit of a reach. Neither policeman could visualize the two victims travelling in the same circles. For Jim to have a case, there had to be a connection. Jim could think of only one.

He wondered if Cooper was the one supplying page proofs to Lane. It was possible but he would reserve judgment. If Cooper was feeding proofs to Lane then Lane should have been paying Cooper instead of the other way around. In his gut this didn't feel right. Why would Lane want these proofs anyway? Jim still hadn't come up with an explanation for that.

However, the appearance and reaction of the vice-president of the printing firm as described by Larry Reyno was unsettling to his detective mind. Reyno suggested Jackson was expecting someone to die. The death didn't come as a surprise, only the name of the victim. Cooper and Lane could have been connected and whatever that connection was could have led to their deaths. Were there others with similar connections? Were more deaths imminent?

Jim thought about Herb Clattenburg and the attempt to make his murder look like an accident. Did it tie in as well? One more thing to check.

He settled back into the seat of his own car. He would have to rethink this upcoming meeting with Claude Jackson. A second fatal accident put everything into a different light. He would follow up on this investigation, check for similarities, and try to find the common links. Perhaps this was the elusive break he was looking for. He could only hope. He decided to put immediate pressure on Claude Jackson. With Cooper's death fresh in everyone's mind let's see what shakes loose.

He walked into Claude's office at the same time that Jean announced him on the intercom. She tried to stop him but an aggressive interview was the path he decided to take. Pushing past the secretary and walking in unannounced would set the tone he was after.

Claude only had time to set the bottle of Captain Morgan on the floor instead of in the drawer. He looked like a kid caught with his hand in the cookie jar.

"Who are you?" His voice contained evident surprise. He had expected the return of the uniformed police officer when

Jean had alerted him of police presence again. In his current state, the arrival of Jim McDonald was unnerving. Plain clothes cops meant trouble.

"Detective Sergeant James McDonald," Jim flashed his identification and put it away. "Homicide." He could see he had the edge and he intended to keep it. "Tell me what you know about this accident on the bridge." He put special emphasis on the word accident.

"Ac-accident on the bridge? Noth-nothing." Claude said.

"Nothing?" Jim said. "Didn't you just meet with Constable Reyno from the traffic division? What was that about? An accident on the bridge?" He paused but didn't wait for an answer. "Now focus. Are you familiar with a man named Matthew Lane?" He saw a flicker of recognition in Claude's eyes. Possibly a flicker of fear which he tried to mask.

"Matthew Lane? No, no I don't think so." The rapid change of direction of the question had Claude unbalanced.

"Yes, Matthew Lane. Think about it. Focus. What's your relationship with him? He's dead too, you know. He was killed in an accident as well." Again he emphasized the word accident.

"I-I am focused," Claude said.

Just then the door burst open and Neil Jackson charged into the room. He looked around and assessed the scene.

"Jean tells me you are a police officer," he said to Jim. "What is this all about?" It was a demand, not a question.

In a long practiced move, the gold shield of the detective appeared in his hand and then disappeared as if by magic.

"Detective Sergeant Jim McDonald and who might you be?" Jim asked although he was pretty sure he knew. Not just anyone would intrude on the office of the vice president of the company, unless of course you were the president. He waited. He had no intention of giving up his advantage. He wanted to continue the myth of I know more than you do.

Neil relaxed. He reached out his hand to the policeman and said: "Neil Jackson, this is my company, along with my brother." He indicated Claude. "Now, what is going on? We don't often have policemen on our premises and Jean tells me you're the second one in half an hour."

Jim took the outstretched hand. He would prefer to interview these two men in separate rooms. But if there was anything going on, and Jim didn't know for sure if there was, he doubted if Neil Jackson was going to let him talk to his brother alone. The two brothers seemed to have nothing in common and he didn't want to have any lawyers involved. If he pushed for separate interviews, he concluded that bringing in a lawyer would be the senior Jackson's next step.

Instead he said to Neil: "Your brother was just telling me about Matthew Lane."

Neil shot a wilting glance at Claude. "Really," he said. "What was he telling you?"

"Nothing," Claude said. "Nothing. I didn't tell him nothing."

Neil smiled at McDonald. Nice move. There was no further sense in trying to deny any knowledge. His brother might as well have spelt out all the details instead of that too enthusiastic denial. "Matthew Lane, killed recently in motor vehicle accident wasn't he? We knew him," he said. "We hired him as a time and motion expert. He came in looked, around and then tried to tell us how to run our business. My opinion is that his intention was to take over our company. The experience suggests there would be hundreds of people out there happy to see him dead. He was a predator when it came to business dealings." Neil paused as if recalling his dealings with the man. "I'd call him a corporate psychopath.

Had absolutely no regard for the victims of his corporate bullying. Strictly interested in his bottom line. The rest of the world be damned. But, be that as it may, the death was an accident, wasn't it? I read about it in the newspaper. Shook up the financial world for a day or two. I don't see why the police are involved unless you are with the commercial crime branch. Are you?"

Again Claude interrupted. "Dan Cooper is dead. He was killed in the car accident. It was his car on the bridge. This cop's from homicide."

"Dan Cooper, I was just talking to him this morning." Neil's face turned ashen. He reached out for a chair and sank into it. "I spoke to him in the parking lot. He was on his way to meet a client and close a big printing deal. This can't be true. It can't be. Not Dan." The concern seemed real.

"Who was he meeting?" McDonald asked. Reyno told him all that had been found in his car were a couple of large, empty manila envelopes. There was nothing there to help them. He told the Jackson brothers about the envelopes and asked what they were for.

"Empty?" Neil was confused. "By large, do you mean 24 inches by 15 inches?" He knew there should have been page negatives in them. Why would they be empty? Cooper should not have been coming back empty-handed. It was a done deal. At 2:00 p.m. Cooper should have been returning from his meeting with a cheque and all the final materials.

Realization dawned on Neil. There never was a catalogue contract. The killer's contingency plans were put in place long before Claude had screwed up. He gave his head a shake. One thing Claude deserved credit for, he had hired the best. Now Neil tried to remember anything he knew about the man Dan Cooper was supposed to be meeting. He realized he knew nothing. Dan had never given him a name.

He would have to check Dan's notes and get back to McDonald.

"It has been suggested Cooper may have been intoxicated," Jim said. "How did he appear to you this morning."

Neil showed surprise at this news. "Just the opposite. I remember thinking to myself how good he looked." The cop looked at him with a quizzical look. Neil realized further explanations were necessary. "Dan has had some problems lately. This morning he looked like everything was in hand. That was only a couple of hours ago, just before lunch."

Jim recalled the report from Larry Reyno. The two stories did not jibe. Jim flipped ahead in his notebook. "Cooper lived in Shad Bay?"

Neil looked confused. "I'm not sure. Sounds right but I can check." Before Jim could stop him, Neil touched the intercom button on Claude's desk. "Jean, find me Dan Cooper's home address."

"No problem," her voice said. "I have the file right here. The other policeman wanted to see it. Has something happened to Dan?" Genuine concern came from the intercom.

Neil ignored the question and walked to the door, opened it and returned with the file open in his hand. "Shad Bay, yes, that's where he lives. Shady Acres Estates. I think it's a new subdivision for people moving up in the housing market. He bought the house in the last year or so." His voice caught. "Lived, I guess we have to say now. Why do you ask?"

Jim shook his head. "Nothing. I talked to him yesterday about another case I'm involved in. Making sure it was the same guy."

"The fishing accident?" Neil said. "Are you involved in any real homicides?"

"What do you know about that death?" Jim searched Neil Jackson's eyes surprised at his knowledge of the event. There was a connection.

"Nothing. Dan told me about it this morning. The victim was his neighbour, just a young man who drowned while fishing. A tragic accident."

Jim glanced at the open notebook. "Do you know Herb Clattenburg?"

Neil thought for a minute before shaking his head. "Doesn't ring any bells."

Jim looked at Claude and raised his eyebrows. Claude wasn't paying attention to the conversation.

"What?" he asked.

Neil spoke first. "Pay attention, Claude. Have you run across Herb Clattenburg in your travels? Is he a client of ours?"

Claude wiped his blood shot eyes with the thumb and fingers of one hand bringing them together over his nose. He appeared to be in deep thought. "I don't know."

"Is this important?" Neil asked. "Dan told me it was an accident."

"It could be," Jim said.

Neil crowded Claude away from the computer on his desk and tapped a few keys. "Nothing comes up in our records. I think he was just a friend and neighbour of Dan's. I know Dan was upset at his death, but he was sober this morning. I'll swear to that"

Jim shrugged. "That's not the initial report I have but we'll see what the autopsy reveals. I still need to know who Cooper was meeting."

While that was being checked out, McDonald got back to Matthew Lane and the Jackson Printing and Publishing connection. He tried to pump Claude for more details. Neil answered most of the questions. When the younger brother was allowed to answer, Claude maintained the story line issued by Neil. The relationship was strictly business. Jim had no real evidence that this was false but he suspected otherwise. He would have to separate the two for the next interview.

There were a series of questions that needed to be answered before he pursued this further with the Jacksons. Was Claude the one showing advance proofs to Lane? These would have been the proofs Ronald Welton, the janitor, told him about. It had to be Jackson. Things were coming together. Why would he be bringing the proofs to Lane? What were they involved in together? What were they arguing about? Was it something that could lead to murder?

More investigation would be required but he was making some progress at last. Jim kept the information about the proofs to himself. He didn't want to play all of his cards too early. He needed some answers before tipping off the Jacksons about what he already knew and about what he already suspected.

Jim decided to check out the accident vehicle for some leads before pushing the Jacksons any further. They thought he knew much more than he did so he would let them worry about that while he tried to find out some of the stuff he was pretending to know. He would be back and he would be expecting answers, he advised them.

Chapter 26

Ironically Matthew Lane did not have to die. That is not to say several, possibly hundreds, didn't want to see him dead. But Claude Jackson had jumped the gun or to be accurate, Neil Jackson had jumped the gun.

Lane was guilty of playing millionaire games, several millions actually, with wannabe millionaires. Unfortunately he was the only one who knew the game had ended.

Back when he found out about Claude's financial problems, he bailed him out. At that time he had no definite plan of attack. It might be nice to own a printing company. Many people already thought he had a license to print money. He might just have been helping out a fellow human being. Claude was a person people could like.

Lane checked out the company with his increased productivity ruse, was impressed with the efficiency of the operation, maybe not how he would have done it, but efficient none the less. It was not publicly traded on the stock market so a hostile takeover was not feasible. That would mean an outright purchase and that was unlikely. Claude's debt of one half million dollars made a kind of takeover possible. That is hostile in the truest sense of the world. Squeeze Jackson's gonads until he handed over his share of the company.

But then Lane came up with another idea. There were lots of volatile stocks out there in technology or mining and oil where a quick profit could be turned. Day traders had their prices making wild swings everyday. Deadly if you didn't know what you were doing but lots of room to make a ton of money in a hurry if you did. Lane did. If you were careful you might even be able to do a little manipulating as long as you didn't get caught. That was called insider trading and that was a crime.

While checking out Jackson Printers, Lane came up with the idea that he could do the same thing with a more stable stock. That would be a challenge to get a blue chip stock to make some controlled fluctuations. He would tackle the grocery market. Millionaire games.

A few weeks later Lane hatched his plan. He summoned Claude to his office on the morning a payment was due. There were several late payments already. Claude's hand held no cheque when he walked through the door, no brown paper bag full of cash bulged under his suit jacket. Claude walked out 20 minutes later with a payment extension and instructions to drop off final grocery ad proofs the following Tuesday night. This was the deadline to get the grocery ads out in time for the weekend deluge of shoppers.

Claude argued that the final prices were not inserted until just before the pages went to press. Grocery stores were a cutthroat business themselves. Lane, however, had done his homework. He knew there were final proof checks before the presses turned over to print even one page. Everyone has to eat. Many shoppers read, no studied, the grocery ads. Accuracy was of the utmost importance and that required one last check after the final changes were made. Lane wanted copies of those proofs. Jackson would provide them.

There are three major grocery chains in this country. Lane owned shares in all of them. It didn't matter to him which share prices went up or which ones went down. He stood to make money regardless.

Ninety per cent of the prices in the flyers for all three companies were the same. They all bought their goods from the same suppliers, most often at the same price. They did the same math on the markup. They came up with the same selling price. The variations were in the items featured as weekly loss leaders, the items designed to get feet across the threshold of the store. These products were sold at a loss to the store just to lure people in.

The experts knew the majority of people would buy much more than the advertised item once in the store. How many times have you dropped into your local supermarket for bread and milk which should have cost less than five bucks and emerged $35 later carrying two grocery bags? Every time, right? The loss leaders were the items people noticed first. These were the ones in which Lane was most interested as he hatched his little scheme.

The loss leaders were featured in the regular pages of the newspaper on the same day the flyers were inserted or "stuffed" into them.

JP&P had one super market's contract to produce these ad pages and supply them to the newspapers all across the country electronically. Others were prepared in Ontario. Lane took advantage of the power he held over one of the ad execs from a previous bailout to raise a couple of prices a couple of cents. It didn't take much.

Later the next day when the ads hit the streets, Jackson was surprised to see the competition's prices were the lower ones. He was confused. He expected Lane to undercut the other stores. This went on for two weeks.

In reality, all the companies dropped their prices to meet the lowest advertised price in their region. Lane knew this but it was the stock market he was interested in, not the food market.

In the stock market, perception was the important factor. It appeared that one company was continually beating the competition in pricing.

Lane had a network that could never be connected to him—Marilyn's Wednesday night party group. If Lane, while sipping a brandy after the steaks, happened to mention to some one close by that Company A was in trouble and it might be a good idea to dump those stocks, you could be sure that anyone in earshot was calling his broker before the market opened in the morning. Not only that, everyone at the party soon had the same message.

These get togethers would generally host about twelve couples. If one member of each couple told only two other people, and those additional 24 each told two people and those 48 told 2 other people, we have a mathematical progression. Now 12 + 24 + 48 + 96 produces 180 people in on the secret. At that point it really takes off. The next step adds 192 new people, then 384, 768 and on into the thousands. And that's if they kept their insider knowledge down to only two other friends. That doesn't allow for the natural tendency of people to brag about who and what they know. Most would not be limited to telling only two other people. Most would send to the entire address book on their computers. The information would be send to hundreds of thousands of people.

With e-mail and the Internet that would happen in minutes not hours. You do the math. Investment advice was travelling at the speed of a broadband link or even faster at the speed of ISDN connection. There were several thousand people across the country selling stocks the next day and one bunch of confused grocery store executives wondering what the hell was happening.

This caused a modest drop, but moved a lot of shares. This amount of activity was only a blip in the big picture. Lane then kicked in the next phase of the plan. He placed a call to the local newspaper where, as it happened, there was a rookie business reporter searching for stories to make his mark. Had he noticed the variations in the prices of the grocery flyers? Were the prices higher in one because that company was in trouble? Check the stock market page for tomorrow's paper to see if the prices have been influenced.

The closing prices from the Toronto Stock Exchange that are reported in the daily paper are put on the Canadian Press wire between six and seven p.m. the night before. This was lots of time for an enterprising young reporter to see the volume of trades but not enough time to do any in-depth checking as to what caused it. He had to make the early deadline to catch the business pages. The tips gave him his lead.

A newspaper says a company is in trouble, especially in the business section, it is in trouble, at least for a short time. Now, make sure this news is picked up in a few stock market type chat rooms on the Internet and a full fledged drop in value is underway. Prices decline. The questioning started among the amateurs.

"Why should I sell those stocks? These are almost blue chip."

"Well suit yourself but Matthew Lane is selling his."

"*The* Matthew Lane? Thanks for the tip."

Never mind price to value ratios or previous performance, follow the herd. Join the sheep. After all, Nortel was supposed to have been safe, wasn't it?

"You can listen to your broker who works from paycheck to paycheck just like you do if you want. I'm going to take my advice from a multi-millionaire," was posted in one chat room. This soon become a mantra on many of the other business related boards. Most who took this advice weren't even sure who the multi-millionaire was. But, hey, you can't argue with that logic.

With the combination of these amateurs and Lane's own strategic sales, on Friday all hell broke loose. Lane sat in his spacious office huddled over his computer watching the action, wishing he could share the moment with someone but not willing to take the chance. Even in millionaire games, there are rules. Manipulating stock prices for your own personal gain violates one of them. He would not set himself up for the actions of some future disgruntled whistle blower. He would revel in the success of his grand scheme all alone. Alone at the top.

On his computer screen, there were two lists of figures: a price people were willing to pay for a stock and a price people were willing to sell a stock for. When these two figures met, a sale took place.

A smile crossed Lane's face as this price dropped from 28.75 to 26.00, the magic ten per cent mark. A flurry of activity occurred at this point. He watched the activity on the ticker tape scrolling along the bottom of his screen, set to the stocks of his choice. Automatic trading kicked in generated by computers monitoring the prices and limiting the loss of their owners. To fuel the flames, he ordered the sale of some more of his private shares.

Lane's smile widened at the 23.25 mark, twenty per cent. Pension fund computers were getting involved. Automatic selling fueled by these large funds kicked in. No more fuel was needed for the fire, it was now a raging inferno. Humans would have known these companies were not in trouble. Computers just do what they are told or think they are told. They sell. The selling triggered a free fall in the stock price. The amateurs were panicking and taking huge losses as they unloaded their shares.

At this point, Lane no longer had to be secretive. As a fund manager, he would be expected to jump in and protect his clients.

Analysts were trying to figure out, with no success, what started the selling. Then the decline stopped. The pros stepped in and the profit taking started.

Lane studied the numbers flashing on his screen. It was time to start buying again. He jumped back in at 18.75, watched the decline continue to 18.00 but that didn't worry him. He knew the price would rise again and he didn't want to be chasing it up. The rapid drop sounded alarms and real people, the pension fund managers, took a look at what was happening. Unlike the computers, they knew a good thing when they saw it and bought huge blocks of stock. The price sky rocketed.

Lane regained his original position as value passed 22.00 on the way back up. He had to be fast. For good measure, he bought an extra 100,000 shares before the selling price settled back in at 29.25, up 50 cents on the day.

Meanwhile, if one grocery chain is in trouble, the other must be doing good. Lane watched these prices as well.

The other company share values climbed from $35.10 to $36.75. Not a huge jump unless you owned over a million and a half shares.

"Time to sell some of them off," he said. The higher prices leveled off then returned to where they started. Lane bought back what he had sold.

He did some rapid calculations. He made a profit, from both the buying and the selling, of slightly over $6.8 million. His holdings in the one company were improved by 100,000 shares at no real expense to himself. No paper trail of the illegal activities existed, only the normal give and take of business in the stock trading world. Most important of all, he proved he could do it. He could influence the market in what should have been a nonvolatile stock. He reached out and turned off his computer, leaned back in his plush, executive chair, closed his eyes and enjoyed his moment of success all by himself. Millionaire games.

Lane turned a profit of more than 12 times what he lent Claude Jackson. Jackson would still have to pay him back, of course, but Lane would put less pressure on him. Lane no longer had any ambitions of taking over Claude's company. In the big picture of things, JP&P was too small to bother with. Jackson did not know this. The call to Robert Crosley had already been placed. This unfortunate lack of knowledge would prove fatal for Matthew Lane.

Later that Friday night, the senior editor of the newspaper that first broke the story sat in the corner of the press club with a glass of brandy in one hand, a curved Carrie pipe in the other. He took a long puff on the pipe, dragging the smoke up past the "magic inch" filter system which cooled it. He smiled at his business editor who shared his cigarette scarred table. Sweet smelling smoke circled his head like a cloud.

"That was a great scoop on the grocery store debacle. I knew young Josh had what it takes to ferret out the good stories."

The business editor sat down his mug of beer and sucked the overflow brew from his mustache, two drinks for the price of one.

"It was a great story. I have to admit that I was skeptical about Josh at first but I'm glad to have been proven wrong. We scooped everyone. It was almost as if we ran the story before it happened. "

The smoking man removed his pipe from his mouth and chuckled, escaping smoke curling around his ears. "Oh well, not everyone can spot talent right off," he said. "That's why they pay me the big bucks."

Business guy takes another drink of the dark draft beer and this time wipes the foam mustache away. "I almost lost a bunch of money on this deal. I read his story in the morning. I own a couple of hundred shares myself, you know. Before I got around to doing anything the price had dropped like a lead balloon and then bounced back up again like an Indian rubber ball. A little procrastination and I missed all the action. It was eerie. Now that we know Josh can do it, what has he got lined up for the Sunday edition?"

In the newspaper industry, today's paper is old news. It's what you are working on for tomorrow's edition that counts. There is no writer's block in the newsroom.

Senior editor swirls the amber liquid in the glass and takes a sip. "Don't worry. It'll be good. What did you assign him?"

"Assign him? Shouldn't I let talent like that run free; find its own inspiration?" There was a hint of sarcasm in the business editor's voice. "He's related to you, isn't he?"

The senior editor looked a little affronted. "Sure, he's my wife's nephew. But that has nothing to do with why I hired him. I don't believe in nepotism. Just watch him, you'll see. The boy's the real thing.

"What do you think of the Blue Jays chances of going all the way this year? They are looking good so far. They're just a couple of trades away from the pennant."

The subject was changed, no one any the wiser of Matthew Lane's intervention in the life of the country and the part played by an unsuspecting media. Several small investors were short a car or mortgage payment this month because they got caught up in the excitement of playing millionaire games on a Kraft Dinner budget. The millions made by Lane would not change his life one iota. To him it was just numbers on a balance sheet, how he kept score.

If only Lane had let Claude in on the game, he would have been able to play again another day. Claude wouldn't have been dodging a hired killer and Sergeant McDonald wouldn't be stymied on this case that seemed to be going nowhere. Unfortunately for everyone, that didn't happen.

Chapter 27

McDonald was at the motor pool, for the second time in a week, studying a wrecked car with Chuck Bezanson.

"The big Caddy was a mess, but this one is a total wreck," Chuck said to him. "But, as I said when we examined the Cadillac, I don't see why we have a homicide dick here. This car doesn't appear to have any real mechanical problems. Just the usual wear and tear for a car this age. It's only two years old so not much has gone wrong yet. I hear the driver was wrecked though. His blood alcohol level was off the meter."

McDonald looked into the remains of the blue Dodge. He didn't know what he hoped to find. Somewhere there had to be some answers. He noticed a Styrofoam cup on the floor amongst the newspapers and garbage. There was no telltale sign of a brown ring on the bottom which would have indicated it was used for a cola or coffee or something similar. He removed the pen from his pocket and used it to deposit the cup into an evidence bag.

"Let's get this thing checked out," he said to Chuck. "I remember we found one of these in the Lane car."

The previous cup had been a dead end. It had been perfectly clean. This one looked the same. There must be some significance to this if indeed there was something going on that was not kosher. Something undetectable must have been in it. They would have to try harder to figure out what.

Chuck took the cup and looked into it.

"It looks empty to me," he said, a smirk on his face.

"Yeah," said Jim. "How many clean cups are lying on the floor of your car?"

"Point taken, the evidence is not what is in the cup, but what is not in it," Chuck nodded. "You could have something here. Who knows? It is a starting point."

"What the hell makes us think there is a case here anyway?" Jim said. "Lane dies in what looks like an obvious accident. Hell, it would have been an accident if I hadn't been there to see it and if the Inspector hadn't received a warning call about a murder plot. You had to see the look on this guy's face, Chuck. Something was going on in his mind that wasn't being seen by the rest of us."

Jim walked over to the nearby work bench and looked at the large empty envelopes that came from the wrecked car.

"This Cooper guy is killed in what looks like an obvious accident, a DUI— driving under the influence. Heaven knows enough people die in them every year. You know, I met him the day before, Sunday morning and he had drunk his breakfast. It makes me shudder. Getting smashed at lunch time doesn't seem like much of a stretch to me. Again, it would have been an obvious accident if this Jackson character hadn't seemed to know about it before we got there. What is going on Chuck?"

"Professional hits," Chuck said agreeing to the tacit implication that McDonald was making. He was not just a mechanic but a forensic mechanic, actually a cop. It was his job to see beyond what appeared to be just simple accidents. In these two cases nothing leapt out at them. Everything seemed routine. And that was what the gifted pros were good at — making everything seem routine.

"OK," Jim said. "Who is the pro and who hired him."

"Answer those two questions and the case is closed," Chuck said. "Sounds simple enough."

"Claude Jackson is not the hitter," he said more to himself than to Chuck. "But he is my favorite candidate for having made the hire. All we have to do is find out why and get him talking. To do this, we have to keep his brother out of the way when we interview him."

He wondered about Neil Jackson. At their previous meeting, he took over. He kept his younger brother from talking. But still McDonald didn't see him as the kind of person to have hired an assassin. He looked more like the kind of person who would have taken care of things himself.

"Then there's this other case I'm working on. Guy drowns while out fishing. Looks innocent enough at first, but Scott Bowen from traffic thinks the whole thing smells fishy, no pun intended. We're investigating it as a homicide. The victim in that case was Dan Cooper's next door neighbour. Raises the obvious question: Is there a connection?"

Chuck pulled a rag from his back pocket and started wiping at his hands. "So you think the fishing guy and the Cadillac guy are connected? The pro hit them both and maybe Cooper found out?"

"No, I don't. Fishing death is too sloppy. Too many mistakes. But I'm not a lover of coincidence. We're still looking for a link."

"Apparent accidental drowning, car accident, drunk driver, you know how to pick 'em."

Jim smiled. "Makes you long for the good old days. Two shots to the back of the head or a knife in the heart. Something that took away the element of doubt in your mind and let you concentrate on solving the murder."

Jim was still in the process of getting himself assigned to the investigation of the Cooper accident in an official capacity. He had to convince a few people that a homicide detective belonged on this DUI case. He wanted a few more facts before he approached Inspector Holland about it.

Three apparent accidents, oh joy.

Chapter 28

Jim pulled in to the parking lot of Kates Kafe at precisely 2:30. The only other vehicle present was Scott Bowen's police cruiser. Jim noticed a knot of men in front of the fire hall having an animated discussion. He recognized two of them from Sunday morning's body retrieval venture: Brad Johnson and Bill Mack. Bill seemed to be recreating the discovery of Herb Clattenburg's grisly remains for the newcomers. It had been a big day for this small village on the outskirts of the city. Tragic death was not a foreigner here, but this time it was different. This was a fishing community. Usually drownings occurred on the high seas, not in the surrounding hills.

Jim entered the cafe and spotted Scott at a window seat. He, too, was taking in the scene across the road. Tragic death was not a stranger to him. He failed to share their excitement.

Jim slipped into the booth across from the uniformed policeman. "Are we still working on a homicide?"

Scott looked away from the window. "Most definitely." He checked to make sure no one else was within hearing range. "The buckles on the chest waders were freshly filed down. They appeared to engage but just the motion of walking caused them to release a little. When the first surge of river water hit them, they just opened up. This was not carelessness on Clattenburg's part and it was not an accident. The waders were deliberately sabotaged."

"You sound pretty definite."

"I am. I have the file and the plastic filings. Crime scene guys found them in Herb Clattenburg's garage with his excess fishing gear. He had a ton of it. Even tied his own flies."

"In the garage? Who all had access to that?"

"Anybody at Friday's party. The door's not locked and besides fishing gear, the garage contained a beer fridge. Periodically someone would grab a couple of six-packs and restock the ice chest near the BBQ with fresh cans. No one in particular was assigned the task. The chest somehow remained full. No one admits to looking after it. They remember Herb doing it once or twice and just assumed he kept it full. He's not around to tell us differently. Occasional showers had them all drifting into the garage at one time or another."

Jim leaned back in his seat and thought about the possibilities. Before he could speak, Kate was at the table with coffee pot in hand. "Sorry," she said, "didn't notice you come in." She plopped a white ceramic mug in front of Jim and filled it with black brew. Two creamers appeared from her apron pocket. Before she could place them on the table, Jim shook his head.

"Black's fine." He noticed the slice of half-eaten pie in front of Scott. "Piece of pie would be good. What kinds do you have?"

Kate pointed towards a glass-doored cooler behind the counter. Several pies were displayed inside. "A picture is worth a thousand words," she said and made a Vanna White type gesture.

Jim's eyes followed the hand. "Wow, in that case, you have a virtual library here. Let's start with the coconut cream and we'll see how it goes from there."

He watched as Kate rounded the counter and procured an appetizing mound of white cream on a light yellow base. Flakes of real toasted coconut were drizzled over the top of the pie. Before the pie even reached his table, he could feel his taste buds coming alive and the saliva building in his mouth. He looked back at Scott. "Eat here often? You must work out five hours a day to keep the weight off."

Scott smiled. "Ten," he said and took another bite of his own pie.

Kate dropped off the slice of pie as two other people came through the door. She grabbed the coffee pot and herded the newcomers to the opposite end of the room. Instinct told her the two cops wanted some privacy. They were here for more than the pie.

When he was sure no one was within earshot, Scott consulted his notes again. "We started with five suspects on our list: Darryl Cooper, the neighbour's brother; Joel Gallant, the partner; Sue Thornton, the mother-in-law; her husband George and of course, you can never leave off the wife, the statistical favorite. All these people were present at Friday night's party. There were a few other neighbours present. Mostly, they were very recent acquaintances who lived in the subdivision. They seem to have no other ties to Herb. It was a low key party. I'll give the neighbours more serious attention later if none of the initial five pans out."

Jim looked up from the coconut cream pie. "I'm listening." He unconsciously stuck out his tongue and captured an errant spot of cream at the corner of his mouth.

Scott suppressed a smile. "They all claim to have alibis, some are better than others. George Thornton was fishing at the tidal water power plant on the Annapolis River. He's sort of a fixture there and several people know him including the local Mounties. They remember talking to him Saturday morning. Some other fisherman caused a bit of commotion when he landed a 52.8 pound bass. Took a couple of hours and much of the town was there to watch at the end."

Jim set down his fork long enough to make a note of Scott's narrative in his own notebook. "Sounds pretty airtight. Could he have set the trap before he went to Annapolis."

"Maybe, but it would have been dark then. It's a three-hour drive to where he was fishing."

"OK, we'll keep him low on the list."

Scott nodded. "I wondered about Joel Gallant. He admits to a previous relationship with the wife. I thought he might be having an affair with Marilyn or at the very least have hopes of reigniting a flame with her. She is an attractive woman." Jim's eyes expressed agreement with that statement. "He claimed to be working on the company books, alone. The computer geeks downtown checked out his story and superficially examined his hard drives. Although it is possible to fake the times, they believe he was truly working in his office on Saturday morning. They gave me more detail than I ever wanted to back up their claims." Scott held up a sheaf of papers. "They are willing to dig deeper if I think it is necessary. For now, I'm holding off on using up their time.

"I talked to some of the employees of the company. Everyone loved Herb. Joel may have been the brains of the organization, but Herb was its heart. He generated the revenue that Joel tracked. Still, they couldn't imagine Joel killing anybody and especially not his partner. I give him a tentative pass for now but I'm going to be watching what happens between him and the widow. Love and money are two powerful motives."

Jim wrote down Joel's name in his book and followed with the word 'pass' followed by a question mark. He looked up at Scott again.

"Dan Cooper did have a brother Darryl. I googled Darryl and found his obituary. Died suddenly at home at the age of 32. Former owner-operator of his own business supply company. Surviving brother named Daniel. Looks like suicide to me brought on by losing his business. The case was never investigated."

"That let's Darryl off the hook but could give Dan a motive if he blamed Herb's company for his brother's death," Jim said. He had finished his pie and pushed back the plate. "Revenge doesn't require logical reasoning. Which one moved into the subdivision first?"

Scott consulted his notes. "Dan Cooper lived there about six months before Herb Clattenburg moved in. Turns out Dan's Saturday morning walk was to the liquor store. Kate confirms Dan spent most of the morning sitting right where you are, probably eating the same kind of pie. He doesn't strike me as the kind of person who gets out of bed too early on a Saturday morning. I'd think this was probably his first stop. Another pass?"

Jim stroked his chin. "I still wonder if there is some connection between Matthew Lane, Herb Clattenburg and Dan Cooper's deaths. As we know, Clattenburg and Cooper were neighbours. Lane spent time working in the same building as Cooper doing a productivity study. Not a great link but they could have been in contact. Besides, their deaths were too similar to be coincidence. There is some sort of a connection." He flipped back and forth through the pages of his notebook. Scott watched and waited. "I can't find a Clattenburg linkage to Lane, though. That's not too surprising. Most of Lane's business dealings are surrounded by secrecy. If you don't object, I'd like to have a little one-on-one with Joel Gallant. See if there is some way to connect these two cases."

Scott gave his hand a dismissive wave. "Go for it."

The two men paused to give this matter some thought. In the short period of silence, Kate arrived with more coffee. "I can smell the wood burning. You boys are into some heavy thinking. Need some more pie to fuel the fires?"

Both men snapped out of their reverie. "Coffee's fine," Jim said. He patted his flat stomach. "No more pie right now but, maybe I'll get one for takeout."

Scott pointed to his coffee cup and waited for Kate to top it up and leave. "Marilyn's only alibi is her husband and he's not telling us much. Obviously the two were having marriage difficulties. No one denies that, but the people I've talked to indicate the problems were generated more by the in-laws than by the couple themselves. Joel confided in me that the Thornton's had offered Herb money if he agreed to end the marriage. That was earlier this year. Joel said Herb was so mad he could hardly speak. His hands were shaking when he told Joel about the offer. His face was red and Joel could see the blood pulsing in his neck. He was afraid Herb was going to have a stroke or something. That was what finally prompted the move out here. Joel said Herb would've moved to BC if it hadn't meant breaking up the company. That would have simply supplied more fuel for the Thornton's to use against him. Instead he resolved to make the company bigger and better than ever."

Jim sipped his new, hot coffee. "That, I suppose meant working longer hours which put more strain on the marriage. He was in a lose-lose situation." Jim studied his notes from the Sunday interviews to see if there was anything there to help.

"What about that phone call Marilyn mentioned? That seemed to be a triggering factor for Herb to go fishing."

Scott's head involuntarily expressed agreement. "My thoughts exactly. The timing suggests that it could have been the killer. Came from a pay phone near the local service station. No one noticed anyone making the call. It's strictly a self-serve operation. One university kid works behind the counter. He's taking a summer course and was working on a report for class. There's no video surveillance and no customers at the time. It's a dead end."

Again Jim scanned his notes. "One thing is certain, Dr. Sue Thornton made no secret of her dislike of Herb. Usually death mellows some of the comments people make about others, but not the doctor. There was no hiding her contempt for her son-in-law. Do you think she could kill him?"

Scott did not answer right away. "Maybe," he said after a minute. He read a couple of pages in his own notebook before going on. "I checked at the university, talked to a couple of her coworkers. She is a published author." Scott looked up from his notes. "Get this. Her book is titled *The Power of Suggestion*. I'm trying to get a copy."

"That could be interesting," Jim said. "Give me a Cole's Notes version of it if there's anything relevant."

Scott grinned. "I struggle through the whole book and then write up an abbreviated report for you. I'll let you read the synopsis on the dust cover."

Jim held up his hands. "OK, OK. If it looks relative, I'll glance through it too. What about her alibi? She was shopping or something?"

"Claimed to be shopping alone in the city. Has a receipt for 9:05 a.m. from Wal-Mart and another for 12:30 p.m., again at Wal-Mart. No offence to Sam and the boys but she doesn't strike me as the Wal-Mart type. That's a long time to be in one store and, as you know, Wal-Mart has check-out lanes. You make all your purchases at once. The store is between here and her house."

Jim tapped his pencil on the table. "I've been in Wal-Mart on a Saturday morning. No way would anyone remember her. Now if she spent three hours in one of her upscale stores, she'd be remembered."

"Her husband was up before dawn to go to Annapolis Royal. Sue knows this, she must have been at least awake.

That gives her plenty of time to prepare her trap before heading out on her supposed shopping trip. Half-hour, 45 minutes from Wal-Mart to Basils Gate. Say an hour-and-a-half round trip. That gives her lots of time to plant the line before Herb arrived on the scene. A quick phone call to the Clattenburg residence on the way out of town would make sure Herb was taking the bait."

Jim was agreeing with the scenario Scott was spelling out as he ticked off the steps. "Please, no more fishing puns," he said, "now all we have to do is prove it. Despite all the things you found wrong at the scene, the plan is pretty intricate and required a huge dose of blind luck to have it actually work. Could she pull it off?"

"That," Scott said, "I'm still working on. Maybe it wasn't her first attempt. She may be content to set up possibilities for the worst case scenario and then let nature take its course. Sooner or later one of them might work. That could explain why it was so haphazard."

"Scary thought," Jim said. "Downright scary."

Chapter 29

Jim tracked down Joel Gallant at his downtown office the following morning.

"Sure, Sergeant, I can give you a couple of minutes," Joel said. He indicated a chair for Jim to sit in. "The office is closed today for Herb's funeral. I'm just clearing up a few details before I head out to give Marilyn a hand. This is going to be a rough day for her."

"Thanks. This won't take long." Jim looked around the office. Everything was neat and orderly. Nothing appeared out of place. In his mind he concurred with Scott Bowen's assessment that Joel did not kill his partner, for either love or money. The murder, which superficially looked like an accident, had too many lose ends to have been committed by someone as dedicated to detail as Joel appeared to be. This made Jim feel safer with the questions he was about to ask.

"Do you know Matthew Lane?"

Joel laughed. "Doesn't everybody?"

"So you were friends?"

"That would be stretching the truth too far. I know of Matthew Lane. We both belong to the City Club. I'm afraid I'm not in his league quite yet. Our little company hasn't appeared on Lane's radar so far."

Jim looked confused. "Could you explain that?"

Joel paused. "I'm not going to be quoted on what I say, am I? Matthew Lane was never a person to cross. I'm not sure which of the vultures have taken over the company since his death, but I don't want to be in their bad books." Again he paused.

Jim said nothing, just waited for Joel to continue. Joel appeared to pick his words carefully. "Matthew Lane has the reputation of being an astute businessman. He was, of course. But his main talent was observing weakness in other companies and pouncing on them at the opportune moment, when they were at their lowest point. Some called him a savior. Those people never owned any of the companies he helped out."

"That's quite an observation for someone not even on Lane's radar screen as you put it. Do you know of someone who was victimized by Lane?"

"Again, I know of them. In my previous life, I worked for one of the big accounting firms. You know the type where the company name is made up of all the partner's names. Matherson, Coughlan, Bentley, Robichaud and it went on and on and on. I never did get to memorize the whole thing. The secretaries' productivity could have been improved by 25% if the company would just choose a simpler name. My favorite was always "ACTS." Stood for Accounting Company Tax Services. That said it all and was close to the top of the list in the phone book.

"Anyway, in those days, I worked on some pretty big accounts. Got to see the inside workings of the operations. I can't go into any details but if a company came upon hard times, Matthew Lane's name seemed to pop up in its recovery. I went to the City Club a lot in those days, still do. It's where all the movers and shakers in the business world hang out. It's a place to meet clients in an informal setting, run up the expense account. Lane seemed to sense when one of these guys was in trouble. He would summon them to his table. He held court there.

"I was never invited to the table but I saw the aftermath of his bailouts. It usually meant more money for Lane in the long run. He was a patient man. The troubled company may or may not have been recognizable after being the recipient of Lane's largess."

Jim nodded. This confirmed what others had told him. "Do you know Claude Jackson?"

Joel let out a soft grunt. "Claude Jackson. There was the poster boy for why you didn't want to get involved with Matthew Lane. I don't know any of the details but I saw the results."

Jim raised his eyebrows. "Results?"

"Claude was one of those guys who had a tongue like a Mountie's boot: highly polished and commanded attention. He was already a regular at the City Club when I started going there. He's in the printing business. Every businessman who entered the building was a potential customer of Claude's and he recruited a lot of them into his fold. The company produced quality products, so that made the selling easier, but Claude could close a deal."

Joel's eyes seemed to lose their focus as he looked at a point on the wall behind Jim's head. He continued. "About three, maybe four years ago, that seemed to change. By then, Herb and I had started our own company. Expense account money came from my own pocket, not someone else's, so I was demoted a few tables at the club. Since I was no longer involved in the day to day lives of other people's companies, I became an observer of people. I noticed Claude became more aggressive, a little harder around the edges, pushed too hard. Whereas before he entertained freely, he started to spend less on his clients and let them do the paying more often. That's an accounting thing most people wouldn't notice like I did.

"Another strange thing he did at the time was to start collecting a fee to book his presses. It wasn't an added cost, he explained, just an advance. It was to deter people from booking press time on spec and then not following through with the final deal. It doesn't make sense when I describe it but Claude could make you believe it was a necessary part of doing business."

Joel looked pensive for a moment as if he was going to take another crack at explaining the process. Then he shook his head and went on. "The decline was slow and gradual until about a month ago. By then, you would hardly recognize him as the same man. You might say the boots were scuffed and worn."

"What has this to do with Matthew Lane?" Jim asked.

Joel looked at the cop again. "The first change, three or four years ago, was abrupt. I thought someone in the family must have died. Lasted about a week, maybe two. I later heard he made some bad investments in the futures market, coffee or something like that. Claude was like a lost puppy. I was there the day he got the summons to the king's table. Like I said, I'm a people watcher so I noticed who Lane talked to. Claude came away from Lane's table with a big smile on his face. He was almost the old Claude for a while. Then the changes I told you about started taking place. Every so often Lane would summon Claude again. These times he wasn't invited to sit down. He just stood like a supplicant at the master's table. He never left happy and as often as not he left the table and went straight out the door. Something was afoot."

Joel leaned forward over his desk towards the detective. "Did Claude have something to do with Matthew Lane's death?"

The question caught Jim off guard. "Why would you ask?"

"You're a homicide detective. You're not here making idle chitchat. Do you think Herb's death is somehow tied in to all this?"

"Did Herb know Jackson and Lane?"

"No, neither one to my knowledge. Herb never went to the City Club. As I said, that was from my previous life, a membership I never relinquished. I invited Herb from time to time but he always refused. To him, the City Club was the domain of the Thornton's and he had no desire to participate in it."

"So the Thornton's knew Matthew Lane?"

"Sure did. George Thornton thought of Matthew Lane as an astute businessman. He approved of his tactics."

"Did he know Claude Jackson?"

"Not really. Claude was a salesman. Not one of the old man's types." Joel slowly shook his head. "Do you know what that son of a bitch asked me? He wanted to know if now that Herb was dead, was I going to give up that silly, little business venture and get back to my true profession." Joel's eyes hardened. "Herb's not even in the ground yet. I told the old bastard to go to hell."

Jim let this comment hang in the air for a few seconds before moving on. "One more question. Did Neil Jackson belong to the City Club?"

Joel gave the matter some thought before shaking his head. "Don't recall the name."

Jim wasn't surprised. Neil would let Claude do all the sucking up. He would be content to simply back up Claude's words with action.

"Thanks for the help," Jim said. He stood up. "See you at the funeral." He had taken three steps towards the door when Joel stopped him.

"Sergeant, was Herb murdered?"

Jim stopped and slowly turned around. "What do you think?"

Joel came around his desk to meet the policeman. "I know that Herb was too good of a fisherman to let his waders fill with water. That's a rookie mistake and Herb was no rookie."

"Oh."

"Every family has a few stories that they tell over and over at family get-togethers. The Thorntons tell of being present when another fisherman drowned the same way Herb did. This was years ago and several people were present at the time of the death, including both Mr. and Mrs. Thornton. The men were fishing in a fast flowing river, the ladies were sitting on the bank drinking sherry or whatever when one of the men tumbled into the water. This was before waders had the tight waist chinch they have today.

"Despite the presence of half a dozen other men on the scene they could not pull the guy from the water before his lungs filled with water and he drowned. The weight in the waders was too much to overcome without filling their own boots. When they finally did get him out they performed the Hogger-Neilson method of resuscitation but it was too late. They also didn't have CPR and defibrillators in those days.

"Sue was shocked by the incident. Never went on one of those trips again. Mr. Thornton had his line back in the water later the same day."

Jim reached out and shook Joel's hand. "Interesting story. Thank you," he said.

Chapter 30

"... we therefore commit his body to the ground; earth to earth, ashes, to ashes, dust to dust..."

A large group of mourners assembled at the little church yard on the outskirts of the city. The sun was shining; the cerulean sky displayed a few wisps of white clouds. Nature was battling the solemnity of the occasion, making it an effort for all but the grieving widow to feel sad. Summer thoughts ruled everyone else's minds. Most had taken the afternoon off to attend the funeral, now they wanted to enjoy the remainder of the day.

The minister droned on. "Marilyn would like to invite you all to drop into her home at Shad Bay for some refreshments. It is a nice day for a drive in the country. I look forward to seeing you there." Herb and Marilyn had not lived in their new community long enough to establish church ties. Thus, the service was held in their old stomping grounds.

Detective-Sergeant Jim McDonald and Corporal Scott Bowen stood back away from those assembled around the open grave now expressing their condolences to Herb's immediate family. A few gray-haired people dotted the crowd. Herb's parents, aunts and uncles, no doubt. The vast majority of the attendees were the thirty-somethings, Herb's peers, clients and employees. They had patiently sat through the service and the committal. Now they were restless. They wanted to move on and get away from this reminder of their own mortality. Quietly, but quickly, they filtered to their cars and drove off.

Soon, only family stood around the grave. Sue Thornton's arms closed around her daughter's waist as she tried to ease her towards the waiting limousine. Marilyn resisted. She was not prepared to say good-bye to her husband. An older man moved in and corralled both women. With brute force, he walked them away from the coffin-filled hole.

"Mr. Thornton," Scott said. "I talked to him briefly but he had nothing to offer. Said a real fisherman would never have been that careless. Rather blunt, but I couldn't disagree with him."

Jim grunted in reply. His attention focused outside the funeral car. The Thornton's appeared to be arguing about something. "Let's get a little closer. I want to hear this."

The two policemen casually walked towards the remaining cars. Sue and her husband had moved back to a black Explorer which was next in line. The approaching cops moved out of their line of sight.

"I told you I'd go to the damn house," George Thornton was saying. "I'll make my token appearance and then I'm going to try that fishing spot. Joel Gallant claims trophy fish can be taken there. Why miss the chance to try and get one when we are all the way out there anyway."

"We are standing in sight of Herbert's grave. Let's give him at least one day's respect."

"Respect." Venom was attached to the word. "I'm no hypocrite, Sue. Being dead doesn't make me like him anymore. I'll show him respect by catching the fish that he couldn't."

The two stood silent for a moment. Jim could see Sue looking around. She still didn't notice the two policemen through the Explorer's tinted windows. "I don't want you to go to that spot. It's not safe. You might trip and fall in too." She studied her husband's reaction. He was not backing down. "If you have to go fishing, please go somewhere else."

The two cops looked at each other. They had released the information that Herb had fallen in, his waders had filled with water and he had drowned. The location of the accident was given as the lower part of the small pool where the body was recovered. They had made no mention of what had caused him to take his tumble or where the tumble had taken place. If Sue was indeed the killer, for all she knew the line was still stretched across the river. She hadn't risked returning to the scene of the crime. Now she feared for the life of her husband.

"Don't be foolish woman," Thornton said. "This is the best spot. Why go elsewhere?" George started to open the SUV's door. "I'm not stupid enough to fall in, that's for sure, and if I did, no water would get into my waders."

Sue gently took hold of the flaps of her husband's suit coat. She looked up into his eyes. Her face softened. "For once, could you just do something for me just because I'm asking you to and for no other reason." She gave an insistent tug on the jacket. "Please come to the house and play the grieving father-in-law. If not for me, do it for Marilyn. She needs you now more than at any other time since she moved out. Please come. We want to welcome her back into our home. This small concession will be the first step."

Jim noticed the older man's shoulders physically sag. A look of defeat came across his face. "OK, I'll do this for Marilyn, but if we have to come back out here this weekend, I'm going fishing."

Sue moved in and gave her husband a big hug. An exasperated look came across his face but he hugged back anyway before climbing into the Explorer. Sue went forward to the other car and joined her mourning daughter.

"Can we stretch that into a confession?" Scott asked.

Jim grimaced. "In light of what we learned this morning, it's good enough for me. I don't think the courts will buy it, though. We've got to get her to admit what she did. I think she's vulnerable. If we question her, she might just break down and tell all."

"Should we grab her at the wake? That might weaken her resolve."

Jim shook his head. "I'd like to." He hesitated. "But if we're wrong, it would be a PR nightmare. It's not as if she's some crazed killer who is going to strike again. For Marilyn's sake, I think we can wait for a day or two. It will give us a chance to get all our ducks in a row for the interrogation."

Chapter 31

Dan Cooper's death knocked the wind out of Claude Jackson. As vice-president in charge of sales he had worked closely with Cooper for a number of years and considered him as much a friend as an employee. Now Dan's death fell squarely on Claude's shoulders. There could be no denying it, no rationalizing it away. It was his fault. Damn it, how could his life have gone to hell in such a short space of time?

Cooper's funeral had been held that morning and both he and Neil attended to show respect for the long time employee. The family pew, he noted, had some interesting characters sitting there, but who was he to judge. Dan's death rested squarely on his shoulders. Claude's emotional response to the burial rivaled those of the family members. Many people noticed this and were moved by his devotion to an employee. It spoke highly for the regard in which Dan had been held by the company, they concluded. No one came to the more accurate conclusion that this bereaved man was the cause of Dan's demise.

As Claude sat at his desk back in his own office, nothing had improved. Crosley was still out there. Things were not going to get better any time soon.

When Crosley called to make arrangements for the final payoff, Claude told him to go to hell. He wouldn't pay. He expected some arguments, some threats, but there was nothing. Crosley just calmly said: "As you wish" and hung up again. That pissed Claude off too. He wanted to hang up on Crosley just once.

Now, as he sat here alone in his office, he was starting to realize he was in deep, deep shit. Crosley never called back.

Did that mean that Claude would be next to have an accident? Of course it did. Even in the depressed state he was in, Claude understood that. There was no ambiguity when Crosley told him that. Claude was next.

He had even given him an exact date, but Claude couldn't dredge that important bit of information from his confused memory of the previous meeting. At the time, he had been overwhelmed by Crosley's threat, no promise, to kill some other acquaintance of Claude's just to prove his ability. Now he sat on his own death watch. His office was his own private version of death row.

Maybe it wouldn't even be an accident. When they had discussed it right after Dan's death, Neil pointed out there was no need for Crosley to be subtle. He would have to make an example of Claude, send a message to future customers what would happen if they reneged on payment. Neil deplored him to just pay and put this part of his life behind him. As usual Neil was right. As usual Claude had screwed up. Now what?

He could run. But where? How far? For how long?

He could go out west or maybe to Europe. Even Australia might not be far enough. He knew nothing about what kind of reach Crosley had.

He could stay and fight. What a joke that was. Matthew Lane with all his security was dead. Everyone except for one homicide cop thought it was an accident. Even Claude, who had ordered it, first believed it was only an accident. What chance did he have against such a formidable foe as Crosley? At last, a question he could answer: None. None at all. He had at least come that far in his thinking.

Then, there was that cop, Sergeant Jim McDonald, what did he know? It wasn't just a coincidence that he had shown up on the same day Dan was killed. He knew more than he was letting on. Claude would have to be wary of him and not walk into any traps he set. That created a double threat, running from the good guys as well as the bad guys.

He reached for the bottom drawer of his desk and withdrew the bottle of Captain Morgan rum hidden there. He was having another liquid lunch. His stash wasn't lasting as long as it used to. He poured a drink, threw it back and poured another. His intercom buzzed.

"Sergeant McDonald from the RCMP is here to see you," Jean's voice told him.

Oh Christ, he thought. "Give me a minute," he told her.

He opened the bottom drawer and set the freshly poured but untouched glass of liquor in beside the bottle. A new bottle of Pepto Bismal lay beside the rum bottle, already half empty. Claude grabbed it and took a slug. He wiped the pink liquid from his lips with the back of his hand and gently closed the drawer again. Then he got up and went over to Neil's adjoining door and knocked. There was no answer. Damn, where was he? We've just buried Dan Cooper and already Neil is back to the grindstone.

Jim McDonald smiled as he sat in the outer office waiting for his audience with Claude. He had followed the Jackson brothers back to the plant after Dan Cooper's funeral. He sat in the parking lot for two and one-half hours waiting to see Neil leave. He wanted to talk to Claude alone. Meeting in Claude's office was fine with him. Any other place Claude led him, if Claude had been the first to leave, would have been equally good. Jim was easy.

Claude stood out as the weak link in this case. The detective was about to shatter that link as if it were made from ice and struck with a firm blow from a hammer. Jim stood by to pick up the pieces and put a plausible scenario of the events together. He felt in his bones Claude was ready to break the last time, the nervousness, the drinking. Only Neil

Jackson's intervention had prevented Jim from getting the whole story then. Add to that, Claude's performance at the funeral, Jim could only feel confident the time was ripe. Due to the policeman's patient waiting in the parking lot, Claude was now on his own.

Whereas, the last time Jim was here, he had burst right in on Claude and caught him off guard, this time he wanted to give him time to stew a little. Let him think about what Jim might know. Let that perceived knowledge multiply and grow in his mind until Claude believed the sergeant had all the answers. In reality, the knowledge was not much more than his last visit, not enough to pin a murder charge on him, but he had learned a few things.

Joel Gallant's observations suggested Matthew Lane and Claude Jackson were involved in some sort of business dealings. Dealings that were having a negative effect on Claude.

Jim had shown a picture of Claude to the chauffeur, James Nelson, who confirmed Claude was the one who visited Lane once a month with cash in hand. There was no doubt in Nelson's mind. It was a positive identification.

Ronald Welton was unable to tie the picture in to the person with the advertising proofs. He had only heard voices and had not seen the source of them. His description of a whiny voice fit in with Claude Jackson. Claude's voice, when he was on the defensive, changed and grated on Jim's nerves as well. Jim would set up a voice lineup if necessary to see if Welton could recognize it, but not right away. Voice recognition after this length of time could be tricky and if Welton failed, it would be in Claude's favor at trial.

Neither man recognized the picture of Neil Jackson, nor did any other investigation into the older brother tie him to Matthew Lane. His only apparent connection to the case was to be the brother of Jim's prime suspect, not a crime, but still worth watching considering the influence he seemed to wield over his sibling.

No pictures were required for Joel to tie the two men together. He was familiar with both of them.

Jim also showed a driver's license photo of Dan Cooper to Nelson and Welton. Dan too, was unfamiliar to both.

The pictures of the Jackson brothers came from a JP&P brochure Jim picked up on his way out from the first trip. It told him a little about the company but, except for the pictures, was not a great deal of use. However he would parrot back some of the facts to Claude to make him think he knew more about the company than he did. It might work.

He also checked out Claude's finances. Claude was in deep financial trouble. Whatever he was doing with Lane was costing him money, not making him money.

One outstanding question, how did Dan Cooper fit into this? That, he hadn't worked out yet. Was it just a serendipitous coincidence that made him look at Jackson a little harder? He didn't think so. Also the death of Herb Clattenburg added to the confusion. Was it somehow connected as well? Again, Jim didn't think so, but he still had no definite proof of Sue Thornton's guilt. He intended to answer all these questions at this meeting.

Claude lowered himself into the chair at his desk again and looked down at the closed drawer.

"Why the hell not?" he asked himself and opened the drawer, took out the glass and drank it down in one quick swallow. He screwed up his mouth and gave a shudder. Black rum failed as a chaser for liquid antacid. He returned the glass to the drawer, squared his shoulders, straightened his tie and punched the intercom button.

"Send the officer in," he said to Jean, a little too loudly, convincing himself that he sounded in control and sober. At least someone was convinced.

Jean looked over at the sergeant and shrugged. This had become a strange place to work in the last week or so. Her employer seemed to be going to hell in a hand-basket right before her eyes.

"You heard him," she said.

The policeman smiled at her and pushed through the door.

"We believe Matthew Lane and Dan Cooper were both murdered," McDonald said as he approached the desk, without any preliminaries. "What was your involvement in their deaths?"

By now, he was standing directly in front of Claude, looking down at him, hands on his hips, a no-nonsense expression on his face. This direct procedure was a gamble. Often if worked on weaker people.

Claude was stunned by this attack. "Wha- what are you saying?" he said. He looked towards the door leading to Neil's office. There was no help forthcoming. He looked down at his empty desk. Again, no help.

"Me, involved in killing Dan Cooper. That's the most ridiculous thing I've ever heard. He was like family. He was family, damn it." Claude was babbling now. His voice died away. Then in a faint, almost inaudible, voice, he added: "I tried to stop him. I just couldn't find the damn slips. Dan was part of our corporate family. I would never hurt him. Never. Oh Christ, what have I done."

McDonald was astounded at what he was hearing. Never in a million years had he expected this sort of a response so fast. He arrived today determined to make Claude talk. Determined to come out of this interview with some concrete facts. Determined to square in his own mind that murder had taken place. But a confession after just two sentences: one a statement, one a question. Was Claude even aware he was speaking out loud? Jim didn't think so. No matter, his job was to act as though he knew everything all along and pump out as much detail as he could before Claude realized what he was saying. His next question would be crucial.

Chapter 32

Crosley sat in his car in the far corner of the printing firm's large parking lot. No additional funds had arrived in his bank account and the day of reckoning had arrived. Claude had until the end of business on this day. If he didn't pay up, the trip home would prove fatal. Only one more step was required to set the wheels of the messenger of God in motion one more time. The time for proper planning was over. Now was the time for action.

Crosley had an excellent view of the entrances to and exits from the plant's main building but at the same time was inconspicuous to anyone who may have looked his way. Nearby was a bus shelter and often people parked here while waiting to pick up an arriving passenger.

He was reading the latest edition of The Herald. Wherever he went he kept up on both the local and national news. This enabled him to make "small talk" with the people he ran into. To him there was no such thing as "small talk." This was how he derived a lot of the information he needed for his work. First you needed to warm people up with innocuous conversation and then dig in to get the details you wanted.

As a result he read both the local paper and at least one national, sometimes two, from front to back. You never knew what subject would help to open his contacts up. With some people it would be sports, others politics or world news and others the field of entertainment. Sometimes he even perused the supermarket tabloids. Not for pleasure, mind you. This was part of his work.

In bars, he would open with a line like "What about those Leafs" if it was hockey season or close to it. In the summer he would substitute Blue Jays for Leafs. It seemed most people had an opinion, one way or the other, on one of Canada's professional sports teams, regardless of the part of the country he was in. Yankees was the name he used in the States. Americans loved or hated the Yanks year round, not just in baseball season. Personally, he couldn't care less, but whatever worked.

With Nelson, the chauffeur, music was the magic key. Crosley kept himself up to speed on all the latest music trends as well as maintaining a conversational knowledge of music dating back to the 40s. This included blues, jazz, popular, rock, hip hop and even rap.

However, even as he read the paper, another part of his mind was contemplating the presence of another car in the parking lot. It was a plain, black Ford. Crosley was a detail man. He took in everything that went on around him and filed the information away for future use. This plain, black Ford was very similar to the one that had just avoided being hit by Lane when he was making his way to the Promised Land. In fact, it was so similar that it could be the same car.

Like McDonald, coincidence was not in Crosley's vocabulary. As he studied the car, it became obvious, so obvious in fact that he couldn't believe he missed it before. This was a police car. That explained the skilled avoidance at the accident scene. Police training turned the driver into an expert.

His mind had been tricked at the accident site by the T-shirt, cargo shorts and sandals, not the attire a cop would be expected to be wearing. The presence of the girl snuggled up beside him completed the deception. That was slack thinking on his part. Even cops get a day off now and then. The car couldn't have been any more obvious as a police vehicle if it had RCMP written in large, white letters down both sides and across the roof. No chrome, no hubcaps, no frills. Real people didn't buy cars like that, only government agencies.

The car was occupied when Crosley arrived. He watched the driver, dressed in Sears Menswear chic, go into the building as soon as Neil Jackson left. Due to the length of time the man had waited in the parking lot before entering the building, the two events seemed to be tied together.

Why were the police here? Did it have anything to do with him? Both incidents were reported as accidents. Both were executed without a hitch. Nothing sloppy, nothing out of the ordinary, nothing different from any number of accidents that took place across the country every day. One was excessive speed, the other excessive drinking. Two of the most common reasons people were killed on the highways.

But if this was indeed the exact same car that almost became part of the Lane collision and Crosley was positive it was, its presence suggested more interest than a routine accident should have. Personal involvement tended to generate more than normal interest in what should have been routine. Routine being: investigated, declared an accident, turned into a statistic, filed and forgotten. This would bear some further examination on his part. Kismet may have dealt a new wrinkle to be handled even if he didn't believe in fate.

The cop, and now he was convinced it was one, could have been anywhere in the building. Crosley reached for his cell phone and dialed the number of Claude Jackson's secretary. Posing as a police officer himself, he would find out if there was a detective talking to Claude at this moment. It may be time to speed up the necessary steps required to end the Jackson problem.

"Good morning," he said in an official sounding voice with just a wee touch of Irish accent. "This is Sergeant O'Reilly of the Metro Police Force. One of our members was going to drop in on Mr. Jackson and I was wondering if he had arrived yet?"

This was a gamble if the policeman was there for some unconnected reason but then again it would give Claude one more thing to worry about when Jean reported it to him. And keeping Claude unbalanced was now part of the game plan. Anything that would inspire him to pay up was in order. Killing him was a last resort.

"Why yes, Sergeant McDonald is talking to Mr. Jackson even as we speak. Shall I get him for you?"

"No, that won't be necessary, lassie. I'll talk to him when he gets back to the station. Sorry to have bothered you and have a nice day." He made a note of the detective's name.

He had invested a considerable amount of time in this job and hated the thought of not being paid. But on the bright side, it was like a vacation being back home. He seldom got to spend this much time on his home turf. He was reluctant about taking the job in the first place because he didn't like to mix work and home life. However, he had even less desire to mix work time and jail time. If the police were investigating the deaths, Jackson would have to be dispensed with and without any further delay.

He put down the cell phone. It was a disposable that he picked up at the local Shoppers Drug Mart. He took another one from his jacket pocket. This one belonged to Cooper. The phone was surprisingly still operative. Once again his finger poked at the tiny figures on the keyboard of the cell phone. He dialed Jackson's private number and waited while the phone rang — once, twice, three times. He could visualize Jackson squirming in front of the police officer, his drawer ringing.

Four, five, six, seven. Crosley was enjoying this.

Chapter 33

"**I** believe your phone is ringing," Sergeant McDonald said to the nervous, perspiring Jackson after several rings. He was peeved at the intrusion at this point just when Jackson was about to break down but he wanted Claude's full attention.

Claude hesitated, opened the drawer and picked up the receiver of the phone. Leaning down behind his desk in a lackluster attempt at privacy, he answered.

"He-hello."

A drop of perspiration landed on the bottle of Captain Morgan in the drawer and ran down the side to land on the overturned glass. The display said Jackson Printers and Publishers. He had seen that before. This could only be one person and he didn't want to be talking to him in front of the police.

"Have you ever heard of a *kundela*?" he heard Crosley ask. "One is being pointed at you right now."

There was a click and once again Jackson was left holding a dead phone. McDonald noticed the stunned, confused look on the other's face.

"Kundela? Kundela? What the hell is a kundela?" Jackson said to no one in particular. Crosley would be surprised, no amazed, to discover Claude would have an answer to that question. His intention was to remind Claude that he was still out there somewhere and perhaps convince him not to talk. To be more afraid of Crosley than the police. He just wanted to make a phone call to Claude, the contents were unimportant. As fate would have it, he increased Claude's fear and apprehension.

"A kundela is the name of a carved killing-bone used by the aborigines in the outback of Australia," McDonald said, surprised at the use of the obscure word. He was a student of various forms of death and killing around the world.

"It is believed that if the *mulunguwa* or tribal executioners make, ritually load and point a kundela at a person, they will die. Since nothing is fired but only pointed at the victim it leaves no trace. It almost never fails. It is used against those who have violated some serious tribal law or custom. Victims have even been rushed to modern day hospitals where nothing is found wrong with them, except a few days later, they die.

"This sounds like a grave intimidation. Who is threatening you with a kundela?"

In his distraught state, Jackson didn't even question the validity of the statement about dying because someone pointed a bone at you. He now believed Crosley might have that power. He looked at the police detective sitting across from him with the knowledge to define these vague terms. He knew what it meant; McDonald should be able to protect him from dying.

"You've got to help me," he said. "There is a maniac killer trying to get me."

"We're here to serve and protect," said McDonald with only a trace of sarcasm in his voice. "Tell me all about it. The last time I was here you were telling me about your connection to Matthew Lane. Has that connection anything to do with this?"

"Lane, yeah Matthew Lane," Claude said. "That son of bitch started this whole thing. He pretends to be your friend and the next thing you know he's trying to take possession of your business and people are dying all over the place, good friends are dying. I wish I had never heard that name."

Once again McDonald was in the position of having to act as though he knew a lot more than he did. Claude admitted there was a link between people dying and what caused it. Now it was up to Jim to connect the dots and find the link. He decided to go for the wide open question.

"Tell me everything you know about Lane's death. I can only help you if I know everything you know. Hold anything back and it could prove fatal to you. Confirm my information and we can protect you." McDonald laid it on thick as if using a trowel.

Claude started with meeting Steve Wilcox, advanced to the coffee futures, proceeded to the hurricane, followed with the bailout by Lane and finished with the shakedown. In his mind he had done nothing wrong and his narrative didn't make it to the hiring of a hit man.

Jim prompted him. "And Lane's supposed accident? How did that come about?"

"Well, he was trying to steal our company right out from underneath us," Claude said. "He had to be stopped."

There was a long pause in which both men remained silent, each in their own thoughts. Claude continued in a low, almost inaudible voice: "I stopped him."

Bingo, Jim thought. "Stopped him how?"

Jackson seemed to snap out of the stupor he was in. The lethargy lifted as he realized what he was saying and to whom. He shifted in his chair. He was unsure of how much he had told McDonald. Damn the booze. What should he do now?

Jim sensed the conversion from scared, confused victim to aware, confused culprit. He stood up and leaned over the desk closing the space between them.

"What do you know about the murder of Matthew Lane? How did YOU stop him?"

This was the second time the word murder was used. The first mention of it started Jackson on his downward spiral. He appeared to be in some kind of a trance at the time unaware of what he was saying. This time he was aware and alert and the effect on Claude was immediate and jarring. He recoiled back in the chair. The colour left his face.

"Murder? Murder? Let me call my brother," he said.

"So, your brother is involved too?" Jim went on, the same firmness in his voice. "Bring him in here so he can be interrogated as well."

"No, no. He is not involved. I did it myself. I think I had better call a lawyer."

"Suit yourself," Jim said, "but I can't help you once you do that."

Claude stopped to think about the offer of help. He got up from his chair and walked over to the stereo in the corner of the office. He turned down the volume then turned and walked over to the window, looking out but not seeing. The preponderance of the events of the previous two weeks weighed heavily on him. He knew he was in deep trouble, knew his arrest was imminent and now just wanted to have everything end.

Jim waited.

"I only met him once and I have only a vague recollection of what he looked like. I was pretty stressed at the time." Claude decided he may as well cooperate. He didn't need two people attacking him and the police seemed the safest option. McDonald wasn't threatening to kill him. Once again he lowered himself into the chair behind his desk, leaned back and closed his eyes as if in deep thought.

"Met who once?" Jim asked after the silence stretched out for over a minute.

"Crosley, the killer," Claude said. He gave his head a shake as if he disbelieved what he was about to say. "I even called a death threat into the police thinking that might scare Lane into leaving me alone. It was a stupid idea. I wasn't thinking straight at the time." He fell silent again.

Jim added this tidbit to his notes. That call had set up the whole police involvement. It had come from Claude Jackson. Without it, Jim would not even be here today.

"Go on with your story," Jim said.

Claude opened his eyes and leaned forward looking straight at the detective. The narrative resumed. He detailed how he first contacted Crosley, the details about the payment, how an accident intervened and let him off the hook, the whole story. He concluded with Crosley demanding the money and him not being able to find the deposit slips.

Jim took copious notes.

"An accident let you off the hook?" he asked at one point. Jim was interrogating the most naive man in the world.

"Well, I guess it wasn't an accident. Crosley must have caused it somehow."

Jim waited for this phase of the story to finish. Again, Claude fell silent. In his mind, he was reliving the events as he described them.

"How does Cooper fit in to all this?" Jim asked prompting Claude to get on with his chronicle.

Claude winced at the sound of Dan Cooper's name. Once again waves of guilt rolled across him.

"Crosley claimed he was going to set up a demonstration to show how he could make an assassination look like an accident. Poor Cooper, who would never hurt anyone, was the victim. It may just have been a coincidence. I don't know. Anyway, if I don't pay, I will be next. That's where we are now. Now he's talking about pointing some magical bone at me."

"Right, a kundela. How did Cooper know Crosley?" Jim asked. He was still trying to link the two deaths and possibly tie in Herb Clattenburg.

This question never occurred to Claude. He turned it over in his mind and again began to think it might have just been a chance occurrence that Cooper died at the exact moment Crosley predicted. Was Crosley just an opportunist who watched the news and cashed in on events as they happened? Was it all serendipity? Don't be stupid, he told himself. It was this kind of thinking that got him to the position he was in now, that got Dan killed. Crosley was a pro and he, Claude, was in his sights.

"I don't know," he said. "Neil said something about Dan having a meeting with a new client just before the accident. There was something strange about it but, well, my thinking hasn't been too clear of late. I didn't pay much attention. Neil was going to check it out. He can tell you what was going on. Ask him."

"I will," Jim said. The older brother—the smart one was how Jim kept them separate in his mind—was supposed to get back to him with this information. Jim would be sure to follow up on this now.

"But," Jim said "if I am to keep you alive you have to tell me the whole story, right from the beginning."

Jim realized Claude was getting more and more in control of his faculties. He wanted to hear the story again, try for more details.

"Don't hold anything back," he said. "Don't hide anything. Don't try to make yourself look like the victim. It's way too late for that."

I am the victim, Claude thought but didn't put it into words. Instead he cooperated. Claude poured out the whole story.

Once again he started with Steve Wilcox and the coffee futures, the hurricane, the debt just as if he hadn't already told McDonald a short time ago. This time, however, no prompting was required when he reached the incriminating part. The story continued with the hiring of Crosley right up to and including the phone call about the kundela which he and McDonald had just discussed.

When he finished, a look of relief was on his face. Just telling the whole story in one sitting had a therapeutic value even if was opening the door to a prison cell. He gestured towards the policeman with his palms facing the ceiling and shrugged.

"That's it. You've heard it all."

Jim was able to compare the two stories given to him in the last few minutes. One when Claude was off in another world and detached and one when he was cooperative and coherent. Both seemed to agree with each other. The facts were essentially the same but there was enough variation to realize it wasn't a planned, memorized fiction.

However, outside of verifying there were suspicious circumstances in both the deaths and Jackson's payment made one happen and nonpayment caused the other, McDonald realized he was no closer to the "how" than when he witnessed Lane's death for himself. Jackson could shed no light on this part of the story. He was as in the dark as Jim. Final outcome was all he had discussed with Crosley, the how was left to come from the mind of the killer. Even though Jim now knew it was not the case, everything still pointed to two separate unrelated accidents. This killer, whoever he was, knew his stuff.

In the distance a car alarm sounded. Jim got up and walked to the window to find the source. A commanding panorama of the Halifax Harbour with its two bridges and the steel blue waters of the Bedford Basin filled his sight. It was a post card view of peninsular Halifax, the kind of view you would expect from an executive office. The parking lot was out of sight at the front of the building. No cars were in sight. Jim resumed his seat.

Chapter 34

Crosley slipped back into his car and withdrew the Slim Jim from the sleeve of his jacket. He put the long thin piece of wire back into the case with the other similar wires and slipped the container under the front seat out of sight. Each wire was designed for a different kind of car. Each was as efficient, if not more so, than an actual car key in the proper hands. Crosley opened the car door, took care of business and relocked and closed the door in less than twenty seconds.

All that time, he listened to the car alarm going through its litany of squeals and beeps. These noises were only of a minor concern to him. No one paid any attention to them any more. To be sure, he glanced up at the office windows as he sauntered away from the area of the car. Only two people bothered to come to the windows to look out, both well after he had left the area of the car. Neither showed any real concern. One looked out, glanced back into the office and turned to the window again, laughing. No doubt he made some comment like the baby is crying again to his fellow staffers.

Crosley had moved up his schedule. Claude's end of day would come much sooner than he anticipated. Crosley would have preferred the rest of his money, but with the police involved that didn't seem to be the path Claude had chosen. Crosley wasn't taking any chances. He was prepared for this eventuality right from the beginning. Part of his operating procedure was to allow for the worst case scenario, the client losing his nerve. Too bad Mr. Jackson, but one of us is going to accept his loses and move on. The other, well let's say he won't be moving on.

Crosley figured this was probably the first meeting with the police. Otherwise it wouldn't be taking place in Jackson's office. The police officer would get a few of the details but he would not start a serious interview until Jackson was downtown at police headquarters. At that point there would be others helping, observing and recording what all was said. He figured Jackson would be an easy target. He lacked the backbone to even protect himself. That meeting could not take place.

Crosley had taken care of one possibility, Jackson getting to drive his own car. More drastic measures would have to be taken if that scenario didn't play out. At the other extreme, a bullet in the head could solve Crosley's problem. If Jackson and the cop got into a police car, the destination would be obvious, police headquarters. The necessary action could take place while the car sat in traffic anywhere along the route. Crosley preferred not to do that.

But just how much could the cop know? In fact, how could he know anything? Jackson was supposed to be a top salesman. Surely he could convince the policeman of his innocence or if not, to let him turn himself in and not be led out of his own building in front of his own staff in handcuffs. Perhaps he should go in and pass himself off as Jackson's attorney and take control of things.

There was someone else who could take control and definitely would if he knew what was going on. On his pervious visits to the company building, it didn't take long to figure out who possessed the brains in the operation. Now he understood why the cop waited so long before going in. He was avoiding Neil Jackson.

Crosley made a few calls and tracked down the elder Jackson. "Call your brother right now," he told him and sat back to wait to see what would happen. In less than five minutes a cream coloured Buick pulled into the parking lot and right up to the main door. Neil jumped out leaving the door open and hustled inside.

Seconds later, an older uniformed man appeared in the doorway. He looked around the parking lot before climbing into the car deserted by the company president. He slowly and carefully drove the car to its designated parking area a few feet away from the door beyond the handicapped spots. One more look around the lot and he returned to the building.

Once more Crosley picked up the cell phone, consulted a worn leather covered notebook and dialed.

"Paul Whitten," a voice drawled in his ear.

"Yeah, Paul," he said. "I've heard there's been a breakthrough in the Matthew Lane case. Claude Jackson of Jackson Printing and Publishing is about to be arrested."

Whitten leaned forward in his chair and reached for his pad and a pencil, the tools of his trade. There was the normal bustle of a big city newsroom getting ready to put out the next edition all around him but his complete attention was on the caller on the phone. He was, however, a bit confused. The call was coming from a Jackson company phone. A whistle-blower? A disgruntled employee?

"The Matthew Lane case?" he asked. "I'm not sure I'm familiar with it. Could you bring me up to speed." His pencil was poised over the notepad waiting for a break in what was a dull day up to that point. Overnight was very quiet which makes it a challenge for a crime writer to fill his news quota for the day. Even the courts were dead today. As a result this caller would get much more attention than he normally would with his anonymous tip.

As a rule, Crosley slipped in to town, did his job and disappeared. Most of the time no one was aware that his hand was even involved. Accidents happened. People were buried. Life went on. But somehow, the fate he didn't believe in, intervened in this case and it was off the tracks. The police were involved. Now it was up to him to manipulate things back into his favor.

"Lane, the multimillionaire, was murdered a while back. Now they've caught the guy and are about to arrest him. Just thought you would be interested, unless of course, you're part of the corporate cover-up too." Crosley hung up.

Paul wrote "Matthew Lane, Claude Jackson and multimillionaire" on his pad. He underlined multimillionaire twice. He rotated his grey upholstered office chair towards a coworker in the crime department who was busy solving the cryptoquote in that morning's paper. It was a slow day.

"Pat, are you working on the Matthew Lane murder?" he asked. There were only two crime reporters working full time for the paper so if it wasn't his story, it must be hers.

"Matthew Lane?" She screwed up her face as she dug into the recesses of her mind for the name. "How long ago?" she asked when nothing came to mind.

"Matthew Lane of Lane Investments?" said a business writer sitting at a nearby desk. "Died in a car accident a week or so ago. Huge waves in the business world. Don't you guys pay any attention to what is going on in the real world? Some rumors have it that it may have been a suicide but no one in the know bought into that story." He was including himself as one of those in the know and his dismissal of the suicide was as good as a confirmation that it hadn't happened.

Paul thought about all the crime scenes he had visited. The blood trails that sometimes ran for blocks along the sidewalk, the death and destruction of human beings, the broken lives from the results of bad drug deals — a redundancy since there were no good drug deals — the aftermath of home invasions and robberies. He was very aware of the "real" world. But for now he wanted information and not a philosophical discussion. He let the comment pass.

While the business reporter brought him up to speed on Matthew Lane's biography and also the fact that it was a car accident, Paul wondered about the corporate cover-up line from the informant. It was possible.

He called his source at the police station. He had talked to him less than an hour ago to find out about the overnight crimes in the city. He had said nothing about an impending arrest, either officially or unofficially. He would have to ask him point blank and then try to interpret the answer.

Interpretation was a part of the job that improved over time. For example if a victim was taken to the hospital and the reporter wanted to know if the person was dead or not, there was no simple yes or no answer from the hospital. If the answer was "we have no one of that name on our patient list" and he knew the injuries were serious enough that the patient would not have been released, that would translate into "the patient had died." Otherwise they could not comment on the patient's condition. Still alive.

The media liaison officer denied any knowledge of an impending arrest. He sounded convincing. But it was a slow news day. Paul had lots of time to keep digging. Who knows, maybe it was a cover-up. He looked up the number of Jackson Printing and Publishing.

Meanwhile Crosley resumed his waiting in the parking lot of the printing company. The call was a long shot. Now was time to see if it produced the desired results.

Chapter 35

Neil Jackson burst into the office of his younger brother without knocking or even acknowledging Jean as she sat at her desk watching him blow by. The strangeness continues, she thought. Coworkers dying, police interviewing her boss, unusual phone calls and now a less than polite Neil Jackson. Something was in the air.

"Stop talking Claude," were the first words out of Neil's mouth. He surveyed the scene, taking in the disheveled look of his brother and the aggressive attitude of the police officer. Was he too late to stop his brother from doing something beyond stupid? It looked that way.

Neil had been visiting a supplier in the industrial park when he received the strange call to phone his brother. The display indicated it came from a company phone but it was not a voice he recognized. Neil's call to Claude's secretary informed him of the police presence in the office and brought Neil on the run. Now he had to do some fire fighting. He had to determine where the situation stood without revealing any additional information that might not have come up to this point. He didn't have to wait long.

Jim turned to face the intruder. He wondered if the older brother ever knocked before entering the younger brother's office. He was two for two in crashing the party in Jim's observations.

"Your brother was just telling me about his part in the death of Matthew Lane," McDonald said. "Would you like to tell me about your part?" For a brief second Neil was stunned by McDonald's accusation. In a flash, he recovered his composure again.

"What in the hell are you talking about? Why would my brother be a part of Lane's death? It was an automobile accident, wasn't it?" Neil sounded convincing.

McDonald was unsure but didn't want to give up his advantage. "Think so? Well, you had better sit down and listen to this little tale of woe." Claude had not implicated his brother in either rendition of events. It was possible Neil was unaware of what happened but McDonald doubted it. Neil was the smart one, Jim reminded himself.

Once again Claude told his story although with more reluctance in his brother's presence. Jim prompted him often to keep the narrative going. Neil managed to look both shocked and surprised as the tale unfolded.

When Claude got to the part about passing page proofs along to Lane, a change came over Neil. He leaned forward to make sure he fully understood what Claude was telling him. Neil's eyes bore into his brother's as if they were suddenly strangers. Disbelief hung in the air like a curtain between the two men.

McDonald studied the older brother's reaction. Neil was either a great actor or outside the loop. McDonald would reserve his decision.

After the chronicle was complete, Neil sat in total silence looking at his brother. This was the first time he had heard the complete story. Time passed. Claude ran out of things to say. Jim was assessing the two men before him, looking for the truth. Neil was weighing his options on how to handle this situation that had gone completely out of control.

The squawk of the intercom jarred all three men out of their individual reverie.

Claude looked at the box on the desk in front of him but made no move to respond. Neil leaned forward and barked into the microphone: "Not now, Jean. Hold all calls."

"I'm sorry Mr. Neil," she said "but there's a reporter from the newspaper on the line looking for a comment on Mr. Claude being arrested for murder." She sounded rattled and waited for the expected denial. It was a strange day and getting stranger.

"Aren't we getting ahead of ourselves?" Neil glared at McDonald and pushed the talk button to connect him to the secretary again. "Tell him that statement is too ludicrous to even comment on," he said. If only that were true, he thought.

The downward spiral continued. Somehow, Neil thought, he had to take command. He looked back at the police detective, about to berate him again when he noticed that McDonald looked equally as surprised and confused about the media involvement.

What was the source of this information, Jim wondered. He had entered this building with no thoughts of making an arrest. He was just searching for leads. No one else was on the case. What forces were in play here? He struggled to hide his surprise. He must maintain control of the interview. He turned to Neil and they both started to speak at the same time.

"Let's continue this downtown," Jim was the louder of the two. He wanted to move this confrontation to familiar turf. He wanted to find out who knew things about his handling of the case that he didn't even know himself. None of this made any sense. He wanted to know who had tipped off the press.

"Let me take Claude home and get cleaned up first. Put on a suit that doesn't look like he slept in it and have a shave. Media will be hanging around all over the place now that they've been tipped off and I'd prefer my brother not be photographed like a criminal before he is even charged.

"He will be your main witness so this is in your best interest as well. You have no case without him regardless of what has been said in this office. Let's face it, he's not going to incriminate himself in court once we get a lawyer involved and anything I know is just hearsay. We'll consult an attorney and then Claude will consent to come down and be interviewed again." Jim could see Neil was stalling for time. He could almost hear the wheels spinning double time in his head.

Jim knew that the case was weak despite all this new knowledge. He still didn't know what happened and as guilty as Claude was, his part was incidental, he wasn't the murderer. Jim would need Claude's cooperation to bring this case to a conclusion with the right person in jail. He wanted the killer not this lame excuse for a man. If he knew any more, Jim would get it out of him once they got into a proper interview room. Cooperation would cost him nothing.

"You can take him home," Jim said, "but I'm going to follow you. I wouldn't want your trip to include a detour to the airport. We are talking murder here."

Neil looked offended but agreed.

"Let's not get too carried away with talk of murder. Our lawyer and the Crown Prosecutor have to get together before we know what, if any, charges will be. The magic of plea bargaining still has to be played out. Even if charged, Claude is still innocent until twelve of his upstanding peers say different.

"Allow me to step into my office and make some arrangements please. You two talk about the weather. We have asked for an attorney to be present for any more questions." With that, Neil went through the adjoining door to his own office.

Once inside he pulled out his cell phone. The anonymous tip that got him here had shown up on his call display. It was one of the company's own phones. Claude had told him the hit man had Dan Cooper's. Neil should have canceled the number but in the confusion had forgotten. He hit the LCR button, last call received, and waited to hear who answered.

Crosley was startled when the phone rang. He was surprised it still worked and that he was able to call out, but never expected anyone to call him. Cooper was dead. Everyone in the company knew that.

A couple of minutes later Neil returned to his brother's office.

"Change of plans," he said. "Claude you drive yourself home and leave your car there. The sergeant will drive you down town and I will meet you there with our attorney. I have a couple of things to work out with him first before we get to police headquarters. Don't say anymore until we get there. Bail may be quite high so I will start working on it as well."

Claude looked surprised at this change. McDonald was skeptical but liked the part where he would bring the accused in himself. That lessened any chances of funny business. The part about the attorney was just the price of doing his job in this new day and age. He would just have to bear up to that component of the plan. As for bail, the charge was going to be murder regardless of what the brothers might think. Bail was a bit optimistic, he thought, but said nothing.

"One more thing," Neil said. "I would like to talk to Claude for a minute alone. Since that unfortunate phone call from the media, rumors in the plant will be rampant. Could you go out to your car and wait? Claude will follow along in a minute or two under his own steam? We are cooperating with you. We are just asking for a little dignity."

Dignity, what a crock, McDonald thought, this joker's being charged with being an accessory before the fact to murder. However, as he told himself before, cooperation would cost him nothing and if it made everyone more amenable to the eventual solution of this case, why not. He left the office with one final warning.

"Just a couple of minutes. Don't you become an accessory after the fact." The last was directed to Neil Jackson.

Chapter 36

The parade to Claude Jackson's estate in Bedford leading up the Magazine Hill from the Jackson Printing and Publishing offices consisted of the black Mercedes of Claude Jackson in the lead, acting as parade marshal, followed by the plain, black Ford of Sergeant Jim McDonald, as the municipal representative, followed by the common looking rental car of Robert Crosley representing the world at large.

Jim noticed the rental car accelerating into the passing lane beside him. He kept a close eye on the other vehicle. From years of using this interchange, Jim knew cars from away often ended up in the wrong lane when the roads diverged. Straight ahead lay the community of Bedford, Jim and Claude's destination. To the right, the road swung towards Highway 101, the community of Sackville and all points west. By some accident of engineering or maybe just Jim's imagination, Sackville-bound cars frequently ended up crossing in front of the Bedford-bound cars to get to their destination. Most frequent users of this road were aware of this quirk and automatically allowed for the confusion. Strangers were simply caught off guard.

Jim tuned back to look at Claude's Mercedes. He hoped Claude was also paying attention to the visitor. Jim couldn't be sure. Claude's hands seemed to firmly grip the steering wheel in the standard 10 to 2 position. He appeared to be hunched forward. His head was pointed directly to the front. Jim feared that Claude might be lost in a world of his own.

Sure enough, the rental sped up and passed in front of Claude and veered off to the right. The Mercedes' brake lights flashed on. The nose of the car dipped. Claude had overreacted. Jim watched the rental speed off towards

Sackville. When he looked to the front again, he couldn't believe his eyes.

White smoke was streaming from both tires of the big Mercedes as it roared up the hill searching for its top speed. Jackson wildly waved his arms about inside the car. It was déjà vu all over again for McDonald.

The black behemoth of a car crashed through the fence at the top of the overpass, dropped down into the path of an oncoming fuel truck chugging up the hill from the opposite direction and exploded in a fiery ball of orange-red flames. The truck driver caught a brief glimpse of something big and black passing over his cab before finding his portion of the vehicle airborne. The cab landed on its side in the ditch, the driver unhurt except he could already feel the heat and see the paint blistering on the engine bonnet in front of him. With adrenaline induced strength he kicked out the windshield and scampered to safety beyond the reach of the spreading flames.

From Jim's perspective, the Mercedes was swallowed up in a pillar of high octane generated fire, the hilly terrain hiding the actual conflagration. The wompf of the explosion caused a shock wave that shook Jim's car.

A bonus, Crosley would think, when he saw the burnt out husk of the car later on the evening news. Sometimes the messenger of God caught a break.

"What the hell did he hit?" Jim asked of no one, still not believing what was happening before his very eyes, knowing there would be no survivors and little left to investigate. In his mind he reviewed the events of the last minute. Nothing indicated a reason for Jackson to act in such a bizarre manner. The rental cut Jackson off but Jim observed nothing further. He wanted to talk to the driver of that car. What had he done?

McDonald grabbed the microphone of his two-way radio and ordered any highway patrol in the area to stop the blue rental car. Hold them until I get there, he demanded after giving a brief description of the car.

If the rental stayed on Highway 101, a limited access road, the patrols would find it. If it went on to the main drag into Sackville, they had a chance. If it disappeared into one of the many nearby subdivisions, it would be gone. McDonald hoped for a respite from the dead ends he had come up against so far.

He jumped out of his car, climbed to the top of the bridge to the gapping hole in the guardrail and looked down at the carnage below. There would be no clues coming from this wreckage. The acrid smoke burned his eyes and fouled his nose. Instinctively he pulled his hands back from the already too hot to touch aluminum fencing. Below the asphalt bubbled around the two vehicles entwined like passionate lovers, their metal parts glowed an iridescent red. The searing heat dried Jim's skin forcing him to move back. In the distance he could hear the fire trucks making their way to the scene. Flames shot high into the air.

Had he received any useful information from Jackson in their discussions back in his office, anything to lead to the killer? Nothing came to mind. Jackson incriminated himself but no one else. His confession no longer mattered. Jim had a name, more than likely false, but nothing to go with it.

His radio crackled. He ran back to the car and reached in for the radio.

"Go ahead," he said, hopping the break had happened.

Sure enough the Mounties managed to stop the sought after rental car innocently driving along the 101 following the speed limit and doing nothing wrong. The driver was getting upset at being held for no apparent reason. The constable, for his part had no idea why he was holding him. McDonald had given him little useful information.

"I'm having a computer problem checking your driver's license," the Mountie told Crosley. "Please be patient. It is an out of province document. The problem could be anywhere along the line." It was a line of bull but it had a nice ring to it he thought. In the distance he could see the flashing lights of McDonald's Ford. Hurry up and get here.

Crosley also caught the winking of the red and blue lights on the front of the approaching car. He recognized it at once as the car from the parking lot. This guy was working hard at becoming his nemesis but Crosley would see to it that that didn't happen. Nothing would be his downfall but his own incompetence and Crosley strove to keep that in check.

He noticed in his mirror that the patrolman was also focusing his attention on the approaching detective. Crosley took advantage of this short space of time to park his pistol under the dash of the car above the heater. A quick look around showed everything else was in order. Now to work on his indignation.

McDonald's frustration built as he roared along the highway reviewing what he knew of these apparent murders. Some fool had hired a pro because he got himself into money trouble and then reneged on paying. A second killing failed to get the message to him because he screwed up the payment option. Maybe this third death was a benefit to everyone as it removed this inept clown from the current gene pool. At once he regretted having that thought, sort of.

Jim felt a small touch of responsibility for this last death. Jackson should have been in his custody, should have been in the back seat of Jim's car. But, if that had been the case, Jim might also be dead now. The killer did not appear to discriminate when choosing victims. He wiped that thought from his mind and focused on the other deaths.

All three died in automobile accidents. No, that was inaccurate. All three died in their cars. None of the deaths were accidents. Proving that became his priority task.

He pulled up behind the patrol car and jumped out. The Mountie met him between the two police cars.

"What have we got?" McDonald said.

The Mountie hesitated. "We have one pissed-off out-of-province driver safely following the speed limit being pulled out from a line of cars for no apparent reason. You tell me what we've got."

McDonald took a deep breath. What was he thinking? Somehow in his mind he was convinced this person, whom he had never seen, was involved in these deaths. There was just so little to work on. He dialed back his aggression.

"Sorry," he said. "There was a fatal accident back there and this car was sort of involved." Once again he cringed at using the word accident. But at this point there was no other word to use. "You say he was driving the speed limit, not hustling away?"

"The speed limit, right on the nose. Had his cruise control set. I had to cut him out of a line of cars like a cowboy after one calf still in need of branding. All the cars in the line were doing the speed limit. It wasn't easy to explain why I only stopped him."

This stretch of road had an excessive number of fatal collisions, 88 in 10 years, and usually caused by speeding. Even though the portion they were on was now twinned, the entire length of the highway had the killer reputation. It was even discussed on the floor of the House of Parliament in Ottawa. Speed limits were known to be strictly enforced. The traffic responded by slowing down on this highly patrolled section.

McDonald thanked his fellow officer for holding the driver and walked up to Crosley's window. Although it was

Robert Crosley behind the wheel, the man's driver's license identified him as Luke Crossman from Markham, Ontario, one of the names Crosley used in Nova Scotia. He had complete sets of ID for use in different parts of the country. This made it harder for his name to come up in routine police searches which might place him in the vicinity of any criminal activity being investigated on a national scale.

"Who are you?" Crosley said to the non-uniformed figure staring in at him. "First I'm stopped for absolutely no reason by the Mounties and now you, whoever you are. Is this some sort of backwater Nova Scotia shakedown? Listen man, I'm some busy today and I don't have time for this shit."

McDonald was taken aback. There was, as a rule, a little respect when a police officer approached your car on the side of the road, at least for the first minute or so. He produced his badge and explained who he was and why he was there.

"You were detained because you caused an accident back down the road," he told Crosley. "You cut across a lane of traffic causing another vehicle to lose control and crash."

"I did not." Crosley slowly stated the words for emphasis. Policemen towering over his car did not intimidate him. "When and where was this supposed to have happened?"

"On the Magazine Hill," McDonald said. "I was in the following car and had to jam on my brakes myself when you cut across the traffic. I saw it all." He countered Crosley's confrontational attitude with an aggressive approach of his own.

Crosley calmed down. He seemed to ponder this bit of information. "Magazine Hill? You mean that terrible bit of road design where the lanes crisscross? I was forced to cut across the lane all right, but I didn't cause any accident. I checked in my rearview mirror. I had lots of room. Everyone was all right."

He observed the few cars passing them, their drivers relieved it was Crosley and not them suffering on the side of the road at the hands of the police.

"I spend most of my time driving the highways around Toronto, the 401, 407, Don Valley Expressway. Places where the traffic is heavy. I know whether I can change a lane safely or not. And I did this safely. Hell, it was only one lane. Any accident that resulted from this wasn't my fault." He paused. "Was anybody hurt?" Both men looked back down the highway to where a spiral of black smoke scarred the horizon.

"I don't know the extent of any injuries yet. I will have to wait for a report from the investigating officer," McDonald said. He studied Crosley. Was that a flicker of disappointment?

Crosley controlled his facial expression. He could only guarantee a horrendous accident. Whether people lived or died was beyond his immediate control. As a rule they died. If not, other steps could be taken such as a sudden infection while being treated for injuries in the hospital. Those places just weren't safe.

Crosley's previously aggressive attitude changed to a contrite demeanor. "Look, officer, I'm sorry if there was an accident back there, but I didn't cause it. I found myself in the wrong lane and it was safer to speed by the traffic than to jam on my brakes. I know I had enough room to cut in."

The man is right, McDonald admitted to himself. There was no obvious reason for Jackson to suddenly take off like an idiot and crash through the barrier and off the overpass into an oncoming truck. Nothing happened there that didn't happen on that stretch of road a hundred times or more every day. However, he didn't like coincidence. The sudden shift by Crosley's car cutting off Jackson and immediately

followed by Jackson's driving crazy act was the closest thing
to a lead he might have with Claude out of the picture.

Perhaps there was also a bit of culpability on Jim's part
as well. Jackson should never have been driving his own car.
Jackson was drinking. Jackson was stressed, really stressed.
He was a murder suspect. He should have been in police
custody. Now McDonald was showing signs of stress himself.

"You've got to be aware of your surroundings while on
the roadway. That way you can avoid sudden and aggressive
moves." Jim felt like a hypocrite.

"Like I said," Crosley said, "I'm sorry. When your daily
commute is through eight lanes of traffic, it takes a little time
to adjust to the more relaxed way of life in the Maritimes."
Now that he realized that the policeman had nothing on him,
he was all cooperation.

With additional questioning, McDonald learned that
Crosley was visiting the province to talk to some antique
dealers. He was on his way to the Annapolis Valley where he
had loosely set up some appointments. This accounted for
his annoyance at being held up. Time was money.

No, he knew nothing about Jackson Printing and
Publishing or Matthew Lane and his investment company.
His interests lie in the buying and selling of antiques.
Perhaps the sergeant had some old items of interest in his
own home. McDonald assured him he did not. He did,
however, take the business card that Crosley offered him. It
was for a central Canadian company. Then out of the blue
McDonald asked Crosley if he minded if McDonald took a
look in his trunk.

"My trunk?" Crosley was surprised. He looked down at
all the switches on the dash of the car for the icon of an open
trunk. "One of these should open it," he said as he searched.
"But remember this is a rental. Any bodies you find in there
are not mine but the previous renters." He laughed. Neither

of the policemen shared his attempt at a joke but the groundwork for deniability was laid if the search continued to the passenger compartment of the car and the gun and Slim Jims were found.

"There." McDonald pointed to the proper switch and walked to the rear of the car while Crosley released the trunk.

"What are we looking for?" the Mountie asked as he peered into the empty trunk.

"I'm not sure. In fact, I'm not sure I would recognize it even if I saw it but this car cut across in front of my suspect back there on the highway. My guy then drove his car at top speed through a guard rail. I'm looking for a radio transmitter or a Laser light or ..." McDonald paused and shrugged his shoulders, "...I don't know, something, anything."

The trunk contained the usual rental car items, spare tire, jack, lug wrench. Otherwise it offered nothing. Jim replaced the floor mat and then looked at the Mountie. "Did you ever hear of a kundela?"

"A what?"

Jim smiled. "Nothing. I guess there's nothing out of the ordinary here."

The Mountie scowled. "Oh look, is that what you're looking for right there, under the Charter of Rights and Freedoms. You had better hope you don't find anything because a good lawyer would never let it see the inside of a courtroom. We have no reason to be searching this trunk."

McDonald knew his fellow lawman was right but he needed a starting point for this case. Something had triggered Claude Jackson's frantic actions. He would take any lead he could get, anyway he could get it just to get things moving in a positive direction. As things were going there was no chance of anything being seen inside a courtroom.

Jim approached the driver's door again.

"Do you have a cell phone?" he asked.

Crosley looked at him for a second before answering. "Doesn't everyone?" He reached into the glove compartment and retrieved the small phone.

"I only carry it for emergencies," he added. Emergencies like nosy cops, he thought.

McDonald turned it on, successfully punched in 1-2-3-4 as the password and checked the history. There were no calls recorded either incoming or outgoing. It had no special features that could have caused Claude's reaction. He passed it back. He was clutching at straws.

Crosley noticed the disappointed look on McDonald's face.

"I've never had to use it, knock on wood."

The other phones were safely tucked inside his jacket pocket. For Jim, another string not tied to anything.

A small stack of Styrofoam cups lay on the passenger side floor. "What's with the cups?" Jim asked.

"Like my coffee but don't like to litter," Crosley told him. "It's against the law. I just haven't gotten around to finding a trash receptacle yet." He flashed Jim a disarming smile.

McDonald nodded and returned to the rear of the car where the Mountie was completing his search by examining the area which gave access to the tail lights.

"Nothing," he reported.

Jim just grunted. The whole stop was becoming a disappointment.

"Have you been stationed in Nova Scotia long?" he asked the patrolman.

"Three months. Was in Alberta before this."

"He claims to be from Ontario but only a Nova Scotian would be 'some busy'. If he was a native Ontarian, he'd be saying 'eh' at least once every two or three sentences. Some as an adjective is a Nova Scotia thing. When he leaves, I want you to follow him. Let's see where he is headed besides visiting antique dealers. He doesn't strike me as the antique-buying type. I'm wondering if he has other community ties and what we might find there if he has."

The Mountie looked around Jim at the long, straight stretch of empty road. "You want me to follow him. I'm driving a marked patrol car. It may be a little conspicuous, don't you think?" The Mountie had been unimpressed with the detective from homicide up to his point. This move did not improve his opinion.

"Just hang back and keep an eye on him. I'll radio for a ghost car to take over and finish the pursuit. There's always one out here somewhere. In the meantime don't lose him. The road goes straight for miles. You are both headed in the same direction, nothing suspicious." Jim smiled at the Mountie and returned to his car.

That patrolman must think I'm nuts, Jim thought, but there's something not right about this guy. I just can't put my finger on it. After 16 years on the force, a large database of information built up in the brain of suspicious behavior. Tones of voice, expressions, body language, intangibles that couldn't be defined. A hunch should count as something. Cases had been solved this way before.

He would follow up on Jackson, make sure he was dead and see if there were any leads in his car or at the accident scene. He was and there wasn't.

Chapter 37

Neil Jackson answered the phone in his office and turned pale at the message he was given. His brother Claude was dead. It was a mere half hour since they were talking and planning his defense. Now, no defense was required.

Jim deplored breaking this news by telephone. Sometimes proper procedures didn't allow for the circumstances. Having Neil get this information when he and his lawyer showed up at police headquarters would be the greater of the two evils. Under these time constraints, the telephone was Jim's only choice.

Besides, Jim wanted to talk to the older brother while the events were still evolving. He needed any information Neil could give him right now. Neil said he would wait for a few moments but he wanted to get out to comfort Claude's family. Had they been informed about Claude's passing? If not, he would like to deliver the message. McDonald understood and was there in less than ten minutes.

Claude Jackson was without a doubt a major player in these deaths, including his own but what about Neil? The jury was still out on him, McDonald decided.

"What do you know about this professional killer your brother hired?" he asked. He studied the older brother's reaction to the question. His face looked blank.

Neil held his hands up in a dismissive gesture. "Nothing. You know more about it than I do. You were there when I found out and you know what I was told." If this was an act, he was good. "I can't believe my brother could even do something like that. Not to speak badly of the dead but it seems like something that would be beyond his ability, a world he wouldn't even know about. I guess I didn't know my brother as well as I thought."

Neil played with some papers on his desk. "I didn't even know about his debt. If I had, we could have worked something out within the family and not gone to a stranger. I told him to stay away from those goddamn futures markets, you know. Told him to leave it for the experts. He always listened to my advice before. At least I thought so. We still have to figure out what kind of dollars he embezzled from the company."

He was rambling and Jim realized that the shock of his brother's death was probably setting in. He would let him get to his family. He did not appear to have any real knowledge that would be of immediate help. When he was more focused he would be able to assist with the investigation. For now Jim just had one more question for him.

"Do you have video surveillance inside your plant and your parking lot?" he asked.

"Just inside, but we don't archive it. Did for a year. Never used them, so we stopped. Risk verses reward." Neil shrugged as if to explain the laxness of the system.

"Now they run on a continuous loop so there would be ten or so hours at any one time. We more or less just monitor the building to help us find people when we need them rather than for security. You don't think Claude's killer was in the building do you?"

"We can only hope. Somehow, someone knew about Claude's movement." Jim would love to find the traffic stop person on a tape inside this building. "Could I have today's tapes and perhaps when you have some time we could go over them together. You could tell me if there is anyone roaming around who doesn't belong in the building."

"I doubt that there is," Neil said. "We do control the entrances, as you know."

Jim declined to argue with the man. He had gained access to the entire building on three separate occasions by just flashing his badge. Someone as smart as this killer appeared to be would have no problem beating these systems.

That said, Neil made the arrangements for the tapes to be given to the sergeant. He then went to Claude's home, bearer of the worst possible news for the family. Jim silently followed Neil down to the security office to get the tapes. There were cameras on each elevator door and on a few isolated areas of the building, six in all. That would be sixty hours of the dullest TV ever.

Chapter 38

A plate of sandwiches and a full pot of coffee shared the table in the small interview room with a stack of videotapes. The TV hung from the wall behind a sheet of Plexiglas. It could be viewed but not touched.

"Well, my son, we have sixty hours worth of reality show to watch," Andre Tiabault said. He picked up a ham and lettuce sandwich. "Let's see if we can vote your bad guy off of the island."

Andre served as head of security at JP&P. He was originally from Cape Breton but had worked at JP&P for over fifteen years. He knew everyone in the company. Regardless of the department they worked in, they had to pass Andre's station at the front door everyday.

Jim plunked himself down in a chair beside Andre. "Sixty hours. That's a week of viewing at ten hours a day and 6 days a week." A huge sigh escaped from his lips. "Let's get started."

"It won't be that bad, my son. Most of it can be skipped over and we'll speed up the tape as much as we possible. Unlike Mr. Jackson, I know who belongs where, a wise decision to use me instead of him to view the tapes."

"You're just trying to cheer me up," Jim said. "How much overtime are you getting for this?" He gave the security guard a friendly tap on the shoulder. "We'll stay until midnight tonight. That should make a big dent in this pile. Where do you recommend we start?"

"Everyone goes through the front door. Let's do it first."

The tape marked main entrance went into the machine. The first hour showed no activity. It was 6 a.m. according to the time stamp. The day's business was yet to begin. At seven the first people showed up, only a trickle, Neil Jackson among them. As eight approached, the numbers built. Claude came in around nine and shortly thereafter he and Neil left again

"Danny Cooper's funeral," Andre said. "A lot of the staff attended that. Sad, sad time."

"Dan was a friend?"

"Everyone's. Always stopped to chat. Called me by name. Some of these jerks don't even know I exist. Too good to talk to the security staff. Not Dan. I know his wife, his kids."

Andre abruptly stopped talking. "You don't realize how lucky you are, my son. Poor Dan. His kids used to stop in every so often. Looking for money, I guess. The last couple of years–" Andre shook his head as he remembered the girl's appearance. He then filled Jim in on Dan's home life. Dan had needed someone to unload on. Andre had listened. Now Jim realized what an easy target Dan would have been for a smooth talker. He needed a big contract. He had to get his life back on track.

"Last time I saw him is how I'll always remember him," Andre said. "He walked out of here that day with a smile that could light up a stadium for a night game. 'Going for Chinese,' he told me 'and then gonna watch those presses roll.' Big contract, I guess."

"Chinese? Chinese food?" Jim said. "I wonder if he had a reservation somewhere. There might be a record of who he was with. The reservation might be in the client's name." He made a note to check out all the Chinese restaurants near the bridge. Five names immediately came to his mind. He would have to visit them all and show pictures of Dan around. With luck, someone would remember him.

The videos droned on. The two brothers returned from the funeral. Claude looked like he was dragged through a wringer. Neil just looked preoccupied. He had work to do.

The lunch crowd came and went and then Neil left the building again. Jim watched as his own image showed up on the screen. He smiled.

"The camera adds ten pounds," he said. He patted his stomach. He would have to make sure it was only the camera adding the weight. They continued to watch.

Neil Jackson burst through the door and ran up to the inside security door. Andre buzzed him through.

"Never saw him look so agitated in all the time I've been here," Andre said. "First time he ever ran in the building. Looked like an angry Jesus after a sinner. I should have known something bad was happening.

"He abandoned his car right outside the door. I had to go and park it properly. I checked the lot at the time but didn't see anything out of the ordinary."

He was tipped off, Jim realized. He knew I was here when he entered the building. Who called him?

More people came and left. Andre put a small wedge under the inside door and disappeared himself for a short time.

"Bathroom break," he said. "Had a beer with my lunch. You don't buy the stuff, you only rent it."

"You were relieved for lunch. Is that the only break you get?"

"No, I get another one around three but sometimes I can't wait. The wedge keeps people from being upset. They don't want to wait the two or three minutes for me to get back. Always complaining about deadlines."

Two people had come in during the time Andre was relieving himself. Andre identified both of them. He saw no security lapse in his practice.

Next, Jim exited the building. He could see the new found optimism on his face that didn't exist on entering the building. That optimistic outlook was short-lived. It burnt to a crisp in a fiery crash on the Magazine Hill.

Two minutes later Claude followed.

"Look at him," Andre said. "He has the weight of the world on his shoulders. He's been carrying it around for a couple of weeks now. I noticed it every day, but this is the worst. He looks terrible."

Jim agreed. Claude looked sick. Jim could see the realization in the man's face that jail time was a real possibility. He must have been hoping for a miracle from his brother. There would be no miracles.

"What a contrast between the two men, "Andre said. "The last time I saw Danny he looked so happy and Mr. Jackson there looks so gloomy. They both go out and die in a car accident. Life can be cruel, my son, life can be cruel."

Jim studied the older man. It can be, he thought, but neither of these two events was a car accident. These were homicides.

"You know," Andre said, "I think I've met the man Danny was going to meet that day. He dropped in here a couple of times to meet Danny. They usually went out to lunch or something. I'm pretty sure he was the one the new contract was with. Danny always treated him like a life saver. He was desperate for a good sale."

Jim perked up. The hours of slogging through the video had worn him down. "You know what the client looks like? Do you know his name?"

Jim's reaction surprised Andre. "I don't know it right off but he would have had to sign in and out. I can get it for you."

"I'll get a sketch artist. Can you describe him."

"Sort of heavy, mustache, wore glasses I think. It's been a couple of weeks."

Jim tried to hide his disappointment. He hoped the description would match up with the man stopped on Highway 101 after Claude's death. Not even close. The driver was trim and clean faced. No one on the first ten hours of security tape matched his description either. He hadn't come through the front door on the day of Claude's death. The man described by Andre was also absent from the tapes for the day.

That didn't let either man off the hook. Perhaps other people in the building had met the client. Maybe they would remember him differently. Jim would return to the plant in the daytime to conduct additional interviews with the people in the sales area. He would check to see if there were other entrances, perhaps through the freight doors. No offense to Andre but security was only a token word at JP&P.

Jim checked his watch. The midnight hour had come and gone. Together they had gone through the front door tapes and the tapes in the freight area. Andre agreed to check the inside tapes himself to see if there was anyone he didn't know in the building. Great idea, Jim though. He thanked the security guard for all his help and insights.

Jim filed his list of things to do and packed it in for the night. Sitting around watching images flashing by on a television screen had zapped his energy. He would start fresh in the morning.

"Can I drop you somewhere?" he asked the guard.

"Thanks," Andre said. He gave Jim an address.

"I'll let you know if I find anything more, my son," Andre said as he exited the car in front of his house. "The other tapes will be faster. Lots of nothing on them." Working with the police made the boring task more exciting for Andre.

Jim dreaded the thought. The first tape was their best hope. It had been a great disappointment. He had learned more by talking to the security guard.

255

Chapter 39

Two messages waited for Jim when he came in to work on Friday morning. Andre called to report that the signatures on the sign up sheet were illegible. There was no name coming for the mystery client. Neil Jackson had supplied a company name from the ad booking. It turned out to be real, but no one from that business had any dealings with JP&P. No new franchises were scheduled in the Halifax area.

A report from the highway patrol was waiting on his desk. The driver of the ghost car followed the subject as requested. There were no trips to antique dealers in the Windsor area. In fact they turned off at exit 4 before reaching Windsor. He then proceeded to a small farm in the Brooklyn area. The address was attached along with a picture. The house sat back from the road in a pastoral setting with lots of trees in the yard. It didn't meet expectations of a killer's hideout. This officer was efficient if nothing else. The police man stayed until dark when the surveillance was abandoned. The subject appeared to be settled in for the night.

It's a good day for a drive in the country, McDonald thought. Claude Jackson's funeral was at two o'clock that afternoon. He would be back in lots of time for it. He would get down to some serious talks with Neil Jackson once the funeral was out of the way. He wanted his undivided attention while he delved into what the older brother might know about the strange events of recent weeks. Going up against Claude Jackson could be compared to engaging in a match of wits with an unarmed man. This would not be the case with Neil Jackson. Jim would give Neil the weekend to properly mourn his brother and then meet with him first thing Monday morning.

McDonald made his way out of the city and swung onto Highway 101. The restricted access road was bordered by verdant trees on both sides. The black ribbon of highway was the only sign of civilization for the half hour ride into the countryside. As he approached exit 4, which would lead him to Brooklyn, a few farms cropped up beside the road. The hay was cut and huge rolls of it lay scattered about the fields, the golden brown standing out in stark contrast to the green fields. Herds of cows observed his passage with disinterest. This short, peaceful drive recharged his batteries and gave him new hope of putting this case behind him.

Upon reaching the address written on the piece of paper on the seat beside him, McDonald took in the long tree-lined driveway leading to the older one and one-half story bungalow. It looked like the attached picture. This was the right place. There were no vehicles in sight. An older, weather beaten, gray barn stood on the property, but the place did not have the look of a working farm. Several apple trees grew along one side of the field, heavy with small, still forming fruit. Old fashioned Gravensteins, McDonald thought. He was no expert on apple varieties but these resembled the ones his mother used to make delicious apple pies every fall when he lived at home. He pulled into the next driveway three hundred feet down the road.

An elderly couple worked in the yard, she in the garden, he trimming the grass along the edge of their well-maintained white house. A pile of hardwood logs waited for processing into firewood at the far end of the driveway. This task awaited the cooler fall weather.

Both old people stopped what they were doing and smiled as his car stopped in front of the house. The man approached the door of McDonald's vehicle. His face was a deep brown from the wind and the sun, wrinkled at the eyes and neck. His hair was graying, but still thick with only slight receding on the sides. White skin could be seen at the vee where the top button of his shirt opened. The skin under the shirt had not been exposed to old Sol. The shirt had long sleeves buttoned at the cuffs. The eyes were keen and intelligent with age.

McDonald flashed his badge and asked if they could give him any information about their neighbour.

"Not much to tell," the old gent said. His voice had a gentle drawl to it. "No one lives there." He paused for effect. "Young fella who owns it drops in every couple of months but can't say he really lives there. Lives in upper Canada now."

"He has been around a bit more this summer," the kindly grandmotherly looking lady inserted into the conversation. Inserts were easy to do as the old man talked so slow you had to work hard to remember the beginning of the sentence by the time he reached the end.

He scowled at his wife. "The man asked me, Martha. I was getting to that part. Been around a bit more this summer than usual. Talked to him a couple of times."

"He brings us honey," Martha said. "He raises his own bees and supplies us with enough to last all year."

"Martha." The old man was getting upset. "I'm talking to this officer. Don't you have work to do in your garden?" He dragged out the first syllable and dropped the 'r' to produce gaahden. "Uses the bees to propagate his apple trees. Lets strangers come in and pick the apples but shares the honey with us neighbours. Gets more than he can use himself, I reckon. I like the honey but I wish those bees of his would stay in his own yard. Neither Martha nor I have much use for them anymore.

"Farm is an old family homestead belonged to his uncle or great-uncle Amos. He showed up when old Amos died here a few years back. Nice enough boy. Keeps to himself though. Pays some of the local kids to keep the grass cut. Seldom shows up in the winter. Likes to play all kinds of music. Out here in the country sound travels pretty good on a quiet night and you can hear him playing different kinds of tunes: long haired stuff, good old country and that rock and roll trash. He plays it all."

Martha looked up from her *gaahdening* and added: "Sometimes he plays the same piece over and over and over like he's making copies or something. That's against the law, isn't it? Is that why you're here?" Her curiosity was piqued by the arrival of the lawman from the city.

McDonald smiled and thanked them for their cooperation but offered no information. He would leave them believing he was investigating something as benign as music theft and not murder for hire. Crossman did not appear to be a threat to his neighbours so why scare them. Indeed, he did not appear to be a threat to anyone but McDonald would ride this hunch to the bitter end. There was nothing else to go on.

He swung into the yard of the empty house and got out of his car. A squirrel chattered from the big maple tree over his head warning everything around of his presence. Blue jays flitted from branch to branch. A string of pigeons sat on the electrical wire leading to the house, staring vacantly at him. Jim knocked on the door, waited and listened. There was no answer. He didn't expect one. The door was locked, unusual in the country but this guy was from Markham, Ontario. Locking the door would be ingrained in him.

McDonald walked around the vinyl-clad white building peering in the windows. Everything was quiet. To Jim's untrained eye, the house appeared to be furnished with antiques. In the living room there appeared to be a large amount of electronic sound equipment. Maybe Martha was right. This did look like it could be used for dubbing tapes and CDs. Perhaps it was related to what the man did for a living. Maybe he was an antique dealer. Jim made a note in his notebook. You never knew what might prove to be important. Further searching revealed nothing relevant.

Had he been lied to? The neighbours confirmed Crossman lived in Ontario. Failing to mention that he owned a house in the area was a lie by omission even if he didn't really live there. Why had he left that detail out? No one asked him could be the innocent answer. McDonald was looking for something more sinister. What happened to the appointments with the antique dealers? Maybe he was detained too long by the police for no apparent reason. That would be a touchy point of discussion.

It is always dangerous to reason from insufficient data. Not his words but those of super sleuth Sherlock Holmes. He had insufficient data. He would have to keep looking

Jim opened the door of his car and started to step inside when his cell phone chirped. Instead, he stood straight and fished the phone from his pocket.

"Sergeant? Scott Bowen here." The corporal's voice bubbled with excitement. "I've just photographed Dr. Sue Thornton splashing through the river at The Tunnel."

Jim could hear the background rush of water as it tumbled over the rocks. "At the tunnel? Is she fishing?"

"Not in the conventional sense. I think she's looking for the salmon line we collected last week. The old broad has got a conscience. It just took a week for it to kick in."

"That and the fact that her husband is going to be fishing there tomorrow. At least, that's what he said at the funeral. Arrest her. I'll meet you at headquarters in about 45 minutes."

Chapter 40

Jim joined Scott Bowen outside the interview room at police headquarters. Scott had a disappointed look on his face.

"She's evoked her right to remain silent and her lawyer is on the way in."

Jim walked over to the one-way window and studied the woman on the other side. Her clothes were still wet and a puddle formed around her chair. She was dressed for the outdoors. Blue jeans, probably stiff by now from the water, soaked hiking boots and a dark, blue sweat shirt, drooping at the shoulders. It clung to her breasts which appeared to be surprisingly firm for a person of her age.

"Did you offer her dry clothes?" Jim asked.

Scott pointed to the orange coveralls on the floor in the corner. "Not her colour. She still thinks she's going to walk out of here today."

"You told her the charge was murder?"

"I told her. Whether or not she heard me is another question."

"Do you have a copy of her book?"

Scott opened his briefcase and extracted a library copy of *The Power of Suggestion*. Jim took the book and hefted it in his hand. "Pretty heavy reading. Written more for professionals than the public. I read the chapters you outlined for me. It does make some valid points."

He flipped the book open to the table of content and scanned through the chapter headings. He paused and read one over to Scott.

Scott nodded. "That chapter is a blueprint for our murder."

Jim closed the book. "Let's go see what she thinks of it."

He opened the door of the interrogation room and the two men walked in. Jim held the book by his side. He sat in the chair opposite Dr. Thornton and placed the book on his lap.

"I have nothing to say," Sue said. "I've called my lawyer. He's on his way."

Jim nodded. "That's your right. We respect those rights. It's what makes this country a great place to live."

Sue gave him a wary look. "Don't try to trick me. I've watched *Law and Order*. I know how you police work."

Jim held up his hands in a surrender position. "No tricks. We won't even talk about the murder until your lawyer gets here. I've read your book." He brought the book up from his lap and placed it on the table in front of him. "Interesting stuff." He looked at Sue and smiled. "I especially enjoyed the chapter on *Negative Suggestion Serves the Same Purpose as Positive Suggestion.*"

Sue visibly blanched. "You've read *my* book."

"Your book." Jim turned the book around to face Sue and slid it across the table. "The subtitle could be *Blueprint for Murder.*" He smiled at Scott as he stole his partner's line. Scott returned the smile and made a gesture with his hand to indicate the line was his to use.

Sue placed her hand on the cover, feeling the texture. "Why would you read my book?"

Jim shook his head. "I'd like to say it was because it was such an interesting read but that wouldn't be factually true. We can't talk about the real reason until your lawyer gets here. You've evoked your right to remain silent."

"Oh, well. What's the use. You've read my book. It's all spelt out there." Sarcasm dripped from her voice. She remained silent for a minute before continuing. "I had no choice. He was ruining her life."

Jim looked up at Scott and then back to Sue. "Are you giving up your right to remain silent, Mrs. Thornton?"

"It's *Doctor* Thornton if you don't mind."

"Excuse me, *Doctor* Thornton." Jim and Scott exchanged a look. "I repeat: are you giving up your right to remain silent?"

"I may as well." Some of the harshness left her voice. "I admit I did convince Herbert to go fishing that morning. Who knew he'd fall in and drown. I suppose I must be guilty of something. My intention was just to show Marilyn how little he actually cared for her. Now he's dead."

Scott picked up a chair from against the wall and brought it over to the table. "She's not only a writer or renown, she's a talented actress."

"Actress? I don't understand."

"What I don't understand is why you did it. Surely, you can't have hated your son-in-law enough to kill him?"

"Can't I? That shows how little you know. He thought he had the key to the kingdom hanging between his legs. Marilyn never could recognize when someone was after her money. She thought she was in love." Sue's voice took on a hard edge. "It wasn't bad enough that he was a gigolo. He started treating Marilyn the same way my no good excuse of a husband has treated me for the last 35 years. Every free minute he gets, he's out fishing somewhere. Every weekend, all summer, and then hunting in the fall."

Sue lowered her voice and looked down at the table. "I brought the money into our marriage. My husband had nothing. Granted, he parlayed my hope chest into a fortune, but I paid the price in loneliness. Marilyn deserved better. She never saw her father. She should at least see her husband."

Sue paused in her tirade and looked up at the two cops, a confused look on her face. Scott's words seemed to sink in.

263

"To say I killed him is a bit of a stretch. My only intention was to get him to go fishing and have Marilyn realize how little she meant to him. Then, she would come home where she belonged."

She sat back in her chair. Neither cop said anything. Sue went on. "I was only trying to save Marilyn from the frustrations I've endured all my life. Goddammit, Herb even moved out to the country to be closer to the action. Marilyn was never going to see him. I did it for her."

The two policemen's eyes met. They had heard just about every excuse going for committing murder. This was another one to add to the list: save your daughter from being a fishing widow by making her a real widow.

"If he had stayed home on his anniversary," Sue said, "he would still be alive today. I didn't drag him out into the woods. It was his choice. And I sure as hell didn't hold his head under water until he drowned."

"His choice? Was it?" Jim tapped the cover of the book. "I've read this, remember. It spells it out pretty clearly. Friday night you goaded him until he had to say he was going fishing just to save face. Then Saturday morning, it was you who called him from the service station. What did you say to him to get him to leave his wife? Did you congratulate him for finally getting wise and taking your advise." Jim picked up the book and slammed it down on the table. "Negative suggestion you call it. Make him do the opposite to what you suggest."

"He still had a choice. You read my book. It tells you how to overcome negative situations. He should have stayed home with Marilyn."

"Yeah, then your little trap might have caught some innocent fisherman," Scott said. He offered no sympathy.

"My little trap?" Marilyn tried to hide her surprise. "I may have pressured him into going fishing so that Marilyn could see what kind of man he was, but his death was an accident? I didn't kill him."

Scott laughed. "Give it up, Dr. Thornton. You're not that good of an actress. Like all criminals you made a few mistakes. You may have spent a lot of time watching your husband fish, but you didn't learn much about the actual sport." He held up his forefinger. "You chose a salmon fly for a trout river."

The second finger went up. "You tied the fly onto a piece of thick bass line."

His ring finger joined the other two. "You didn't use a fisherman's knot to connect the two lines."

Up popped his little finger. "And there were loops in what should have been the reel end of the line where you tied the rock before you threw it across the river to set the trip line."

Scott waved the four outstretched fingers in front of her. "Not even close to looking like an accident."

"It was creative," Jim said, "but to a true fisherman, it was all wrong. The final clue was the little, broken, plastic teeth from the buckle of the waders. The crime scene techs found them on the floor in Herb's garage. It was obvious the waders were deliberately sabotaged. That narrowed the suspect pool to someone who had access to the garage. It turns out that it was you who kept the beer tub stocked the night of the party. No one questioned your frequent trips to the garage. At least they didn't until we questioned them. Then, what they remembered was the silences when you weren't there."

Once again Jim reached out and picked up the book. "How long were you planning this?" he asked. Despite what he had read, he found it hard to believe that a man's actions could be controlled that easily. It must have taken a long time to work that effectively.

Sue's voice lowered to barely a whisper. "I didn't really plan it at all. It just sort of happened. I knew all about the power of suggestion. It was the subject of my doctoral thesis. Over time, I noticed that Herb seemed to go out of his way to do the opposite of anything I suggested. Who can blame him? We didn't want him as part of the family. Marilyn could have done so much better."

Jim opened the book to the chapter on negative suggestion and scanned as he listened.

"The final straw came when they moved out into the middle of nowhere. I knew I had to act to save Marilyn from the fate I had endured. I began to actively apply the principles from my book. I measured the results in a clinical way. When the time was ripe, I knew it. Last weekend, I started turning the screws. That drunk from next door was an added bonus. He agreed with everything I said. Wanted to help save Herb's marriage, he said. This upset Herb even more than if it was just me. To an ordinary person, the things I was saying made sense. But with our history, they were a huge aggravation to Herb. He bought it hook, line and sinker, pun intended."

By now, Sue's eyes were sparkling. Her voice had climbed above its normal timbre. She appeared excited by her success.

"And it doesn't bother you that your daughter loved this man?" Scott was shaking his head in disbelief. "I hope they lock you up and throw away the key."

Sue looked shocked by the statement. "Where's my damn lawyer? You're twisting my words to sound like a confession. It will never stand up in court. I didn't murder Herbert."

Jim slid back his chair and stood up. "We don't need your confession, lady. We have all the evidence we need." He held up the book. "It's right here in your own words."

266

Chapter 41

Monday morning found Neil Jackson at his desk studying a sheaf of yellow papers. He had the company auditor dig in to Claude's finances and put this package together for him. Although preliminary, the results were not good. Neil knew Claude was skimming from the company, he didn't realize the extent of the larceny. Now he was waiting for a visit from the detective investigating the murders. How much should he tell him? This was family business. Should he keep it in the family?

There was very little time to decide. The intercom on his desk buzzed and Jean announced the presence of Detective Sergeant Jim McDonald. She showed him in. They met the previous Friday at Claude's funeral so the awkwardness about what to say regarding a death in the immediate family was behind them. They could get right to business.

In the corner of Neil's office was a stuffed blue leather chair, matching chesterfield and a low coffee table. Neil offered tea or coffee to Jim and Jean left to fill the orders. They sat in the less formal setting rather than across the desk. Neil had the papers in his hand.

Jim was going to take the "give him the benefit of the doubt" route with Neil. Assume he was also a victim in this crime and see where it took him.

When they both had beverages in hand Neil opened the discussion. He held up the documents and said: "I had no idea how deep Claude was involved in this. He owed hundreds of thousands of dollars to Matthew Lane. Despite that I still can't wrap my mind around the concept of Claude hiring someone to have him killed. Violence wasn't in his nature."

He scanned the papers, flipped to the last page and shook his head.

"We have no idea of the true amount of debt. There is nothing in writing that we have found. All we know is how much was needed to bail him out of the coffee fiasco and assume Lane put up at least that much money." This was all information the police could easily find out for themselves. There was no point in hiding it. Neil looked down at the papers and shook his head. "I told him to stay away from the commodities market. He was in way over his head. Then to get caught selling short." The look of despair told the whole story of Neil's disappointment in his brother.

Jim cleared his throat. He wanted to word this question in a delicate manner but he still wanted an answer. The answer would go a long way towards who knew what and when.

"He was making his payments to Lane, right? Large payments from what I gather. That money was somehow being siphoned from the company without showing up in the books. How is that possible?" He looked Neil right in the eye as he asked. Neither flinched.

"Most of the money was in the books. Claude set up an elaborate scheme where he created a false company on paper. He was getting expense receipts from and making payments to this company, receipts that JP&P printed themselves, and presenting them as legitimate expenses. He was a co-owner. No one questioned his expense claims too closely, a costly mistake I guess.

"He also set up a parallel bank account where he was depositing some of the cheques he collected. He cashed these without them ever showing up on our books. We're still investigating. It was an intricate connivance; there may be more twists and turns yet to be discovered. I just wish he had come to me. We could have worked something out." Jackson looked downcast. His brother's unscrupulous actions were taking a toll on him.

Jim took notes. This sounded like a plausible answer but he would talk to the forensic accountants with the department to see if such a machination could work in the real world. It was beyond his scope of understanding.

"This man Crosley, what do you know about him?" he asked without looking up from his notebook. He thought he would just slip the question in. Jackson did not rise to the bait.

"I'm sorry, who is Crosley?" he asked.

"Crosley, the hit man your brother hired," said a disappointed McDonald. Jackson seemed to have no knowledge of the alleged killer.

"Crosley, sorry I don't think I ever heard the name before or if I did I guess it didn't register. I know absolutely nothing about him. This world of murder and intrigue is new to me. As I'm sure I told you before I can't believe my brother would even know how to contact a contract killer. I still find the whole affair sort of surreal. The story Claude spewed out the other day still seems like fiction to me. What does your department know about Crosley?" Jackson was shifting the onus onto McDonald to provide some information, information which did not exist.

"I'm sorry but the investigation is ongoing. I can't answer that question at this time," Jim said. "Your brother has a phone in his desk drawer. We would like to check the record of calls to it. I was there the other day when the killer called him. He said something about a kundela." McDonald involuntarily shivered. There was no truth to that hocus pocus. This was not how these people were killed. Tell that to Claude Jackson. He was the one who was dead. Dead for no apparent reason except he suddenly drove his car through a railing and into an oncoming truck.

Neil was looking at him with a questioning look.

"Kundela," Jim said. "It comes from Australia. The aborigines take a bone, shape it, attach some hair to it, say some magic words, point it at someone and they die." Admit it or not, this was the best explanation of events he currently had. He would not even go there. These things only worked if the victim was aware he was supposed to die. These three casualties had been killed by something else. "Forget it. It was just something your brother said. I will need those records though."

"I'm not sure what phone you're talking about, but no problem. Anything we can do to help we will do."

The discussion turned to Dan Cooper. Did Neil know anything about the mystery client? Neil only knew of his existence and that a big order was supposed to be in the works. He had already passed this information along to the sergeant. Negotiations took place over a period of time but Dan appeared to have won the contract. Printing was a competitive business and sometimes several meetings were required to seal a deal. Neil wished he was more closely involved but he was trying to let Dan regain his confidence. Things were not going that well for him of late but he was a good salesman and just needed to get his act together again. Neil thought that was happening. It would appear this Crosley made contingency plans well in advance of there being a need for them.

Jim scribbled that fact in his notebook. Whatever method Crosley was using did not seem to be random or compulsive. Planning was required. Planning should leave a trail. He would find it. His only hope was that the word Kundela was not part of any explanation. Witnessing victims possessed by the devil had earned him a few gibes around the station house, suggesting they were killed by a Kundela could be a career ending move.

Jim left the president's office. The meeting had added a little insight to how Claude had operated but did little to advance the case. He took out the log of things to do that he and the security officer had compiled. He was in the plant anyway. He may as well start on it.

Andre had finished viewing the security tapes. He found nothing of interest on any of them.

Interviews of other people working in the area of Dan Cooper's desk produced little results. Some people could vaguely remember someone talking to Dan but few paid any attention. They all had their own concerns to concentrate on. It was unusual to have a client in their work area. Meetings most often were held in the customer's office. But even the uniqueness of the situation didn't trigger any worthwhile descriptions. Heavy, might have worn glasses, might not, maybe a mustache, maybe not, definitely a mustache, definitely clean shaven. The lead that promised so much hope the previous week died a slow agonizing death with each disappointing interview. It was time to move on.

Over the weekend, a search of local Chinese restaurants found one waitress that sort of remembered someone looking like Cooper. He had been drinking triples, his buddy ginger ale. Nothing new there, Cooper's blood-alcohol level had been over the moon. The vague description of his dinner partner fit the vague description received from the printing plant. He paid cash, tipped generously. Seemed like a nice guy. Would she be able to pick him out of a line up if necessary? Sure, as long as the lineup didn't include any of the hundreds of other customers she served in the last few months. He wasn't memorable.

But there was a fly in the ointment. The man identified as Cooper left in a taxi, not driving his own automobile. The waitress remembered calling the cab herself thinking it was a good idea at the time. McDonald didn't want to hear this but recorded it in notebook anyway. There must be an explanation and that was one more thing for him to work on. His investigation didn't include interviewing the bartender. Why should it, the man had no direct contact with the patrons.

The taxi wrinkle suggested the pair in question might be two other guys doing business on the company tab and not Cooper and his killer. No one at the cab company remembered either of the men. Jim suspected it was an off the books fare but could find no way to prove that. Everyone seemed able to account for their time when the pickup was supposed to be made.

The actual driver lucked into another fare who was walking towards the taxi office as the driver returned. He picked her up out of turn and that fare did show on the books in place of his restaurant pickup. Rather than admit he took a fare out of rotation, the driver kept his mouth shut. Jim would spend hours doing the legwork to track down all the cab company customers for the period. All the drivers' stories were verified as true. None of the clientele had been in the restaurant and could offer no insight into the case. No Cooper, No assassin. More bad luck for McDonald.

Interviews with security guards at Lane's office building were equally as fruitless. No unauthorized people got into that part of the parking garage. Hours of viewing security tapes verified that fact. No one had gone near Lane's car on that fateful day other than Lane himself.

Chapter 42

Crosley was in the process of closing up his house in Brooklyn when a knock came at the door. He pulled back the plain white curtains and looked out the kitchen window. There was Martha, the elderly lady from next door. This was not the first time she had called on him but she was not a frequent visitor. Her close cropped silver hair was fluttering in the ever present west wind that blew through his elevated yard. There was a Sobey's grocery bag in her hand with many strange bulges in it. It looked heavy.

Crosley opened the door to the smiling face. She passed the bag to Crosley and said: "I've brought your honey bottles back. That was a delicious crop last year. We sure want to thank you for keeping us in mind at harvest time." Subtlety was not one of Martha's strong suits.

It was almost time to spin off this summer's load of sticky sweetness and he would refill the bottles and send them back to the friendly couple next door. Despite the elaborate security system installed, the old couple kept an eye on the place for him in his absence. The local kids knew this and were probably more deterred by that fact than by any of the electronics. The Young Offenders act wouldn't protect them from these watchdogs either. Trespassers would be marched home to their parents instead of the police and in most cases justice would be meted out swiftly and harshly with no appeal.

"Great, thanks. I'll refill them and get them back to you soon." He was about to close the door but Martha stood her ground. Obviously something was on her mind. "Would you like to come in for a cup of tea?" he asked.

"Well I am pretty busy," she said as she pushed past him into the kitchen and thus Crosley learned that the police were poking around his house. Not a uniformed policeman but one wearing a suit and tie driving a plain, black car. Soon Crosley heard about the conversation between her husband and the policeman word for word and she wondered what he made of it. Any mention of Martha suggesting her neighbour might be involved in producing illegal music was omitted from the discussion. Crosley admitted he was baffled. There was no logical reason for the visit he could think of. It must have been a case of mistaken identity he concluded as he ushered his source of the unwelcome information out the door.

By the description he knew which police officer had been there, but how had he found out about this house and why was this officer targeting him? Sure he was guilty as sin but that was irrelevant. There was no good reason he could think of. Merely being in the vicinity of a fatal accident shouldn't brand him as a killer. It appeared he would not be heading west any time soon.

Crosley had been in the killing business for a number of years. He was good at it. Never had the police been this involved in one of his "accidental" killings before. This was a loose end and he did not leave loose ends. It was time to roll out the 7-Ps once more. Proper previous planning prevents piss poor performance.

When he left the scene of the recent traffic stop he saw the Ford heading back to the city. He would have noticed a marked police car following him through the little village to where he kept the house on the outskirts of Brooklyn. There must have been another car. Being at home was making him careless. That would end.

The excuse for heading to the valley to check out antique dealers was a spur of the moment thought and he believed it was a good one. Perhaps he should have followed through on it. He racked his brain to think of who else might have been around and watching him. No one came to mind. Be that as it may, he now had to decide what steps to take to halt this investigation.

He would go on the offensive. What was the name of the police officer who had accused him of causing the accident? Jackson's secretary had told him and he noted it was the same name on the ID of the plainclothes policeman who had been involved in the traffic stop. Yes, he remembered when he consulted his notes. Tracking down Detective Sergeant James McDonald would be the place to start.

Things had taken a strange turn and he had been paid for his work here after all. Now he would have to decide if McDonald was just floundering around or if he really knew what he was doing. He would give his new benefactor a call and see what light he could shine on the investigation.

The Martha-Crosley meeting and the Jackson-McDonald meeting took place at approximately the same time only separated by 40 kilometres of distance. The topics discussed would become the focus of attention of both Crosley and McDonald for the next couple of weeks.

McDonald discovered the calls to Claude Jackson's private phone line came from either M. F. Lane Investments, pay phones or surprisingly since Neil Jackson claimed no knowledge of the phone, a company cell phone. The calls from the investment company stopped just prior to the death of Matthew Lane. There was a call a month before Lane's death, an airport pay phone; a call around the time of Matthew Lane's accident from the Hubbards area, a pay phone. Jim would have to check to see if it was the same pay phone that called the radio station. There was a call a week before Cooper's death, another pay phone. There was a call at the time of the Dan Cooper's accident and the kundela call, both from a company cell phone. All the later calls were less than a minute in duration. The kundela call that came in while he was in the office was from a cell phone being used in the vicinity of the Jackson Printers and Publishers' building.

The telephone company could tell them from which cell tower the call had originated. The tower stood just outside the plant building. The signal was strong. McDonald's first thought was the call came from inside the building. The long tedious hours of viewing the surveillance tapes produced no positive results. Could they have missed someone. He dreaded the thought.

Further investigation showed the phone was registered to Dan Cooper. This would have been a real long distance call. The hit man must have Cooper's phone. When asked, Neil Jackson confirmed the phone had not shown up anywhere.

The killer was most likely sitting in the parking lot when he made the call. More leg work to see if anyone noticed someone out of the ordinary sitting out there. A long shot at best, but it had to be done.

For his part, Crosley was not worried about any of these calls. No one observed him at any of the phone booths he used. Although there was a chance of being seen at one of these locations, this was still safer than using his cell phone. Cell phone calls could be plucked out of the air without his knowledge by people with scanners. You never knew what kook might be listening and who they might call or what they might record.

He wasn't worried about any calls he made to Claude Jackson. The cell phone belonged to the Jackson Printing and Publishing Company anyway. He had taken it from Dan Cooper before sending him to his death.

He knew the video cameras at the printing plant were on a loop. He knew they were not outside. He would not be seen on any of them. He was not inside within the latest looping period. When he was in the building, he was in disguise. The disguise was not always exactly the same. Eye witness descriptions were faulty at the best of times.

His introduced discrepancies would make them even less reliable, a variety of facial hair, shoe lifts for extra height, slight alterations in colouring. Dan Cooper focused so much on winning the printing contract that he failed to notice the gaps in Crosley's appearance. Anyone who happened to have noticed him would be at a loss to come up with an accurate description of a disguise let alone a description of him.

McDonald returned to the office of Neil Jackson after the police auditors checked the plan used by Claude to hide his duplicity. In the process they discovered that the firm of Jackson Printers and Publishers was now owned by only one Jackson family. Claude Jackson's share was transferred to his brother.

There was an automatic succession clause in the agreement between the two brothers. The firm immediately passed to the remaining brother in the event of the death of the other. The company carried insurance on the two men which would compensate the family of the deceased plus pay any capital gains taxes resulting from the transfer. In this way there would be no forced sale of the assets to cover an unexpected tax burden caused by the death.

If the dead man's family decided to fight over the proceeds of the estate instead of running a successful company, operations would continue smoothly. Bereavement caused actions that were not always in everyone's best interest. McDonald didn't have to stretch his mind too hard to decide whose idea that had been.

With Neil and his wife now being sole owners, he was considerably less cooperative with McDonald's investigation. He was a victim here too, he pointed out. A great deal of money was embezzled from the company which would not be recovered. He was not going to sue the estate of his brother. He just wanted to forget it and move on. No obstacles were placed in the way of the investigation but no help was forthcoming either. McDonald found the turn around rather surprising.

"What about your brother's killer? Don't you want him brought to justice?" He confronted the elder Jackson.

"It would be nice but if he's a pro, that's unlikely. No offence. I just want to move on. I have no more energy to expend on this matter." There may have been a tear forming in the corner of his eye. Good luck, but please leave us alone was the implied message. Was he that good of an actor? McDonald wasn't sure. Regardless, that was the end of help from that source. McDonald was on his own again.

Crosley knew his tracks were well covered. It took McDonald a lot of time and effort to come to the same conclusion.

Chapter 43

At last Jim's day off rolled around. The case was going nowhere. Every clue, every lead was beaten to death. Despite all his efforts, he had nothing to show for his hard work. He was glad for the break. He agreed to meet Stella in Point Pleasant Park for a picnic and was looking forward to it with great delight. The food would be good but that was not the delight part. Two weeks had passed since they had seen each other. Jim spent those two weeks interviewing people, searching for Chinese restaurants and viewing endless surveillance tapes from both Lane Investments and JP&P, chasing down taxi drivers and their fares and tracking down telephone calls. Much to his regret, there were no hours left in the day or energy in the body to devote to Stella in a meaningful way. Today he would make up for lost time.

Once again he was humming along to the Beatle's song playing on his tape deck. Recently the tape played all the way through without sticking. I knew this tape wasn't really broken he thought. The second side started playing. It has healed itself. He smiled at this thought and started singing the next song. He had the entire tape more or less memorized. As long as it was playing, he could sing along with it. If it stopped and he tried to sing the words alone, Scott Lennon would be flipping over in his grave to hear the meaningless phrases being strung together in time to his tunes. Jim excelled at the last part of McCartney's *Hey Jude*. The la la la's he had perfected. For now he was just looking forward to a relaxing day in the park.

This would really take his mind off his work. He found in the past that often the best way to solve a problem was to completely forget about it. Let the subconscious find the answers. That was a laugh. This case held such a hold on him he could never completely forget it. No matter what he was doing it was on his mind, sometimes lurking in the background, sometimes standing tall in the foreground, but always on his mind.

He arrived at the park ahead of Stella. He checked his watch to discover he was 15 minutes early. I am more anxious than I realized he thought and settled back on a picnic table bench with his elbows on the table and his feet stretching out into the grass. Contrails ran across the sky from east to west. The bright sun shone down from overhead. Jim closed his eyes momentarily and just let nature flow over him. The setting was tranquil and he needed some tranquility at this moment.

Stella approached from the western edge of the park. She left her car in the lower lot where the food concessions were located and strolled up to their prearranged meeting place. A picnic basket dangled from her arm with a red and white checked cloth tucked in on all sides.

She slowed down and picked her way quietly through the lush green grass which was almost as dark as the green plaid of the kilt she was wearing. It broke a couple of inches above her knees and showed off her slender tanned legs at their best. When she was right on top of him, she saw that Jim's eyes were still closed and he was unaware of her arrival. Easing the basket on to the ground beside the table, she put one foot on the bench where he was seated and took his cheeks in both of her hands and squeezed. His eyes opened with a start. He had been dozing.

However, a smile broke across his face as he saw who had awakened him. This was the way to wake up. The kilt flowed in a gentle arc down from the top of her outstretched leg, not quite reaching her other knee. Slowly Jim brought his hand up along the back of her calf, rotated over her knee and rested on her thigh. From there it travelled steadily along the side of the leg and slid under the coarse wool material to encompass a smooth rounded bottom. To his surprise he only encountered the warmth of flesh.

"Wearing a thong?" he asked, the smile widening.

She smiled impishly. "Regimental. My dear old Daddy used to say 'If you're gonna wear a kilt lass, you gotta wear it properly,'" she said with her best Scottish accent. And properly was with nothing underneath. Or as the Scottish soldiers called it: regimental. She doubted her father intended for her to follow that advice. He was referring to male kilt wearers of the military persuasion, not his virginal young daughter. Oh well, times they were a-changing. She leaned forward to give Jim a kiss on the lips. The top two buttons of her blouse were undone allowing a full view of the bounty hidden there. Regimental as well. She leaned back and smiled.

"However, I didn't lug this basket all the way up here for nothing. I picked up a couple of Cokes at the store down by the beach so they are still cold. Let's eat and then we'll see what comes up." She put her foot back on to the ground, the kilt draping over Jim's wrist stayed elevated almost to her waist. "Oh look," she said, "something has come up already. Wait there's something else coming up." She looked down at Jim and laughed. Then she stepped back and placed the picnic basket on the table.

They sat side by side on the bench as Stella unloaded the goodies hiding in the basket. There were two roast beef sandwiches on whole wheat bread, piled high with meat and lettuce. One with mustard, one with mayonnaise. They did not agree on everything. For dessert there were two Macintosh apples grown in the Annapolis Valley of Nova Scotia.

The picnic was in the courtyard of an old, crumbling, seventeenth century fort deep within the park. Huge squares of interlocking granite formed walls around them growing out of the grassy terrain. It was a quiet intimate location. In the distance, others passed by along the multitude of trails enjoying the interlude of quietness in their lives and not noticing the lovers. They were alone in the midst of a crowd.

They were crunching down of the sweet white flesh of the fruit when a bee passed between them. Stella ducked as usual. She did not like flying insects with yellow and black stripes. Jim's reaction was way over the top. He gave Stella a push causing her to fall from the bench. She fell hard. More shocked than surprised, she looked up to see Jim running wildly across the quadrangle flapping his arms in the air. The bee was no longer anywhere to be seen. What was going on here?

Stella got to her feet. Her initial anger at the unexpected rough treatment was replaced with fear. She could not believe what she was seeing. Calling Jim's name, she ran after him, finally catching him at the top of the fort collapsed in a heap on the ground. Sweat was pouring from his face and hair. He was struggling to get his breathing under control. Adrenaline surged through his body's systems. The fight or flight reflex had not offered an option. There was not even a millisecond's consideration of a fight. This was purely flight.

"I don't know what caused that," he said as he gasped for air. His eyes were still wide open and searching the air around them, his heart pounded in his chest. "Suddenly and for no reason I thought this bee is going to kill us. I'm not even afraid of bees. It makes no sense whatsoever."

Stella was also afraid but for a different reason.

"You looked exactly like that guy who was killed when we were coming back from Bayswater a month or so ago. You had that same wild look in your eyes. You still have it, in fact. Are you sure you're all right?"

Jim put a more concentrated effort into controlling himself. He took several deep breaths and forced himself to be calm.

"You're right," he said. "But why would I act like that all of a sudden and for no reason. This makes absolutely no sense. Bees can't kill us, but I can't get the thought out of my mind that it would."

He started to get up but Stella pushed him back down and sat beside him. "Just relax," she said. "There has to be a reason. It has to be related to the bee."

Relaxation was the furthermost thing from Jim's mind. He didn't know what happened there in the park but he did know it was significant. Now he must figure out why. Forget about the day off. His mind was fully back into the case. He would re-interview everyone and find out if they were afraid of bees. This did not make a lot of sense on further thought. He, himself, was not afraid of bees, at least not until a few minutes ago. He would give Neil Jackson a call to see if he could shed any light on his actions.

Stella brought him back to the present. "You know, you're lucky you weren't behind the wheel of your car. You had lost complete control of yourself. You could be dead."

He grabbed Stella by the shoulders and kissed her, hard.

"Of course. That's it," he said. "That explains everything."

Stella gave him a strange look. "What explains everything?"

Somehow there were bees in those cars. An assassin could not depend on a bee flying into the car in a random chance of fate. He had to have somehow put the bees in the car and then turned them loose at the proper moment to do the most damage. Trained bees? That was foolish. His mind raced with possibilities.

Also why were he and the others so afraid of bees? Was there something you could eat that would bring that about? Nothing he had ever heard about.

"You're right. None of this makes any sense whatsoever," he said. "I don't understand what could make me react in that manner. I need a computer." He reached out and took Stella's hand. "Come on. I've got to read up on bees and their behavior." He started for his car picking up the picnic basket on the way.

Stella resisted the pull on her arm. "Where are we going?"

"I'll drive you back to your car."

"Back to my car?" Stella yanked her hand free. She had other plans for the day. "It's your day off."

"This is important," Jim said. "I have to follow up on it right away." Stella said nothing. Jim again took her and hand and pulled her along. His mind was completely on the case. He didn't even notice her reluctance to follow him. He just powered her along behind him.

When they got into Jim's car, the words of *Let It Be* filled the air as the tape player came on with the key.

"Please," Stella said. "Take out that broken tape and put something else in there." She was still annoyed and was lashing out at anything in sight.

Jim laughed. "It's not broken anymore. It plays all the way through now. It has healed its–" He let the words trail off. Of course the tape hadn't healed itself.

Stella looked over at him. "What?" she asked. Jim's face had taken on a look of revelation.

Jim looked back at her, grabbed again and kissed her hard on the lips, once more. "You're a genius," he said. "That tape is no longer broken. Someone has altered it. It's worked perfect for a couple of weeks. I thought it had healed itself but obviously someone has tampered with it."

Stella gave him a confused look. "I don't get it," she said.

Jim thought hard for a minute running various options through his mind unaware of the glares coming from his girlfriend.

"I read a book a couple of weeks ago about the power of suggestion. The killer used it to dictate what her son-in-law's reactions would be to certain stimuli. She used it to maneuver him into doing her bidding. He followed the suggestions to his death."

Stella shrugged her shoulders. "What has that got to do with you being afraid of bees? The only suggestions you've been getting today are about the birds and the bees." She forced a smile. "And you're ignoring them."

Jim flashed a lewd grin. "Not all of them." He placed his hand on her leg but his eyes were still far away. "This book gave me a whole new perspective on how susceptible we are to proposals from other people." Again he stopped to think. "There was one small chapter on something called subliminal suggestion. Professor Thornton didn't give it much credence, but she acknowledged that others believed it existed."

"Subliminal suggestion? Never heard of it."

"Some conspiracy theorists believe advertisers use secret powers in commercials, have funny images buried in print ads. People tend to ignore them. We don't want to believe we can be manipulated that easily." Jim's eyes were sparkling now. "Maybe they are not nuts after all. The professor listed a couple of sources for more information. I've got to check them out."

Jim started the car and took off with a new purpose. Stella accepted the reality of dating a single-minded detective. She had no choice. The case would always come first. She knew she would have to accept that or move on to someone else. Moving on was not in the cards for her.

Further down in the parking lot sat Robert Crosley, a pair of binoculars in his hand. What an unfortunate turn of events he thought. Plan A had been triggered prematurely. Time for Plan B. Part of the 7Ps allowed for Plan A to go awry. There was always a Plan B.

Chapter 44

Subliminal suggestion. This would not be an easy sell. There were massive amounts of evidence on both sides. For every study proving it worked there was an equally convincing one proving it was just a crock. Joe Citizen didn't want to believe he could be swayed that easily.

It would be twelve Joe and Jane Citizens who would make up any jury that would have to be convinced, convinced that it not only could happen but it did happen. Convinced to the extent that they believed someone could react violently enough to kill themselves. Yesterday, Jim would have been a hard sell. Today, he was a believer. He had been attacked by a killer bee.

The first known experiments occurred in 1956. A movie theatre in Fort Lee, New Jersey had a special projector installed. The motion picture being shown at the time was *Picnic* staring William Holden, Kim Novak, Cliff Robertson and Rosaland Russell among others. It tells the story of a drifter who crashes a small town's Labour Day picnic and romances a girl who's already spoken for.

During the movie every five seconds the words "Eat Popcorn" and "Drink Coca-Cola" were flashed on the screen for 1/3000 of a second. The Subliminal Projection Co., owners of the equipment, claimed the sales of popcorn and Coke went up 18 percent. Later it was claimed the whole thing was a hoax and had never happened but many believe this denial was the result of the bad public relations brought on by upset theatre goers. No one likes to be manipulated.

A study not denied was carried out by Dr. Kenneth Parker at Queens College in New York. He showed the word PLASTIC to testees for such a short period of time though they had no conscious perception of having seen it. He then asked them to form a word using the letters PLA. They all gave the word PLASTIC. Other choices of common words like plant or place were not suggested by anyone. Also when asked to form a word using ELA they formed the word ELASTIC and not words like elated or elaborate.

Next McDonald needed to find out what messages were planted on his tape and how. He sought out a local recording studio. They would be able to dissect his Beatles tape into its various tracks. Squeezed into the gaps in the music were the messages: "Bees will kill you" and "run, run, run" repeated over and over through the entire tape. He shuddered at the thought of how easily he was converted into a mindless idiot by a little insect. Someone took over his rational thinking.

Choosing a bee was a smart move. Many people had a preexisting fear of these tiny workers whether they admit it or not. Fear trumps reason. Make a man afraid enough and all rational thought and action goes out the door, or through the windshield. The subliminal repetition just reinforced these primal fears.

Jim's subliminal messages came from his car stereo. The hit man was in his car at least twice. Once to get the tape or at least to see what kind of music he listened to and once to replace it with the doctored tape. Had he used the same method with the other three?

James Nelson was Matthew Lane's chauffeur. He controlled the music although Lane did listen to it. Was Nelson involved? He would find out where he got his music.

Claude Jackson always played the same music in the background in his office Jim recalled. Some sort of classical stuff. He would get a copy of that to examine as well. That also raised the question of how the tampered music would have been placed in Claude's office. Then he reflected on the slackness of the security system at JP&P and realized the office was as vulnerable as his car parked in an open parking lot.

As for Dan Cooper his car was still in the police impound. It was a total write-off and was just junk waiting to be disposed of. He would start with it.

The next step would be to get a warrant to search the Brooklyn property. He had no idea what grounds he would be able to come up with to persuade a judge to issue that. As convinced as he was, he knew he still had no case.

"Your honour, he raises bees in his yard and has stereo equipment in his living room."

The judge would be looking at him expectantly. "And this shows what?" he would ask.

"That's what I need the warrant for. I have to check out this equipment."

"Nice try Sergeant," he would say. "Come back when you have probable cause and not just a wild hunch. Try tying the man, the bees and the music to the cars, the victims and the accidents." If only I could, Judge, I wouldn't need you or your warrants, he thought. Preparing the paperwork for the warrant would take hours of his time.

He still had to get the "trained bees" into the car and then flying around at the exact moment they were supposed to. This would take some deliberation. Knowing what had happened might prove as frustrating as not knowing when it came time to make others believe him.

He started reviewing the notes taken since the superintendent first assigned him to the case, what is known as the critical first 48 hours. Here it was way back at the beginning. The only thing found in Matthew Lane's car was a Styrofoam cup, a sheet of plastic and a small wedge shaped stick. A similar cup was found in Dan Cooper's car. Nothing was recovered from Claude Jackson's burned out Mercedes.

Everything had been incinerated. There could have been a Styrofoam cup there as well.

The bees must have been in the covered cup and balanced on the wedge. Now, how did the killer tip it over? He recalled the circumstances of each crash.

Claude Jackson was cut off and had to rapidly brake and swerve to avoid hitting the car of that guy from Ontario. The man who actually owned a house in Nova Scotia, his prime and only suspect.

Matthew Lane had just come around a leg of a clover leaf exchange, probably at a high rate of speed if what the Mountie who responded to the call said was true. Lane always travelled too fast and he had a slack rear tire according to Jim's notes. This could cause the car to swerve a bit.

Cooper had just swung off the Bedford Highway and on to the bridge approach, a 90 degree turn adding to the fact he was drunk.

All of these things could cause the cup to tip if the angle of the wedge was right. Judging from what McDonald had seen so far, the angles would have been perfect. The man was a professional. Jim would have to run some tests to prove this theory. As for getting the bees into the car: Lane stopped at Tim Horton's and left the car standing alone, Jackson's was parked in an unsupervised parking lot and Cooper was coming from a meeting with the killer. There was lots of opportunity.

He now had the why, money; how, bees; but he still needed evidence to tie in the who.

Since he was targeted himself, the hit man must still be in the area. Caution would be required. He would have to force the killer's hand. The first thing to do was to get over his fear of bees.

He picked up the phone and punched in the number of the police impound yard. When a voice answered he identified himself and asked for Chuck Bezanson.

"Chuck, that car wrecked on the bridge a few weeks back. Could you check and see if there is a tape in the tape deck and hold it for me if there is?"

"No can do," came back the cheerful voice of the mechanic. "Someone picked the car up for scrap sometime last week. Bought it from the insurance company. Sorry, but it's probably just a little cube of metal by now on its way to Korea to come back to haunt us as a Hyundai. They don't usually store those old wrecks. Take up too much space. Crush 'em and ship 'em."

"Yeah, thanks." McDonald tried not to sound too despondent. He flipped through the pages of his notebook and found the number of James Nelson. Within minutes he discovered Nelson had become what is known as collateral damage.

He dialed Nelson's number and listened as the phone rang five times followed by a click and another ring. The call was transferred to another phone he surmised.

"M. F. Lane Investments." Jim had the switchboard.

"James Nelson, please."

There was a long pause before the receptionist asked: "Who is calling please and what is your relationship to Mr. Nelson?"

Man, Jim thought, they still have the barriers up. Even the chauffeur has his calls screened. "Detective-Sergeant James McDonald, RCMP," he said.

Another pause.

"I'm sorry Sergeant, Mr. Nelson is dead. He drowned while vacationing in California."

"Drowned? How? When?" Jim was taken aback.

"Last week. With Mr. Lane gone, everyone with a title thought James should be their chauffeur. He finally had enough and took the vacation time owed to him and went to California. I don't know where these wild stories come from but it has been reported he was chased into the ocean by a swarm of bees and drowned. Of course, that's ridiculous but he did drown. It's all so sudden and so sad. First Mr. Lane, and now James. He was such a nice boy."

McDonald couldn't believe his bad luck. He got a contact number for the police in the California town Nelson was visiting. He sympathized with Nelson. The receptionist may think it ridiculous but Jim knew it could be true. *The bees will kill you, run, run, run.* It must have been a horrific way to die. Who alive would believe it besides Jim?

"The RCMP in Halifax? Let me call you back," was the response from the officer answering the phone in California. Jim tried to give him a number to call but he insisted he would look it up. The phone went dead. Within a minute the connection was made again.

"Sorry, Sergeant. Ever since this story broke about a swarm of bees drowning this poor lad the phone has been ringing off the hook from tabloids looking for a quote. It adds authenticity to their story to be able to quote the investigating officer. Investigating officer, that's a laugh. It should be the poor schnook who happened to be patrolling closest to the scene of the drowning and got his name involved with these wild stories. It looks like an accidental drowning. What's your interest?"

"I was dealing with Mr. Nelson regarding another case and the subject of a swarm of bees came up—"

"No. Please, no," said the officer. "There are no killer bees involved. In fact there are no killer bees. Two people who witnessed the drowning said there were a couple of bees, that's two bees, flying around the beach when the kid suddenly jumped up and went screaming into the water, went under and never surfaced again. I repeat, two bees. Not a swarm. This is California. We grow fruit. Bees pollinate the fruit trees. We encourage them. There are some of them flying around all the time."

"It was more his demeanor I'm interested in," said Jim. "You say he was screaming? He looked terrified?" Terrified that *the bees were going to kill him*; that he had to *run, run, run*. Jim empathized.

"Yeah, terrified. The medical examiner said it looked like he was still screaming underwater. His lungs were full of sea water."

"And there were a couple of bees in the area?"

"Yeah. Two bees. Two ordinary, domestic honey bees. Not killer bees. Not a swarm."

"Right," Jim said and laughed. Killer bees made a much more interesting story than the reality. "Two honey bees. You've got two of your major industries at odds with each other out there. The movie industry is convincing everyone killer bees exist and are out to get you. The tourist industry convincing them they don't and it's safe to visit."

"It appears that way," the officer said. "Because of the victim's age, we did an autopsy. Figured he must be high on some hallucinogenic drug but couldn't find anything in his system. That could just mean there's something new out there we're not testing for. It's hard to keep up with kids these days. This young fella didn't really fit the profile of a drug user. He was healthy, fit, not a needle user. Something made him snap but I'll be honest with you, there won't be a serious investigation done here. It will be ruled accidental and forgotten about. There's no family in the area to push the case and we are just too busy to pursue it."

"I understand. Like every force in both our countries, we have too many crimes and too few investigators," Jim said. "Thanks for the information."

"Would you like me to forward you a copy of the autopsy report?"

"No thanks, that won't be necessary," Jim said. It would contain nothing helpful. The contents of his brain would still be a mystery. Nelson was just collateral damage to the Lane killing, a victim of his love of country music.

"I could give you the names of the witnesses who started the whole bee story but I can't guarantee much cooperation. They only want to talk to the highest bidder these days."

"The highest bidder? I'm sorry I don't follow."

"The tabloids, print and TV. They will pay them for an exclusive version of the killer bee swarming story. Probably have their picture on the beach pointing to where it happened. The others tabs will just make up a version of their own to print. The actual facts aren't too important. Two bees have grown into a swarm. That's why they want quotes from me. I've been offered money for my version as well."

"Well," Jim said, "I guess I can read their version in the super market line up when I get my groceries next week. Save me talking to them."

"Or you could fly out and interview them. The weather's pretty good here this time of year."

Jim laughed. "Sounds great but I don't think that's in the budget. Thanks for your help. If I have any more questions I'll call you." With that Jim broke off the connection, another lead gone down a hole. It did however, confirm that bees probably led to Lane's wild driving and ultimately his death. Both sat in the same car listening to the subliminal messages. Both knew the *bees will kill you* and you have to *run, run, run.* Jim shivered at the thought.

Chapter 45

Next, Jim decided to head over to Jackson Printing and Publishing. There was a question of a large sum of money being transferred by the company on the day Claude died. The forensic auditors didn't think it was any big deal but it was a strange coincidence. He would make some inquires while he picked up the tape or CD or whatever Claude listened to all the time in his office.

Neil Jackson gave him a cold reception. Claude was out of his company, out of his life and out of his thoughts. Please leave it that way. The brotherly love so apparent before the death seemed to die with the brother. Embezzling family members are a disappointment, especially embezzlers who are also involved in murder, but this was going to extremes.

If truth be told, Neil might have been able to forgive the embezzlement and the hiring of the hit man, well especially the hiring of the hit man. Good business sense dictated that move. No, Claude's sin was putting his personal concerns ahead of those of the company. He jeopardized the integrity of Jackson Printing and Publishing. Giving up confidential information to an outsider could not be tolerated. If this fact came out, either in a trial or some other way, the client list of JP&P would dry up overnight.

Clients put their faith in the printing company to keep their ad campaigns secret until the time destined for the campaign kick off, to keep the information in annual reports secret until the annual meeting was held, to keep sale prices quiet until the sale started. If this confidentiality could not be guaranteed, the clients would go someplace where it could. If the vice president and co-owner of the printing concern was coughing up this information to competitors and strangers, the time to move on to a new printer had arrived. Neil had spent a lifetime building up this trust. He would do anything to protect it.

Claude had not only put his own career at risk, but the career of every employee of JP&P from the president down to the guy who cleaned the toilets. Neil could never forgive this outright disregard for the well being of all the staff and their families. Claude had to go. His indiscretions had to remain suppressed. No other choice presented itself. Above all, the business came first. Claude never grasped that concept. Neil never forgot it.

Claude's office had been packed up and cleared out. There was a new head of the sales and promotion staff and she put her own touches on her working space. Any trace of Claude was gone forever.

Neil wasn't sure what Claude's wife did with the stuff. She sold their Bedford house and moved to British Columbia. There were too many bad memories here for her to face. The news about Claude being an embezzler was too much for her to bear. His involvement in Lane's murder was the final straw. As well, there were lingering doubts about Claude's death being accidental or was it really a suicide? She wanted distance between herself and these memories of the man she loved for so many years, the man she thought she knew. The music was probably sold in one of the many yard sales they held before leaving.

Another door slammed shut. McDonald couldn't believe it.

Neil was surprised McDonald knew about the money transfer from his own private account. It was a business expense, he explained. It came from my account because I'm a hands on kind of guy. Let him make a phone call and Neil would produce some paper work to verify all this. Not necessary, McDonald said. Paper work is what you printers excel at. Claude had shown that.

The only thing left to do was go to Brooklyn and confront Crossman-Crosley himself. Let him know he was on to him. See what he could shake out. Perhaps force a mistake. It was a long shot. He had been told Crossman only lived there some of the time, the rest of the time he was in Ontario. Secretly he hoped for the latter. If the house was empty he would go in and look around, warrant or no warrant.

He left the printing plant and headed for the country planning his strategy as he drove, oblivious to the changing scenery around him. This time instead of luscious green leaves on the trees, they were starting to take on their fall hues. Traces of red, yellow and orange were mixing in with the greens. The honey should be ready he thought for no apparent reason.

He noticed the apples had grown since his last visit, larger with a reddish tinge kissing the soft green. A light blue van with Ontario plates was parked in the yard. There would be no furtive searching. He psyched himself up for the meeting of minds. Crossman had proven to be a staunch adversary. He was prepared.

The door opened and his preparedness started to wane. Standing in front of him was a balding, middle-aged black man with a slight paunch forming around his waist. He was dressed in a checked shirt and wore medium blue work pants, common among the farmers in the area. There was an inquisitive look in his eye.

"Yes?" he asked.

McDonald settled back a little. He was ready for a confrontation. "Luke Crossman? I'm looking for Luke Crossman."

The man in the doorway smiled. "You've got him."

"Luke, Luke Crossman from Markham, Ontario," McDonald said. This must be a cousin or something although the colouring was confusing.

"That's me," the smiling face said. "Only one that I know of. And who might you be?"

McDonald produced his identification.

The smile on Crossman's face faded a little. "Martha, from next door, told me there were some cops around a while back. Been wondering what it was all about ever since. Guess you're here to tell me. Come on in." The inherent distrust of the black race for white police was faintly apparent.

McDonald entered the house. "You wouldn't mind showing me some ID would you?" His mind was trying to figure out what was going on. This was too crazy.

Crossman reached in the rear pocket of his pants and brought out a worn, brown leather wallet. He flipped through the credit cards and came up with a driver's license, the same driver's license McDonald had seen before only this one bore a likeness of the man in front of him in the picture window. He turned the card over in his hand and examined it. It was the real thing.

McDonald returned the piece of plastic. He was at a loss for something to do so he flipped open his notebook to his previous visit and glanced through the pages.

"You have to excuse me Mr. Crossman but your neighbours referred to you as a young fellow. That's the Luke Crossman I'm looking for."

Crossman chuckled. "Well now Sergeant, age is a funny thing. Martha said the same thing about you. When you're looking at eighty from the other side, there are a lot more young fellas in the world than when you're looking at it from where we stand. I have known them for a while and was a lot younger when I first moved here. They just keep me in that class I guess. I'm kind of flattered. I don't live here much of the time but when I do, I live here alone." He shook his head and smiled. "Young fella, that is rich.

"Too bad I can't thank her for the compliment but they've gone on a cruise or something. She was telling me about it the last time I was here. Then she said they were thinking about moving in to a condo somewhere. Too old to put up with another winter in that old house. They heat it with wood you know. Lot of work cutting and splitting it. Haven't seen them this time around so I guess they're gone. Now just what it is you wanted to talk to me about?"

Crossman's eyes twinkled as he talked, his face was animated, enjoying the conversation. Jim could see the man had few visitors and made the most of them when they arrived.

McDonald, on the other hand felt like someone punched him in the head. Not only was this not the person he expected to interview, his source for confirmation that someone else lived or was here prior to his last visit also disappeared. He looked for a chair and lowered himself uninvited into it.

Crossman picked up the white Corral teapot with the blue flowers around the edge that sat on the stove and offered it to McDonald. "Let me heat this up a bit and we'll have a cup." He turned on the heat and the blue propane flame flickered up around the edge of the pot. He added some water and another tea bag without removing those already in the pot. In no time steam was coming from the spout. He filled two big mugs with brown stains permanently colouring their insides and sat down.

"Hope you like it strong. Milk or sugar?" he asked. He set a cardboard carton of milk on the table and indicated the plastic sugar dish with a wave of his hand. "I wasn't here the last time you came by. When Martha told me there was a policeman here I was thinking maybe my house had been broken in to. There was nothing missing but I just had a feeling. Then I just chalked it up an overactive imagination and let it slide. Is that why you were here?"

The question hung in the air. Or did a crime take place somewhere within twenty miles of this place and look here's a black man? Crossman's voice didn't ask that question but his eyes did.

"No," McDonald said. "Do you mind if I look around? These old houses fascinate me." He wanted a closer look at the electronics he observed through the window on his last trip. Another disappointment. The stereos were nothing out of the ordinary, more designed for playing than recording. Definitely not advanced enough for high tech dubbing of subliminal messages.

"What makes you think someone was in your house?" McDonald asked as they went back into the kitchen.

"Oh, I don't know. Chairs looked like they were in different places, things moved, the newspaper was open on the table. Nothing was missing. Like I said, just a feeling. Forget it, I did." McDonald couldn't. It might be true.

Was the Crossman he stopped on the 101 highway aware he was being followed and broke into this house until his tail gave up and went home? If he was familiar with the area, he would know this house was usually deserted. He would have to know the name of the owner to have the phony license made up with his picture on it. That could happen. Professionals covered their tails. One other thing, why didn't Martha mention her neighbour was black? Why should she? That was big city thinking. Besides, this wasn't the only black man in the neighbourhood. Former Canadian welterweight boxing champion Clyde Gray used to live just down the road from here.

"Were you living here at the end of July?" Jim asked.

Crossman rubbed his chin. "I was here in the middle of July. Then I went back to Ontario and came back last week."

"So, to be clear, you weren't here on July 28th?"

"Twenty-eighth? No, that would have been between visits."

Jim snapped his notebook shut. "Thanks for your time," he said.

He made his way out the door and back to his car. His head hung down and a dejected look was painted on his face. Every lead had just fizzled out.

Crosley watched the frustrated policeman walking across the yard. He had followed the cop from the city, placing a quick call to the Crossman actor when the final destination became apparent. He let the binoculars fall back to his chest from the neck strap. They bounced against the cassette in his shirt pocket.

Crosley had followed McDonald to the recording studio where Jim had taken his Beatle tape to be examined. He would have liked to have gotten his hands on it before it was analyzed, but that didn't happen. He settled for breaking in later in the week and replacing it with an identical looking tape that had been erased. The studio technicians offered profuse apologies. They could not understand how it could have happened, but there was no recovery.

The tapes from Jackson's office and Lane's and Cooper's cars were tossed into a roaring hardwood fire in the living room wood stove along with the cell phone unused from the time he had last called Claude except for one surprising and rewarding incoming call from Claude's brother. The resulting ashes were stirred, re-burnt and then sprinkled in the driveway. There were no loose ends.

If McDonald managed to track down James Nelson, Claude Jackson's family or Cooper's wrecked automobile, alas they would all be dead ends. Superb detective work, no reward. Crosley was unaware that Nelson wasn't available to be tracked down. He would have been indifferent to the news. Crosley's business was death.

Neil Jackson turned out to be the ever practical business man. There was a way to recover the money embezzled from the company or if not collect the actual cash, that went to Claude's family, to invoke the succession clause in their partnership. Now the business was all his.

He was willing if not happy to pay to have his brother taken care of. Claude had become a detriment to the company, a liability. He was out of control. Neil covered the fees and expenses owed to Crosley by Claude, a small price to acquire twenty-five per cent of a prosperous, successful business. This would be the last time he would have to clean up a mess left by his younger brother. As a bonus to Crosley, Neil stopped cooperating with the police and even threw up a couple of fences. Nothing to raise suspicion, but enough to confound McDonald's investigation.

Crosley would pick up the bill for the expenses of his friend down in the house. He had put on a stellar performance for the confused cop. A small audience, but his acting job was first rate. The solitary fan attending the show was convinced he was the real deal, the reward every actor seeks. The change of race was the crowning touch. It was Crosley's idea.

Martha was happy in her new condo. There was a garden plot on the balcony where she could grow her flowers and a few tomatoes in large round containers. They could even afford to purchase it themselves once Neil Jackson agreed to help with a generous down payment. Crosley didn't charge him for the hit on his brother. That was going to happen anyway. The old folks just needing a little convincing. Crosley could be persuasive. It truly was time for them to move out at least for the winters. Good neighbour that he was, he pointed out all the benefits of moving to a warmer clime and leaving the snow shoveling and wood splitting behind—enjoying their golden years.

The old man, opposed at first to moving, spent part of each day playing card games with three other old fellows of his vintage. They played auction 45s. They dealt the cards, bid, took in tricks, marked score, but that was all incidental to what they were really doing.

The discussions they held each day were designed to save the world. All the issues of importance were talked through until solutions, only available to those who have the wisdom of the ages, were found. Comparisons to how the world was when they were younger were made and argued over. Each man had his own recollection of the historical events and boisterously argued their accuracy.

One topic never came up, personal finances. The others would have been shocked at how little the old man from Nova Scotia paid for his condo. Crosley had friends everywhere. They were happy to do him a favor when asked.

I'll have to get together a case of honey and send it off to them, Crosley thought as he looked out at the stack of white boxes where he kept his bees. They enjoy it more than anyone else I know. It must keep them young."

He took the music tape out of his pocket and looked at it. I like the Beatles, he thought. At least once I clean up the tape I will. Plan A would have been instantly fatal for Detective Sergeant Jim McDonald. Plan B would haunt him for the rest of his life. Cops shouldn't get too emotionally attached to their cases. Even the best can't solve them all, especially when all their hard sought evidence disappears in smoke up a wood stove chimney.

Epilogue

Jim and Stella lay on the green plaid blanket on the beach. Although the two lay motionless, sand mysteriously crept from the area around them onto the blanket and worked its way under the two prone bodies. The waves crashed in and the white foam rolled just short of where they were stretched out above the high water mark. The calendar called it spring, but summer had come early to Bayswater Beach.

High overhead the sun beat down giving their bodies a comfortable glowing feeling. Wispy cirrus clouds painted on the blue canvas of sky drifted out to the horizon. Phosphoresce specks of silica glinted in the sand. Despite the warmth of the day, the blue-green ocean water was definitely too cold for swimming. It was way beyond refreshing. The nearly deserted beach supported a few other early season sunbathers jump-starting their tans. It was a great day for just relaxing.

"I'm glad you've forgotten about Claude Jackson. It was time to put that case behind you," Stella said in a low voice. She was too comfortable and contented for loud talking. "Lying here on the beach reminded me of it again."

"That was a dead horse. I whipped it to death over the winter. The house in Brooklyn turned out to be owned by a management company. Records show they've owned it for about ten years. They have no idea who Uncle Amos was. They have never met the tenant. He has a rent book and pays cash at any branch of the Royal Bank he happens to be near. Pays once a year and payments are from all over the country. Didn't have a clue what his race was and didn't care as long as the payments were made."

Jim remained silent for a moment. He ran over the case in his mind.

"The car was rented with a phony credit card using a real number, but the renter ended up paying cash anyway. No questions were ever asked. No one knew the card was phony until I followed up to find out where they were sending the bills. The name registered to the number was not the name used in the rental office. Bills were never sent because no charges were made against the card.

"The rental company simply confirmed the card number was valid and not maxed out. They reserved a block of the card's credit limit in case it was needed. In the end, they tore up the slip when the payment was made in cash."

Inspector Holland lost interest in the case as well. New crimes demanded his attention. Claude Jackson was technically responsible for the death of Matthew Lane and he was dead himself. The hit man was only a means to carry out his plan, a weapon, so to speak.

Matthew Lane's family still lived in the dream world where the family head died in an accident. Jackson's family just wanted to forget about the whole ordeal. Cooper's family was never given the details about the suspected murder. There was nothing to tell them really. It was all speculation. JP&P carried a generous insurance policy on its employees. Life for the Cooper's went on. The two neighbouring widows shared their grief and aided in each other's recovery.

With no new leads and the actual killer, a pro, long gone from their jurisdiction, it was time to move on. Holland had other cases for Jim to pursue, cases where people cared if someone was caught.

Jim rolled over onto his side, facing Stella. "It was time to forget about Claude Jackson and put that case behind me."

"Yes," Stella said. "That's what I was saying."

Jim continued. "I fretted about that all winter. It was driving me crazy. It was strange you know. Around the time you replaced my missing Beatles tape at Easter, and by the way I never thanked you for that, I started realizing it was time to forget about Claude Jackson and put that case behind me."

Stella rolled over and faced him. Her cleavage, hidden all winter, showed a little pink from the unaccustomed sun. Noticing this, his eyes were naturally drawn to the area, he touched the mound of her breast leaving a white finger mark which quickly blended back to pink. Stella removed her sunglasses, twisted her neck and looked down at her shoulders. The telltale pink, which if left unattended would evolve to a burning, bright red by nightfall, stared back at her. She pulled on her light blue blouse and buttoned it up.

"It's too early in the year to burn," she said. "Maybe we should get out of this sun before it's too late. No sense turning into a couple of lobsters."

Jim got up, brushed the sand off his shoulders and put on his shirt. "You've got that right. Let's find some shade." One arm around her waist, he directed her towards the trees.

"This is where it all started," Stell said. "Coming back from here." She looked out over the ocean at the white caps breaking on the waves offshore and went on: "By the way, I never replaced your Beatles tape. I like John and Paul as much as the next guy, but not every time I get into your car. Give me a break. I rejoiced when the recording studio accidently crased it. I was as glad to see it go as I was that you forgot about Claude Jackson and put that case behind you."

They looked at each other. Recognition of what they were saying dawned on them both at the same time.

"No, it can't be," Jim said. "He can't have done this to me again, to both of us. I've forgotten about him and put that case behind me." He paused and looked deeply into Stella's eyes. It had been a miserable winter for both of them. Their lives were dominated with Jim's compulsive interest in solving this crime. Now he forgot about it most days. What caused him to lose interest in a case that so dominated his life? Where had the mystery tape come from? What secret messages did it hold?

"*Paul is dead. Paul is dead. Paul is dead.*" Or was it something more sinister? "*Forget about me. Forget about me. Forget about me.*"

Stella saw the fear in his eyes and knew what he was thinking. She did not want this investigation reopened. It was best to forget it, put it behind them.

"I'm glad you have," she said. "You know, I'm tired of listening to that tape anyway. What do you say we just chuck it away? Deep six it. Your father will forgive you. It's time."

Jim took her into his arms and kissed her deeply. "Consider it chucked." He smiled, reached down and picked her up and turned back towards the ocean. Too late, Stella realized his intention. Jim hustled to the water's edge amid her kicking legs and pounding fists. A wave came rolling in bringing the water up to his thighs. Goose bumps instantly pebbled his legs. He dropped her into the ocean amid her squeals of don't you dare, then stumbled and fell on top of her as the next surging wave came crashing over them.

"Oh man, that is cold." His voice went up a couple of octaves. They scrambled to their feet and bee-lined it to shore.

Claude Jackson was forgotten, and so was Robert Crosley—as least for now.

The End

ABOUT THE AUTHOR

Art Burton lives in Latties Brook, Nova Scotia, Canada with his wife, Flame and dog, Charley.

He took an early retirement from The Halifax Herald at the end of 2002 where he had been a printer for 26 years before joining the IT Department. When he left the hustle and bustle of life in the big city for the more relaxed, laid-back lifestyle of rural Nova Scotia, he decided it was time to move up from printing to writing.

He has written four mystery novels as well as two books of related-short stories about the hobos who passed through Central Nova Scotia during the Great Depression.

For more information on these books, visit his web page at users.eastlink.ca/~artburton.

www.ingramcontent.com/pod-product-compliance
Lightning Source LLC
Chambersburg PA
CBHW022136170626
46807CB00005B/1956